Sorcerer's World

May you soar
with the Dragons!,

H. Gary Northcott

Dec. 94

Sorcerer's World

H. Gary Northcott

NPI

Northwest Publishing Inc.
Salt Lake City, Utah

Sorcerer's World

For information address: Northwest Publishing,
5949 South 350 West, Salt Lake City, Utah 84107
JAC 1.6.94

PRINTING HISTORY
First Printing 1994

ISBN: 1-56901-156-7

NPI books are published by Northwest Publishing Incorporated,
5949 South 350 West, Salt Lake City, Utah 84107.
The name "NPI" and the "NPI" logo are trademarks belonging to
Northwest Publishing, Incorporated.

PRINTED IN THE UNITED STATES OF AMERICA.
10 9 8 7 6 5 4 3 2 1

To Opal and Bert Northcott,
better known as:
The Dowager-Empress and her Consort.

One

"To take action, is to be responsible, even when the results are unforeseen."

— The Chronicles of Deathwind.

He really didn't look very much like a powerful sorcerer, at least not like the great Star-mages known to the commoners. He was instead rather plain looking, of medium stature, with a full red beard and wearing a simple blue robe with no ornamentation at all. The staff he picked up as he turned to leave the underground laboratory was plain, black in color, and was one of those short staffs that templars call rods. It, too, had no decorations of any kind.

At the very beginning of his career, he had chosen to adopt a plain and simple appearance, partly as disguise and partly as silent reproof of those practitioners of the Art who affected dramatic dress and showy wealth as proof of their powers. He found amusement in being thought a humble pilgrim. It was a persona he had perfected over the many centuries.

Few indeed, would discern that this wizard, with his simple staff, had traveled to hundreds of different worlds, both upstream and downstream in the River of Time. He had taken care that he was not well-known, always preferring to work in the shadows and give credit to those others who were eager to accept it.

Now, as he elected to walk up the long underground tunnel rather than crossing the dimensional warp and flashing the distance in an instant, he was troubled. In routinely checking the timelines of the world where he now made his home, he had experienced a major vision, and he wanted to walk and think about it.

He turned and as was his custom, fused the door to the laboratory, transmuting it into a solid slab of lead and sealing the laboratory from any unwanted intruders. He very deliberately paced up the long tunnel, unmindful of the many traps he had designed into it, traps that could completely seal his mountain retreat in solid rock in an instant.

The tunnel led to his personal living quarters, and then another tunnelled to the grand salon, which in turn opened out onto a large balcony overlooking a beautiful mountain valley. This valley he had named Xanadu after some legendary place that he had heard about on one of his early journeys. For himself, he used many names but was known on this world primarily as Deathwind, a name that amused him when he wished to make an awesome impression for the foolish. To a very select few, he was known as Sahm-el.

Today, he did not feel awesome. He had glimpsed the approach to disaster and was giving thought as to what he should do. After several long moments of sightless staring out at the valley, he abruptly smiled the grim half smile that had struck terror in foes for over thirty generations.

He carefully formed a mental image in his mind, as precise and detailed as only a master mage could do, then sent a flash of light from his staff streaking off through the mountains bearing his message to an old friend. After pausing for a few seconds, he sent a second message flashing off in a totally different direction. Then he turned and entered the grand salon.

A dark-haired woman dressed in a purple gown approached silently and softly inquired, "Is there anything needed, Master?"

He settled into a wide comfortable chair, cradling his staff in his elbow. "Miranda, we shall have guests soon, Master Chiang and Sinueh the Elf. Please have the cooks fix an entire ox for Chiang, leaving it whole the way he likes it. And bring some of the Wildflower Wine for the elf. I will have the fruit drink, chilled." And he handed her the goblin mug, made from the skull and hand bones of a goblin defeated in a long ago war on another world.

Miranda hurried to the kitchen and gave orders to the household staff for her Master's wants. Upon refection, she dispatched one of the servants to the floor of the valley to give warning to the Dwarven Colony that lived underneath the mountains at the far end of the valley. The occasion of Chiang's last unannounced visit had caused the Dwarves to sound the alarm and seal up their mountain. They were surly for weeks afterward.

Just after the mid-day meal, a huge shadow swept down the long valley towards the Balcony. The Dwarves on watch muttered to themselves, but forewarned, they restrained their natural impulse to raise the alarm, and watched silently as this visitor landed on the balcony and then, in a swirl of color, changed into human form and entered the home of the mighty sorcerer Deathwind.

The arrival of the second visitor caused much less stir among the dwarf guards as it was merely an elf flying on one of those giant bumblebees that only they could ride. Why anyone would want to fly at all was beyond Dwarven thinking, but then all Dwarves knew that Elves were about as dependable as butterflies and just as unpredictable.

The giant bee landed somewhat clumsily on the balcony and the slight form of an elf, dressed in gray leather, nimbly leaped from the saddle and skipped inside with a carefree air about him such as only an elf could maintain. He quietly entered the mountain (Elves do everything quietly) and walked through a zigzag tunnel that was designed to make unwanted intrusion very difficult. This led to an entryway where the elf unhesitatingly turned to the right hand door and entered.

Ordinarily, an elf would be feeling a bit uncomfortable

going deeper and deeper underground like a dwarf. However, the grand salon that he entered was so spacious and comfortable that one forgot one was underground. This effect was achieved by a high vaulted ceiling that faded into light blue nothingness creating an illusion of day. There was a large circular fireplace in the middle of the room. Tapestries adorned the walls and there were thick fur rugs of deep green and orange.

In wide leather covered chairs facing the fireplace, he saw his host, the Sorcerer Deathwind, and a tall human male with bald head and drooping mustache who was wearing robes of golden silk. The aura of light broadcast by the human's emotions was primarily blue, but it had flashes of scarlet and black clouds in it, and was discernible only to an elf. This gave him warning that the mighty Deathwind was angry about something. The fact that he could read no aura at all from the other person was proof positive to the elf that this was not a human but rather something in human form.

As the elf approached these two, his typical elven carefree mood abruptly left him for he heard the sorcerer say, "I have seen the return of the Outsiders."

Deep inside the mountain, in the personal library of the Sorcerer Deathwind, a small bald man with a pot belly was sitting at the main desk absorbed in study. His name was Murdoch, a name he had chosen for himself upon becoming free. Mounted on the wall above his desk there was an iron collar, kept there to constantly remind him of his beginnings. Like the rest of the household staff, three women and two other creatures that were hard to define, he had been rescued from slavery by Deathwind. From making mud bricks on a riverbank, he had been freed and then trained as a sage. His devotion to Deathwind was well earned.

Murdoch was currently working on *The Chronicles*, Deathwind's own diaries, spanning some 1500 years of activity.

He was working in *Volume 12* and comparing the memories of Deathwind of the event known as The Great Cataclysm with the legendary account from *The Run of the Rill*, the Elven epic poem.

"The weapon of the Outsiders flashed down from the sky striking our world with the fire of suns. Our very best effort could only parry the attack, deflecting it from a dead hit to a glancing blow. Still, this glancing blow all but destroyed us.

"This bolt of energy did catastrophic damage and caused major changes in the land masses, creating new river routes, and several new mountain ranges, and the Great Rift which some call 'The Edge of the World.' Most of the known civilizations, countries, cities, and kingdoms were simply wiped out. We learned later that of all the people who were living on this world, three out of every five died that day. The Cataclysm undid the work of the Council of Sorcerers and released the bound Demons back into the world. Only those Elves who had withdrawn completely into hiding remained untouched by it. This accounts for our current calendar dating from the time of the Cataclysm."

It was a familiar tale to Murdoch, and he was struck once again at the wonder of working for someone who actually lived through it. He was about to check the description given in the Elven poem when Elizabeth came in and told him the Master wanted him to join he and his guests in the Laboratory.

Murdoch carefully returned the massive scroll of the Elven poem to its proper rack and then closed and locked Volume 12 of The Chronicles before returning it to the vault. He paused long enough to straighten the edges of a stack of cut parchment and to neatly align the quill pens, always preferring things to be neat and orderly. Then he betook himself to the laboratory, all the while curious as to what guests would be admitted to Deathwind's Laboratory.

The laboratory had been carved out of the bedrock of the

mountain and its walls, floor and ceiling were lined with an unbroken layer of solid lead, transmuted directly from the rock. It had the usual pentagram inlaid mosaically into the floor as well as stone working tables and counters, and racks and shelves full of the strange and the exotic. Off to one side, there was a comfortable study area where Murdoch found his master and guests.

Murdoch knew that only the most trusted of close friends would be allowed into this laboratory so he was intensely curious about these two guests. He had seen elves before and, of course, from his scholarly training he knew his emotions would be easily read by this one. Out of courtesy, he tried to compose himself, for strong human emotions were often painful to elves.

Under the circumstances, this was hard to do, for he noticed the other guest was sitting in the stone chair. This chair was specially constructed to support great weight and from the way the leather cushion was completely flattened by the body of this stranger, Murdoch surmised that it was indeed bearing great weight. That meant this person was probably not human. Most interesting.

His Master made curt introductions and Murdoch became aware that the one called Chiang was in some sort of trance. Murdoch leaned back in his chair, and copied his master and the elf by fishing a pipe from his boot and tobacco from a sleeve pocket and quietly packing his pipe while all three of them waited for the trance to end.

They smoked their long-stemmed pipes quietly, and the smoke from the elf's pipe blended in the air with the other two adding a flowery fragrance to the incense floating in the air. Chiang was simply sitting with his eyes closed murmuring something softly to himself.

The sound of the massive stone door to the laboratory lifting up into its recess in the ceiling startled Murdoch and he twisted around in time to see the cat who had come to be called Fang calmly walk into the secret room, absolutely sure of his welcome as only a cat can be. This one was the favorite of the

Master and was a striped cat, black and silver with pale blue eyes. Deathwind had grown tired of constantly having to interrupt his work to open a door for the cat so he had enchanted the cat with the ability to open doors by doing a silent meow in front of any door he wished to pass through. As the cat entered, the door slid gratingly back down into place. Fang walked over to the four seated "men" and sniffed each one, then jumped into Deathwind's lap and curled up to nap while they waited for Chiang to complete his trance.

At long last, Master Chiang opened his eyes. Murdoch was startled to see vertical slit pupils. This combined with a faint whisper of sulfurous smoke coming from Chiang's nostrils (when he had *not* been smoking a pipe) suddenly informed Murdoch of who, or rather what, Master Chiang was. Murdoch leaped out of his chair and made a very awkward, if heartfelt, bow of respect to the mysterious one in the golden robes. Master Chiang waved his hand in a gesture of acceptance and turned to Deathwind as a flustered Murdoch seated himself once more.

With just the barest twitch of humor at the corners of his mouth, Chiang spoke to Deathwind. "As you said, Sahm-el, he is a well trained scholar indeed." But then the faint trace of humor disappeared as he continued, "Alas, you were correct. I, too, see the return of the Outsiders, downstream in the River of Time."

Upon hearing this, Murdoch fumbled with his pipe in an effort to control himself. He was thinking, "I must be lit up like a fireworks display for the poor elf." Indeed, the elf was clenching his teeth as if in pain. Murdoch employed the three slow breaths of the Ritual of Calming, noting that both Deathwind and Master Chiang were fully aware of his reaction to this news.

A softer voice spoke on his other side. "It would appear that disaster approaches the World of the Three Suns once more, Sahm-el." It was an uncharacteristic insight for an elf and his voice was clearly lacking it usual merriment; understandable to Murdoch given the nature of this sudden crisis.

The Elf, whose name Murdoch now remembered was Sinueh, then asked the question that Murdoch did not have the nerve to ask. "How soon?"

Master Chiang looked at his longtime friend Sahm-el and said, "Ten to twenty?" Sahm-el nodded agreement.

Chiang turned to Sinueh and said, "Sometime in the next ten to twenty years. One cannot be precise at this time. But they are definitely coming back."

Murdoch leaned back in his chair, relaxing a bit. He had feared they were speaking of tomorrow or perhaps next week.

There was a moment of silence as the wizard absently stroked the cat sleeping in his lap. He and Sinueh and Master Chiang all seemed to be remembering the past, and it occurred to Murdoch that, given the natures of those present, he might be the only one here who had not actually lived through the first visit of the Outsiders.

The moment of silence was broken by a rumble from Master Chiang that sounded almost like a growl. (The cat opened one eye, then resumed his nap.) "It must not happen again!" Murdoch caught another whiff of sulfurous smoke.

Sinueh's musical voice sounded odd in contrast. "Do you think such great things can actually be prevented? My people do not believe so. One can alter the passage of a single drop of water in the River of Time, but one cannot change the river. We elves have always known the wisdom of drifting with the current instead of contending with it. This event is too great for even humans to alter. It is folly to think otherwise. You will spend your strength dashing blindly against a stone wall."

Chiang rumbled again, his voice sounding like thunder heard through distant mountain passes. "Nonsense! Nothing is impossible! We may be few and weak compared to these monsters with their strange ships and infernal machines, but we can still oppose them. Even a small amount of power can be effective if used with determination and subtlety. Only an elf would crawl away and hide in such circumstances."

Murdoch had heard of the Wrath of Elves, but he had never actually seen an elf who was angry. Sinueh's face became hard, and his pale gray eyes took on the aspect of granite. With a toss of his head, he flipped his long fair hair back, and his voice now had steel in it as he answered Master Chiang. "Oh Great One, speak not of Elves in this manner. Even you are not invulnerable to our war arrows. I would remind you that Elven magic is unique and just as effective on the great as the small."

The cat woke up and jumped down from Sahm-el's lap, and without pausing for his usual stretching routine, scampered off to one of the dark corners of the laboratory. Murdoch thought it quite sensible of him.

Sinueh continued, turning to Sahm-el, "What would you do? Lead your race in a futile war that brings about their utter destruction? Only a human would do such a thing. You with your fly-speck short lifespans and storms of overpowering emotions. How can you throw away the precious gift of life so wantonly? T'would be far better to follow us and simply go into hiding and wait until this ugliness passes from the scene."

Sahm-el held up his hand in the finger-talk gesture for a parley and waited quietly while Sinueh and Chiang glared at each other. When he spoke, it was in the soft and gentle tones that Murdoch knew could be most persuasive. "Sir elf, all present know the high regard that Elves have for Beauty. Moreover, we understand that Beauty and Truth are but two sides of the same statue. There is much truth in your words.

"I am loath to face this test. I have learned the wisdom of inaction and the dangers of intervention into great events. Twice, I have assisted in the overthrow of evil kings only to see even worse creatures take their place. I bear some responsibility for the crimes of these successors, for my actions led them to power. Certainly we have the ability to protect those most dear to us and stand aside until that point is reached downstream in the River of Time where these Outsiders can no longer threaten us. It is a great temptation.

"And yet, how many could we thus save in this way? And what of all those who do not have the ability to cross the timelines to safety? Do we let their precious gift of life simply cease? I fear we cannot do so. Even though it may be folly, we must engage in this folly or lose that which is most valuable to us. It is a mater of integrity. Most humans do not have the luxury of the long view enjoyed by Elves and others. (Here, his glance flicked to Master Chiang.) They must spend their brief fiery lives as best they can. Sagesse Oblige! Those of us who are able have an obligation to help them do this."

It was the longest speech Murdoch had ever heard his master speak. Tension did seem to have eased a bit in the room because of it.

Sahm-el continued, "We have a saying among our people. It is: 'No man has the right to tell another man what to do.' Elves must follow their own path, and no-one can gainsay them this right. But the same is true for us. We must pursue this folly, even though the Elven Council may not understand it. We will risk making things worse in order to hope to make them better."

"Good!" came from Master Chiang, a bit louder than he intended, for both Sinueh and Murdoch winced at the noise.

When the elf spoke again, it was in a sad and quiet voice. "And what is it that you think you can do?"

Sahm-el leaned back in his chair, absently stroking his beard and was silent for a long moment before answering. Murdoch noticed that neither Master Chiang nor Sinueh interrupted his thought, but rather both waited quietly for him to speak. Murdoch was reminded of something from an old ballad. It was a line that said, "Only true friends can sit in silence and wait upon each other's thoughts."

Sahm-el smiled a wintry smile and admitted, "I do not know. It may well be too great an event for us to alter. We can only search for a way."

The elf made the finger-talk gesture of acquiescence, indicating all was in the hands of fate and he would travel the river wherever the current took him. Sahm-el and Master Chiang nodded in agreement.

Sinueh stood up. "I must fly to Lundunegal and convene the Elven Council. This matter affects the entire world."

Sahm-el stood up and gripped his hand. "Agreed. We shall

remain here. Friend Murdoch will begin some research in the library." Murdoch warmed at the term "friend," and thought he was probably blushing.

"And the Mighty Deathwind and I will consult our art and see if some suggestion does not present itself," rumbled Master Chiang. Murdoch noticed that Chiang gave the briefest of winks when he referred to "The Mighty Deathwind."

Sahm-el smiled and nodded. Murdoch felt the cat rub against his leg, unconcerned about the weighty events of their discussion.

Two

"Thrust power only upon those who do not seek it, for the seeking of power is a sure sign of being unworthy of it."

—The Chronicles of Deathwind, Volume IX.

Several thousand leagues to the northwest of the valley of Xanadu lies the Great Rift Continent, scarred by the gargantuan cut down its middle. Seen from afar one might think some unbelievable giant had slashed the land with some god-like sword. Such an image would not be far from the truth.

A high mountain range divides the continent down the middle, just to the east of the Rift. A fast and deep river, known as the Dire River runs from this mountain range to the eastern seacoast. This river separates the two countries of Ruritania and Telluria. The Dire River is spanned by a bridge at only one point, that is the walled city of Caprice, capital of Telluria.

The Palace of Telluria rests upon a small island created by a loop of the Dire River at Caprice. It is thus protected not only from attack without but also from attack from within the city. Revolts have been common in the long and bloody history of Caprice.

At the moment, a few hours before dawn and the rising of the first of the three suns, the Palace was quiet. King Elric the Dark, whom some have called in whispers Elric the Nasty or

Elric the Cursed, was sleeping in his private chamber with one of the harem girls.

By the side of his bed, on a special stand, there was the black DemonSword that had brought him to power. It was a heavy bladed broadsword that often looked out of place in these days of the cup-hilt rapier and slender dagger, yet Elric carried it everywhere (even into the privy) and it had warned him and saved his life on many occasions. The sword was well known to be enchanted and the Sorcery Guild had quietly passed the word among their friends that the black metal indicated it actually contained a living being of some kind. Hence the name DemonSword.

It was about to prove its worth to Elric once again. As he slumbered in the arms of the naked girl, three black shadows appeared to rise up, right out of the floor of his chamber. Each of these black shadows suddenly thickened and took on the form of men with swords.

As the shadowy assassins began to move toward the King's bed, there was a piercing shriek from the DemonSword. Elric rolled over in the bed, thrusting one hand free of the furs.

The black-bladed sword rose into the air, of its own accord and flashed to his hand, in time for him to make a back-hand parry at the first of the assassins to reach him. The DemonSword twisted in Elric's hand bending into a curve around the other blade and drank the life of the assassin.

The second man was on the opposite side of the bed, leaning across it to swing at him over the huddled and crying harem girl. Elric swung the sword again, amazingly light for its size, and struck the second man, drinking his life from him and then, before Elric could prevent it, striking at the girl like a serpent and taking her life too. By now the DemonSword was humming as if for sheer pleasure at the death it was causing.

King Elric rolled off the bed, having no trouble keeping the sword in his hand, for it seemed to cling to him, and faced the third assassin. One swing and the DemonSword drank that life as well. The killings of all three assassins, and the girl, had taken but a few seconds, and the only sound that lingered in the room was the humming of the sword.

King Elric felt a chill and suddenly realized he was standing naked in his bedchamber, bathed in sweat. He glanced quickly around the room, but the gradually quieting sword told him there were no more enemies present. He waited until the sword stopped humming, then replaced it in its scabbard. He pulled a dressing gown on and belted the sword's scabbard around his middle. Then stepping over one of the bodies, he rang the bellcord.

The night servant came in, sleepily carrying a lantern, and stood speechless at the sight of bodies and blood and weapons in the King's bedchamber. Elric looked at the gaping old man and snarled, "Send for my Chamberlain, my Spymaster, and some servants to clean up this mess. I shall require other chambers for the rest of the night.

The servant became aware that his mouth was still hanging open. He closed it with a gulp and quickly bowed acknowledgment of the orders and hurried from the room that was taking on the stench of death.

Elric was amused to hear the castle alarm sounded and the rush of booted feet and shouts that accompanied it. *Fools! Raise the alarm after the assassins have gotten in and to my very own bedchamber*, he thought to himself. *I shall make sure someone pays for this.* He suddenly felt a wave of shakes pass through him as reaction set in from the attempt on his life.

Calming himself with an act of will, King Elric reminded himself that this was no time to show weakness. In sooth, as he looked at the bodies of three dead assassins, he even smiled a little. *This will make a pretty lesson,* he thought. *They will have been of very high rank in the Assassins Guild, and I have killed them all, even after they gained admittance to my chamber. This should make the fees of assassins rise.* Cheered by the thought, King Elric left the chamber to speak with his lackeys and advisors. He gave no thought at all to the dead harem girl.

In a very few minutes, the outer chamber was filled with

guards and servants, all striving to look efficient and capable and surrounding him with concern that he knew they wore like masks. He despised them all, and they held him in dread. Both facts were a source of satisfaction to Elric.

By the mid-morning meeting of the Privy Council, much had been done. Bodies were examined and then disposed of, servants and guards punished for their laxity, and the chamber cleansed. The Royal Wizard, whose magic shields were supposed to prevent exactly the kind of intrusion that had taken place, was experiencing new levels of pain in the torture chamber.

The Privy Council Chamber was located high in one of the round towers of the Palace. It was a simple circular chamber with a large stone table, round in shape. Six heavy wooden chairs with high backs were arranged around the table. Four were occupied.

Just to the right of the ornate chair the King would use when he arrived, there sat the King's Spymaster, an attractive dark-haired woman in a burgundy gown. She had high cheekbones and very pale skin and would have been a stunning beauty were it not for the cold steel of her gaze. Her name was Miriam and she wore the mantle of power with the ease of long practice and the firm belief that it was her right to decide life or death for other people.

To the right of Miriam, sat General Montrose, heavy set, dressed in fancy chain mail in the green and gold colors of the royal house of Telluria. Montrose was Commander of the Legions. He habitually chewed on one end of his long brown mustache. The whisperers at Court said that Montrose was almost as intelligent as the horse he rode.

The chair to General Montrose's right was empty. Sitting directly across the table from the King, this place belonged to the Royal Wizard and Guildmaster of the Wizard's Guild, Master Fairchilde. Master Fairchilde would not be participating in this meeting as he was otherwise engaged in the Chamber of Chastisement for allowing assassins entry into the Palace. His life was safe, of course, since Elric the Dark was not so foolish as to waste something as valuable as a wizard.

The next chair was also empty, but would soon be filled by the Earl of Lancaster, representing the noble families of Telluria, at least those noble families who were in favor with King Elric.

To the immediate left of the King's chair, there sat the Royal Chamberlain, a gray-haired man dressed in very rich robes trimmed in rare furs. His name was Pollux and he concealed a shrewd mind and thirst for power behind a simple face. Throughout his career, he had often been underestimated by rivals, to their eventual sorrow.

If an independent observer had somehow managed to penetrate the layer upon layer of magic shields and deadly traps that surrounded this chamber, and furthermore had the empathic gift to read beneath the surface of things, such an observer would instantly be aware that the mood in this chamber was not one of friendly camaraderie, but rather one of alert tension. The observer might be reminded of the skittish tension and violence held barely in check when two great lions meet in the forest, watching each other warily, muscles tight and ready to pounce. In sooth, King Elric's Privy Council had much in common with a group of lions.

There was a sudden blare of trumpets and the Privy Chamber door was thrust open by a guard. Three guards with drawn weapons entered the room and quickly sent their gaze flicking over the occupants. Then they stood back and Elric entered, as always, wearing the black sword. He was followed by a thin, almost waspish looking man dressed in the yellow doublet that he always affected. This was the Earl of Lancaster. He wore yellow, the color of mourning, in memory of his dead wife. He had worn it ever since the night he had strangled her in her bed.

The corner of Elric's mouth twitched in private mirth as he strode into the room and signaled the guards to leave. He seated himself and in an apologetic tone said dryly, "The fools insist on accompanying me everywhere now that the threat is past. I should think I made it plain last night that I do not really need guards." He stroked the haft of the black sword and all present heard it hum in response.

Naturally all had risen and bowed when he entered the room, and he gestured for them to be seated with a lazy wave of his hand. The Earl of Lancaster took his place with the others and they all looked expectantly at Elric.

He turned to his Spymaster and said curtly, "Report!"

Miriam met his gaze with a calm and icy one of her own, then started speaking in the soft low voice that had proved most effective in dealing with men. "Before reporting to the Chamber of Chastisement, Master Fairchilde cast some knowledge spells in an attempt to learn who backed this play. He learned nothing. He told me he encountered the kind of wall of fog that usually indicates one of the Temples is involved and preventing knowledge of this deed from being learned."

She went on, patiently explaining as if to a child. "You will recall that if one of the Temples gave its blessing to this venture, knowledge of it would be sealed under the Great Covenant among the various Temples whereby they have agreed not to tell each others secrets. If this be the case here, then knowledge of this deed cannot be gained through magic."

Elric nodded as if he had expected this. He was amused at her patronizing tone, knowing full well that it was not directed at him but at the other men at the table, whom Miriam considered to be her inferiors. Elric was quite certain that Miriam did not think so of him. She stood in mortal terror of him, for good reason.

Miriam continued, "We have confirmed this through prayers of intercession at both the Temple of Baalsha and the Temple of Vhulchurus. If one of the Temples is involved, it would most likely be the Temple of Leto with their archaic beliefs in chivalry and honor."

The King nodded again, indicating that he had already reached the same conclusion. Miriam allowed to show the briefest of smiles, then continued, "Without the aid of magic, more mundane methods have been employed. The reports of spies, informants and the logic of the situation suggests House

Lyestehr is behind this attempt."

Again the King's mouth twitched, indicating confirmation of his own thoughts. However, to make the point, he asked, "Why Lyestehr?"

Miriam ticked points off on the tips of slender fingers as she spoke, "First, Lyestehr is well known to be an enemy of your Majesty, since you banished his family from Caprice.

"Second, the Earl of Lyestehr has a major sorcerer in his household in his first born son, Rhastus. This Master Rhastus is thought to have achieved the fifth or sixth Circle of Mastery. If so, he would be fully capable of the dimensional magic that Fairchilde says was required to transport assassins into the Palace and through the barriers that Fairchilde had created.

"Third, House of Lyestehr is known to be members of the Temple of Leto and to follow the ridiculous code of conduct espoused by Leto.

"They are certainly the driving force behind this attempt on your life. In addition, there are certain to be a scattering of underlings, merchants and minor houses lending support to House Lyestehr in this matter. We know some of these and can easily ferret out the rest with judicious use of the Chamber of Chastisement. House Lyestehr is the head of this particular monster and I would recommend a strike directly at the Earl."

Elric thought for a moment, pleased to have been advised to do the very thing he had been considering for a very long time. Then he turned to the Earl of Lancaster. "How would the other Noble Houses react to the House of Lyestehr being brought down?"

Lancaster stroked the thin black line of a mustache that adorned his upper lip and paused only for the briefest moment. This was a chance to get rid of a powerful and hated rival. "The Earl of Lyestehr is popular with a few of the minor Ducal Houses, like the DeGrasses and the Mayerlings. But he is more feared for his wealth and power then liked by the significant nobility. There would be no serious objections."

Elric directed his gaze at the corpulent general. "And what of Lyestehr Keep, can it be taken?"

Even though General Montrose was reputed to be slow of thought, he was not that slow. He had been contemplating Lyestehr Keep ever since the name of the Earl had been mentioned. He knew his monarch well and thus was prepared when asked the inevitable question.

"My Liege, any castle can be taken if enough force is used. Lyestehr Keep is strong, well built and well defended. In an ordinary battle it would require close to two full legions to breach the walls and put it to the torch. But of course, this would not be an ordinary battle. There is the sorcerer Rhastus. He could defend Lyestehr Keep by himself against our army.

The King nodded, "Agreed. But what if the sorcerer is removed? Without magic defenses, could it be taken by ordinary assault?"

"Given that, I can take it with two full legions; one if I have the assistance of our own wizard." The general seemed perfectly confident.

Elric thought for a moment and then said, "I believe both conditions can be met. Miriam, you will see to the removal of the sorcerer. General, prepare your legion to march on Lyestehr Keep. I am certain that our Master Fairchilde will be eager to prove his worth to us with this little task." Elric grinned his wolfish grin. Power was so enjoyable when it was used.

Elric's movement to adjourn was interrupted by the chamberlain, Pollux, who had been silently weaving his own little web of intrigue while he listened to the others. "My Liege. Might this be a rare opportunity to haul in some of the little fish along with the big one in the net?" He smiled blandly.

Elric sat back in his chair. "I dare say. Could it be that you have someone in mind?"

Pollux made a deprecating gesture. "Only that there have been a lot of little gnats buzzing about us recently, complaining and criticizing your Majesty's wise policies. Why not be rid of them all? If they were not directly involved in this plot, surely many of them would at least be sympathetic to it. It is an opportune time to order mass arrests."

Elric laughed aloud. "'Tis a droll idea, good Pollux. We

could get some real profit out of this sorry business. Naturally all property could be confiscated and held forfeit to the Crown."

He warned to the subject. "There are quite a few merchants and minor households that have been a positive pain to me recently. Remember that petition to do away with slavery? We also had a letter from some friends of Elves protesting the cutting of trees in the Faery Wood. As if I could build my navy without logs. Yes...a capital idea."

So saying, Elric the Dark slapped his hand on the table, indicating the meeting was at an end, and rose to leave. The others hurried to follow, each composing a private list of old slights, insults, and imagined injuries that had lain stored in memory for a very long time, awaiting just such an occasion.

Three

"The ultimate poison, Bai Hara Chi, also known as WizardBane, was developed during the Sorcery Wars to counter the effects of certain magic rings. It so thoroughly destroys the very mind pattern and personality of the victim, that it meets the major challenge in assassinating a wizard, that of insuring that the killed wizard remains dead."

—Nigel's Apothecary, Sourcebook For Alchemists.

Some two days march north of the city of Caprice, there stood the castle of the Earl of Lyestehr, known as Lyestehr Keep. It was a large and well built castle with moat, formidable gatehouse, five major towers, a citadel, and the Manor house. Lyestehr Keep had both magical and mundane defenses.

The heart of the magical defenses was the Sorcerer of the Fifth Circle, Master Rhastus, who was also the eldest son of the Earl. On this night, Master Rhastus was alone in his laboratory, located in the East Tower. Like all sorcerers above the Third Circle, Master Rhastus had an ageless look that comes only with at least partial mastery of the River of Time. Were he not a sorcerer, one would think he was in his late thirties, with fair complexion, blond hair, and a narrow face that hinted at an elf ancestor somewhere.

At the moment, Master Rhastus was taking great care in going over the layer upon layer of magic shields he had placed around Lyestehr Keep, using his seeing crystal to go over them, inch by inch to insure there were no accidental gaps whereby an enemy might gain entrance to the castle.

Master Rhastus well knew that this was the most elementary precaution that could be taken, and defenses of greater subtlety were required to really make the castle safe. He, himself, had made use of crossing the dimensional plane in order to bypass exactly the same kind of shields at the Palace in Caprice, in order to place in position the assassins his father had hired.

Therefore, layered underneath this outermost shell of protection came layer after layer of magic shields. Some were designed to detect the presence of magical energy, others to give alarm at any disturbance of the dimensional plane, still others were designed to reflect back bursts of magic, returning them to the caster. Yet still others were designed to take an approaching magic spell and consume it, adding that energy to the castle's defenses and thus gaining strength by the very attack.

All this, Master Rhastus carefully wove together into one intricate sphere enclosing Lyestehr Keep. Since the news had reached them that the assassination attempt on Elric the Nasty had failed, he and his father, the Earl, had agreed that sooner or later Elric would strike at House Lyestehr. Thus the castle was being prepared for siege.

Upon satisfying himself that his preparations were as complete as he could make them, Master Rhastus leaned back in his chair and sipped a cup of lukewarm tea. He would report to his father and then have servants make up a bed in the laboratory. It was, by far, the safest place for him to be, and since the magic protection he had just created for his family would unravel upon his death, protecting his own life was of prime importance. He would be living in his laboratory until the crisis passed.

As he began to finally relax from the strain of the last few days, knowing full well that his family's safety was in his hands and he had prepared for any threat, Master Rhastus let his eyes drift lazily around the laboratory. He was quietly going over one more time all of his precautions, trying to find any overlooked detail when something caught his attention.

At first he could not quite identify what it was other than a vague feeling of having noticed some small thing that seemed to cry for his attention. He ran his gaze around the brightly lit laboratory again, trying to rediscover whatever it was. All seemed normal, nothing was out of place. There were the usual counters and cabinets, work tables and instruments, chests of various things and chairs to use at various places in the laboratory.

Suddenly Master Rhastus stiffened. The chairs. Something about the chairs. He looked around again. He clearly saw three different chairs, all in normal positions at different tables. What was it? Something about the chairs.

Then, with a cold chill, Rhastus realized what it was, and that it might already be too late. His laboratory only had three chairs. If he could see all three, then he was sitting in a fourth chair that he had never placed in this most protected sanctuary of his life.

Master Rhastus tried to throw himself immediately out of the mysterious chair and knew a moment of despair as he felt the sting of the poison needle in his back, clearly originating from the chair. As the cold blackness closed around him his last thoughts were of his family. He ended his time in this reality with the fading thought, "Father! I am sorry!"

It was old Grampus who found the body.

Grampus had once been steward to House Lyestehr, but age had now rounded his shoulders and lengthened his beard. The Earl would have retired him long ago, but Grampus insisted on his right to earn his keep. His one duty was to go about the castle thrice daily, and tend the thirty-seven different fireplaces, feeding them and banking the coals each evening.

He shuffled about the castle, painfully climbing stone steps with an iron fireplace poker that he used as a walking stick. Grampus was one of the very few people that could pass the wards to Master Rhastus's laboratory.

On this night, when he slowly made his way toward the fireplace in the Sorcerer's laboratory, he became aware of something amiss. Looking about, he noticed what he thought at first was a pile of rags on the floor in front of the desk. Coming closer, he saw that it was a body, hideously transformed.

Grampus had sufficient wits to know not to touch the thing and instead leaned closer to peer at it. The body looked like Master Rhastus but it was as black as volcanic glass all over. The face was twisted into a rictus grin. He prodded it with his poker and found it was hard as rock.

Grampus hissed in both fright and surprise and backed away. He started toward the bellcord to raise the alarm but then bethought himself and stayed his action. This was not what one would call a natural death. Whoever had caused it might still be within the castle.

He quickly looked around the room, but could see nothing amiss, other than the thing on the floor. then he turned and hurried from the room, bearing evil tidings indeed to the head of the family he had served for so long.

The youngest member of the Lyestehr Family was the daughter Twila, who was awakened by one of her handmaids and told she was needed. It was something that happened rather frequently to Twila and she thought one of the servants must have come down with a fever as she quickly dressed in her white wool robe and picked up the leather shoulder bag that a Healer always carried.

It was only when she was told to go to the laboratory of her brother that Twila began to realize something might be really serious. She moved quickly through the long passages and down spiral staircases, her slender form and long blonde hair a familiar sight to the night staff and guards.

This night, however, Twila noticed the castle was astir. It

looked like the Blademaster, Oscar Wyndham had ordered some king of search. Men were going about with torches and drawn swords and their was an air of tension. Twila had spent the last few days aiding families on some of the outlying farms and had returned home tired and gone straight to her chamber. It was obvious to her that important events of some kind were occurring.

She climbed the spiral stone stairs of the East Tower, with her handmaid going before and carrying the lantern. By now, she was not surprised to see her father, the Earl, in the open doorway to the laboratory, but the presence of her mother and two older sisters, along with a host of guards and servants, was extraordinary.

Twila's mother and both her sisters were crying and the look on her father's face could only be described as grim. Her worst fears were confirmed when her father said, "Something has happened to Rhastus. See if there is anything you can do."

Twila hurried past them and entered the laboratory to find Oscar Wyndham and several guards standing over a pile of rags. She was about to ask Oscar to show her Rhastus when she realized the pile of rags was what was left of her brother.

The men stood back quietly while she examined the body, being careful not to touch it. Naturally, her first thought was of some kind of mishap with the powerful forces of magic. It was a hazard she and Rhastus had often discussed and he had repeatedly assured her that he took elaborate precautions against that very thing.

Closer examination revealed the strained facial muscles, the glossy black skin, and a tentative probe with a pair of tongs that were specially designed for handling dangerous magic, revealed the solid rock like composition of the body. Twila was both Healer and Alchemist and she knew what this meant. It could not possibly be worse.

With tears on her cheeks, Twila stood up and backed away from the body and announced, "He bears all the signs of Bai Hara Chi, a most powerful assassins poison. I know of nothing that can be done. He is gone."

There was a tangible wave of revulsion that swept through the crowd at that announcement, although Oscar Wyndham did not seem to be surprised. The Earl gritted his teeth and nodded as though he too had guessed the same answer. Lady Lyestehr sobbed and asked about the use of magic restoratives or possibly the intervention of the Church since it was well known that death need not be permanent to one of resources.

Twila could only wordlessly shake her head, knowing that no such remedy could have any affect on her dear brother. Finally the Earl explained to Lady Lyestehr and the rest of those present the nature of this evil substance and that there was no known remedy. He then began issuing orders.

The body was to be cremated on the spot since it was dangerous to even touch such a body. Furniture would be moved, and a funeral service conducted right there, in the morning. Meanwhile, the laboratory was to be sealed.

Oscar Wyndham, as Blademaster, commanded the castle garrison. Without needing to consult the Earl, he ordered the sentries be doubled on the battlements and one third of the garrison to stand at ready for the rest of the night.

Twila turned to leave this sorry place and then turned back again, looking once more at the body on the floor in front of the table. She was struck with the thought that something was out of place in the room. She thought for a moment, but could not quite identify what it was. Then she returned to her sleeping chamber for a night of tears on her pillow for her lost brother.

Twila was awakened just before dawn by the castle alarm. She could hear men shouting and the roar of explosions as she hastily donned a robe and went to her window. Twila's sleeping chamber was on the fifth level of the Manor and thus high enough to safely have a narrow window that overlooked most of the castle. However, even this window was protected by shutters and an ornate iron grate.

Upon opening the shutters, Twila discovered the Castle under full scale attack. It was hard to see by torchlight, but there were a great many armed men surrounding the portions of the castle that she could see. There was a loud clunk as one of the catapults was fired, sending a ball of flame out over the curtain wall to land amidst what looked like at least several hundred soldiers revealed by its burning light.

Twila closed and barred the shutters to her window, just in time to hear what must have been an arrow thud against the stone wall outside, the shot attracted by the light of the open window.

Then following her training, Twila exchanged her white wool robe for a suit of hunting leathers, complete with a small dagger tucked in one soft boot. She folded her robe and carefully packed it in her shoulder bag and filled the small water flask from the standing pitcher. Then shouldering her bag she left her sleeping chamber to join the rest of her family.

Twila's father and Oscar Wyndham had conducted drills to teach everyone what must be done in this kind of emergency. Lyestehr Keep had not come under siege for over one hundred years and very few of the people in it had actually been in a battle before this night. Certainly, Twila had never experienced such and she was amazed at the great din of noise as she hurried through the Manor to the Salon. It sounded like the voices of everyone she had ever met, all moaning and yelling themselves hoarse. Mixed in were the loud clanks of catapults and the roars of great fires.

When she arrived at the Salon, Twila found her mother there along with a small group of Oscar Wyndham's very best men who had been ordered to serve as bodyguards for the family. Her sisters had not yet arrived. Twila rushed to her mother and gave her a hug. Lady Lyestehr correctly interpreted the unspoken question in Twila's eyes and said, "Your father has donned his armor and joined Oscar on the battlements. He wishes us to remain here for the time being.

"But who...? Why are we being attacked?"

"Your father could no longer tolerate the injustices of

Elric, and for the sake of the people made an attempt on him. It failed, we know not how. Now the King strikes back."

Twila closed her eyes in pain as she digested this. She had complete faith in her father's judgment and well understood the justice of his cause. Yet, the wrath of Elric the Dark knew no limits and had now been brought down on her family. The death of her brother was no longer a mystery.

She was then struck with a new thought and addressed her mother once more. "There will be men injured. I will be needed on the battlements."

"Your father was very firm about this and wishes you to remain safely inside. He will be very angry."

"Mother, these are our people. Surely you see that I must help. I will take one of Oscar's warriors with me to guard my safety, but I must help!"

Fear warred with pride in Lady Lyestehr as she looked upon her youngest daughter. In all honor, there was no real answer she could give, so she nodded wordlessly.

Twila looked around at the bodyguards. She really did not know any of them. Selecting one at random she announced, "You will accompany me and do what you may to guard my person." Then turned to the door, followed by the guard.

Four

"Courage is not the absence of fear.
It is proceeding in spite of the fear."

—The Decree of Salamanca,
Sacred Text for the Temple of Leto.

Twila paid no attention to her bodyguard beyond noticing that he bore a cup-hilt rapier and was dressed in leather rather than chain mail. She knew this indicated he must be one of Oscar's prize pupils for only these were trained in the delicate and subtle rapier.

Twila's first reaction to seeing a battle close-up was to get violently sick. As she stepped out on the little porch at the main entrance to the Manor, she saw one of her father's soldiers burning to death as he fell from a high tower. She found death by violence to be quite different from death by illness or accident and she felt herself get nauseous and had to lean over the edge of the porch to vomit. Out here in the courtyard, there was a stench of blood and excrement that was not noticeable inside yet. When added to the head pounding roar of noise it made the place a nightmare.

Her bodyguard was an experienced warrior and while he waited for the young mistress to regain control of herself he looked at the same scene with a warrior's eye. It was immediately apparent to him that their situation was rapidly growing serious.

So long as Master Rhastus had been available to add his sorcery to the strength of the castle walls, Lyestehr Keep could have withstood virtually any siege. With the sorcerer dead, however, it became a matter of numbers. Oscar had planned the defenses based on a factor of five, that is, an enemy would have to have at least five times the number of the castle's defenders in order to take it. It was thought extremely unlikely that an army that size would ever be brought against Lyestehr Keep.

However, it was easily observed that all sides of the castle were engaged by attackers and in sufficient numbers so that it would be imprudent to take defenders from one wall section and shift them to another. If the attacking force had enough additional men in reserve to create an extra push at one section of wall, they may well be able to breach the castle defenses and come pouring in. Twila's bodyguard did some swift computations in his mind and came to the disturbing conclusion that they might be facing nearly an entire legion. If so, they were in trouble.

Twila recovered herself and tried to conceal her embarrassment behind a stoicism she did not feel. The bodyguard must think her an awful fool for pompously insisting on helping in the battle and then vomiting at her first sight of it. She gritted her teeth and started down the steps to the courtyard. Her guard silently followed.

As soldiers of the garrison were wounded or killed, they were being unceremoniously tossed off the wall walk into the courtyard below to quickly make room for more fighters to take their place. There was a growing pile of dead and dying men and a spreading pool of blood. Twila made her way across the courtyard to the nearest of these men, stepping carefully to try to keep from getting blood on her soft leather boots.

The first man she came to was lying in a pool of blood with a crossbow bolt protruding from his belly. His glassy stare at nothing proclaimed him clearly dead even in the flickering torchlight. Twila felt nauseous again but forced herself to go on.

The light was too dim for her to see the second man clearly, so she got into her shoulder bag, rummaging for her lantern. It had been a gift from Rhastus and was very special. He had taken one of the ordinary shuttered lanterns and replaced the wick and oil with enchantment so that when she opened the lantern, bright sunlight flowed forth, either in a beam or all around to light an entire room, depending on which of the shutters were opened.

Twila started to open the lantern full, to light up the entire courtyard when the bodyguard stopped her and suggested she use the smallest bit of light possible. Recalling the arrow shot at her window, Twila felt foolish and complied. The finger of light showed the man to have a broken arm, with bones protruding from his flesh. He was clammy to the touch and breathing very shallowly, and his forehead was cool to her touch. Twila had seen this condition before and went right to work on him, shutting out the surrounding horror of the battle, while sweat dropped from her forehead.

Her bodyguard picked up one of the discarded round shields from the fallen men-at-arms and sheltered her with it. He kept his eyes roving around in all directions observing the progress of the battle. The steady clank of the catapults was followed by balls of fire that arced outward over the walls. These were met by smaller bits of fire coming into the castle in the form of fire arrows. Some of them were landing quite close to them, and he noticed the Young Mistress was quite aware of them, but did not falter in her ministrations to the soldier. She gritted her teeth and kept her attention on his wounds, even when a fire arrow landed next to her, hissing in the pool of blood. By now, Twila's boots and leggings were covered with red stains from the dead and dying, but she no longer cared about such things.

Twila was also too busy to notice a change in the tenor of the battle, but her bodyguard saw Oscar signal with a torch, and soldiers leaving their stations on the battlements of the inner bailey and rushing down the ramps and into the courtyard. The soldiers formed a shield-wall that ran from the corner of the Bailey Tower diagonally across the courtyard to the corner of the Manor. He and the girl were a few meters in front of this line as she knelt bandaging the soldier.

Oscar came running up and yelled as he went past them. "Get her to the safe-room in the citadel! They are about to breach the wall!" He then took command of the line and formed them into a phalanx as a rear guard while everyone who could retreated into the large corner tower that was the last refuge in the event the castle should be taken.

Twila heard the bodyguard tell her they must leave, but ignored him, shining her lantern at the next body on the ground. Suddenly Twila felt herself lifted off the ground and slung over his shoulder, while he dropped the shield he had been holding and grabbed up her shoulder bag with his free hand. She was barely able to keep hold of her little lantern as he carried her bodily through the formation of men and up the narrow stairs into the corner tower, just as the outer wall was breached.

As the bodyguard paused to slam the iron door, still carrying Twila over his shoulder, the last view Twila had of the courtyard was of Oscar Wyndham being struck by a battle ax in the shoulder and falling. Then the door closed and the bolts were thrown and she was carried further into the tower.

Twila was furious and started yelling at the big brute while kicking vigorously, to no avail. He carried her down two flights of stairs and through an iron doorway into the safe-room in the basement of the tower. Twila never saw her father, the Earl of Lyestehr fall, cleaved by a great sword, on the battlements, as the Kings legionaries came over the wall from scaling ladders.

The rear guard phalanx delayed the Royal Legionaries and slowly, step-by-step backed up until they formed a final formation at the base of the Citadel. There most of them died. Soon Twila heard banging on the iron door as the Royal Forces tried to batter their way into the safe-room.

Once inside the safe-room, the bodyguard had put her down and closed a second heavy iron door, barring it by shooting four bolts home. Events had moved too fast for Twila and she was feeling a bit befuddled. But she had enough wits about her to know they were the only people in the safe-room, however, and thus she rushed to the door and began trying to remove the heavy bolts to open it again.

"By the Gods girl! What are ye doing?"

"What of the others? We cannot shut them out! This is the only means of escape! Where is my mother? My sisters? My father? What about all the servants…?"

He gently but firmly pulled her from the door, making sure it was still secure. "Lass, it is too late. There are no others. They are all gone. You and I are the only ones who have a chance to escape from here. Elric has turned it into a place of death."

Twila did not want to believe him. Out of nearly nine hundred people, she did not want to believe only two were left, in such a short amount of time. Her parents, her sisters, servants and friends, all gone. It was too much.

Suddenly there was a pounding on the door. "Open in the name of the King!" Immediately a rhythmic battering began on this door. Twila looked about wildly for some miracle. The battering continued.

Her bodyguard took her by the arm and pulled her towards the large fireplace across the room. The fire was burning and Twila had a fleeting thought of poor old Grampus, no doubt lying dead somewhere else in the castle. Then she helped the guard reach up inside the chimney and find the proper stone to press to open the escape tunnel.

The back of the fireplace slid to one side and both of them jumped through the fire and into the escape passage. The guard pressed another stone and the fireplace closed with a grating sound. They were momentarily in pitch darkness until Twila bethought herself of the lantern she was still clutching. Her brother's gift. Her dead brother's gift. She opened the lantern and they both started down the long secret tunnel, she going first with the bodyguard behind her listening for pursuit.

They paused only once in traveling that long dark tunnel. The guard halted her and pointed to a tiny chalk mark on the floor of the passage, small enough to be overlooked if one were not actively seeking it. He pressed another stone just above the mark, and the ceiling of the long tunnel behind them started lowering, closing off the passage.

The tunnel ceiling appeared to be made of one huge block of stone and Twila thought it must weigh hundreds of tons. When the tunnel was completely sealed, the guard gave a sigh and seemed to relax. "Now Lass, we are safe. They cannot follow us through that.

Twila looked at him in the bright lamplight and saw him for the first time as an individual. He was quite a bit older than her first impression of him, probably ten to fifteen years older than she. There were wrinkles around his eyes that hinted at laughter in other circumstances. He had short dark hair with a fine mustache and a small beard. He was carefully preening the green plume on his broad-brimmed hat.

"Sir, I should thank you. You have saved my life and I do not even know your name."

He gave her a roguish smile and said, "I am called Finnegin, and for the moment at least, I am at your service."

Twila took a long deep breath and began to really collect her wits for the first time since being awakened by the alarm. This stranger had earned her trust. It was time she faced the truth of the circumstances and began thinking about what must be done next. She would mourn later.

Five

"The mere appearance of power can actually increase a Prince's power, at least until a genuine crisis occurs."

—Drury's Primer for Princes.

Four days later, King Elric received reports from his minions in the Audience Chamber, in front of the whole court. He always enjoyed these little lessons and preferred have them be as public as possible.

First to report was General Montrose, who upon being announced by the Seneschal, tried to walk with great dignity and self-importance down the long open aisle between the various nobles and hangers-on who were attending court that day. He did not quite succeed and there were many small smiles hidden behind fans and whispered comments about the oft repeated jest of his being almost as smart as his horse.

Montrose was in court finery, festooned with medals and ribbons. He bowed and began his report to His Majesty.

"Your Majesty. I have the honor to report complete success in the punitive expedition to the traitor Lyestehr. Lyestehr Keep has been breached and put to fire and sword. The Earl, and all his family died in the engagement. What few survivors there were, have been brought to you in chains and are available to be sold into slavery. One of the Earl's chief lieutenants, his Blademaster, was severely wounded and now lies a prisoner in your Majesty's..."

He stopped abruptly as King Elric raised his hand, and waited for the King to speak.

"You are certain that Lyestehr and his whole family are dead? Have the bodies been found? None of them escaped?"

"We have brought you the head of the Earl of Lyestehr. There was a large fire and his wife and children were consumed in the flames. We were most careful Sire. No-one escaped."

"I want that confirmed. Master Fairchilde can add this task to his penance." Elric stroked the thin dark beard on his chin and paused, eyeing the court and finding himself pleased with the impression he was making. He then continued questioning his general, who was beginning to sweat through his fine clothes.

"And what of our losses, good general?"

Montrose swallowed hard and replied like a puppet whose string as just been jerked. "Alas, our losses were heavy. Lyestehr Keep put up a stiff fight, even without magical defenses. We lost 2,800 men in taking it."

Elric concealed a smile and thought to himself, "Now let them see the power of a king." Then he casually asked aloud, "And did you follow my plan of attack?"

Montrose dutifully replied, "As you ordered, the six hundred men of the Fourth Cohort led the attack against the walls. The Fourth Cohort was completely wiped out."

There were gasps and whispers rippling through the court. Elric paused to let the effect sink in. Everyone present knew the Fourth Cohort had been the heart of a growing dissatisfaction in the army of the King. Now he was rid of them.

Elric raised his voice and announced, "We cannot let such a noble unit of my army cease to exist. General, you shall raise a new Fourth Cohort, paid for out of my private funds. Furthermore, you will insure that the Fourth Cohort's traditions of bravery and loyalty shall be maintained and even surpassed in this new unit as it serves King and country."

There was dead silence in the Audience Chamber, and

Elric knew that with the elimination of Lyestehr and the removal of the troublesome army unit, he had just taught a lesson that would be well remembered.

Montrose was still standing at rigid attention before him. "Good General, you have done well. I am well served by you. You may now resume your duties." Montrose visibly relaxed and carefully backed away from His Majesty the required three steps before turning and hastily departing the chamber.

Elric smiled and the members of the court also seemed to relax. He let them enjoy it for a full minute, pretending to be distracted for the moment. Then tension in the chamber rose again, as he called for his Spymaster.

Miriam strode forth confidently, wearing a gown of deep purple trimmed in gold that set her dark good looks to best advantage. She paused and made a deep curtsy before His Majesty.

Elric signaled for her to rise and Miriam began her report in that low deep throaty voice that had such an affect on men. "Your most Gracious Majesty. Upon your order, I dispatched one of my assistants, a shapedancer, to Lyestehr Keep. He was ordered to remove the sorcerer Rhastus, who was also son of the Earl.

"Our agent managed to enter the Keep as a slab of meat on a grocery cart. He then took the form of a servant, a carpet, a guard, and finally a chair, in turn. He was thus able to dispatch the sorcerer in his own laboratory. He then took on the form of a guard, a sentry dog, and briefly a large stone fallen from the battlements before becoming one of our soldiers in order to make his escape. His mission was a complete success."

Elric grinned and asked mockingly, "And will this sorcerer remain dead? You know how troublesome they can be that way."

Miriam spoke in the same light tone, using the ritual thrice repetition. "My Lord, he is dead, dead, dead."

Elric clapped his hands in approval and said, "Well done! Reward our loyal agent."

Miriam bowed in acknowledgment, and at a hand signal

from the Seneschal, she withdrew.

Having accomplished all that he sought to accomplish, Elric suddenly rose from the throne, and griping the DemonSword with his left hand, he strode from the Audience Chamber, leaving his courtiers with much to think about.

Master Fairchilde, the King's Sorcerer, walked with somewhat shaky steps towards his laboratory. His trembling was, in part, from, the punishment he had just endured and in part from his rage at having to endure it from the master he was bound to. Sorcerers do not bear bondage well under any conditions, and this case was no exception. However, so long as Elric held his soul, Fairchilde must bend the knee and bow the head to him.

His laboratory, located in the octagonal tower within the Palace grounds, was undisturbed since his last visit. He carefully pressed certain stones in the wall that put to sleep certain guardians who were there to insure that. There was a bit of dust, since no cleaning had occurred in his absence. Ever since the time three servants had been turned to stone because they tried to sweep his floor, Master Fairchilde had done all of his own cleaning.

He set two brooms and a mop to doing just that, moving by themselves in widening circles around the floor while he had some tea and went through a ritual of calming in preparation for a spell.

This was to be a seeking spell and it was knowledge that was being sought. Thus, after connecting with the continuum field for power, Master Fairchilde began forming in his mind a personification concept of the Lyestehr family in order to insure they were no longer a threat to Elric. Then he hesitated momentarily and let that concept dissipate harmlessly.

Fairchilde started again, this time broadening and refining the concept to show him any threat to Elric. He enlarged the range of his spell to cover the entire world and added the activators "sense" and "designate", then went on to include principles from the Minor Arcana. These included "knowledge," "locus," and "personification." He poured a massive amount of power into the spell from the continuum field and then released it.

Visible only to him, a purple ring of light formed around him and began expanding in size until it disappeared through the walls of the tower. In his mind's eye, Fairchilde watched the circle continue to expand beyond the Palace, beyond the city, and eventually beyond the country until it swept throughout the world of Eridani. He then sat back and waited for results.

Images began to flash through his mind quickly, one following another. Some were faces he could identify, others were allegorical in nature. One image of windblown sleet and snow was particularly disturbing but he could not fathom its meaning. That image faded from this thoughts when it was followed by reptilian faces well-known in legend. Indeed, it was these images that caused Fairchilde to spend several hours pouring over old scrolls in the archives and sitting in brooding thought before he at last decided to report to the King.

Elric was having a most enjoyable afternoon and was not pleased to have it interrupted by the Mage's request for an audience. Through a special secret panel, he had been watching the painful executions of some of his minor enemies.

His Spymaster, Miriam, had been able to show a connection between the recent plot and virtually every individual who had incurred His Majesty's displeasure. They had been arrested in the hundreds.

The fate of each individual depended in part upon whether he might be of some use to Elric in the future, and in part, on Elric's mood of the moment. Having just watched the hands being burned off of a boy of sixteen who was then disemboweled and had his own liver forced into his mouth before he finally went into shock and died, Elric was feeling quite cheerful. Then the Page interrupted his pleasure.

Were it not that Elric knew Master Fairchilde would not dare call him at such a time without very good reason, the page delivering the message might have been at some risk from the King's wrath. However, as has been noted before, Elric was not a fool. He ordered that events in the Chamber of Chastisement be suspended until he could return to them, closed the observation panel and retired to his private chamber to hear what the Mage had to say.

The look on Master Fairchilde's face indicated that he had news of some import, as he entered the chamber. In sooth, were he not a major sorcerer, King Elric might have thought Fairchilde was actually afraid.

Fairchilde started speaking even before he sat down. "My Liege, I have seen something extraordinary…"

Elric raised his hand, as was his custom, and the Mage fell silent in mid-sentence. "First things first. What have you learned of House Lyestehr?"

Fairchilde hesitated, wrenching his thoughts away from what was filling his mind and turning now to the most trivial of matters. He swallowed hard and answered. "As you commanded, I have searched for survivors of House Lyestehr and can report that there are no remnants of that Ducal House to inconvenience Your Majesty."

Fairchilde thought it a small lie, not worth burdening this temperamental King with. He had, in fact, seen the face of the youngest daughter of Lyestehr, but she was known to be a healer and could pose no possible threat to anyone. Besides, he had been unable to locate her, due in part to interference from the Temple of Leto. Best not burden His Majesty with that fact. Fairchilde, himself, could order a quiet search for the girl without having to admit another failure.

He went on smoothly, "In the process of this search I discovered something much more important. My Liege, I do fear the Outsiders are going to return." He stopped, knowing full well that Elric would understand what he meant.

Elric felt a chill go through him. No wonder the mage was so upset. The Great Destroyers themselves, returning after a thousand years. This required careful thought. Both men sat in silence for a very long period.

Elric broke the silence with a flashing glance at Fairchilde and a totally unexpected smile. "Fairchilde, you are a fool! This is more to be welcomed than feared." And he laughed.

Fairchilde groped beneath the folds of his robe for the protective medallion that he always wore, thinking this king who held him in thrall had just gone mad.

Elric laughed again and seemed to read his mind. "Nay! I have not lost my wits. I do but see more in this than you." He paused to let the Mage try and collect himself, then continued. "Think man! Would you not agree that the Outsiders are the most powerful beings you or I or anyone have ever heard of? If even half the tales are true about them, they rival the Gods themselves in strength."

Fairchilde, still bewildered, nodded. "You speak truly, My Liege. I have reason to believe the tales are much more than half true and the power of the Outsiders knows no limit. That is why they are feared."

Elric chuckled and seemed more mad than ever, and Fairchilde wondered if the DemonSword was exerting influence over him. The King continued, "What if we could ally ourselves with the Outsiders, and agree to be their servants on this world?"

Fairchilde's mouth came open and no sound came forth. He was now certain the DemonSword must be controlling Elric. He tried to speak again. "This is madness! They destroy all! They will destroy us!"

Elric laughed again, a laugh that seemed too loud and yet hollow somehow. "Think fool! No one destroys for no purpose. I think it more likely that these Outsiders actually do have some purpose that we have not discovered. We do not know what might have happened if they had not been turned away at the Cataclysm. Suppose they seek slaves, or even food stock for themselves? Could they not have a use for a good strong servant from this world?"

Fairchilde could only shake his head and mutter, "Madness…utter madness," under his breath. He knew Elric the Dark well enough to know Elric had made his decision and would pay no attention to disputation now. To ally with the Outsiders. A thought to freeze the soul, if he still had one.

And yet, if anyone could do it, Elric was certainly the one. If such an alliance could be struck, it would bring immense power to his King, and to those loyal servants of the King. Great risk, but equally great reward. And…chances for survival would at least be better at Elric's side. An alliance with the Outsiders! Fairchilde took a long slow breath and prepared to assist his King.

Six

> "Knowing what thou knowest not
> is the first step on the path to wisdom."
>
> —The Divine Thesis,
> Sacred Text for the Temple of Chardain.

Thousands of leagues to the south and east, in the mountain valley of Xanadu, the scholar Murdoch worked at his desk, deep under the mountain. He was reading another portion of The Chronicles.

"I was soon able to confirm the information brought by Lord Figharoe. I used the black staff to reach out and seek them beyon our world, much as he had done. These creatures we were beginning to call the Outsiders existed in vast numbers on countless worlds. They appeared to know nothing of The Art, but rather traveled about in metal ships through the emptiness between the worlds.

"In appearance they resembled both lizardmen and trolls, being reptilian in nature. I watched as they conquered world after world, enslaving the peoples or, in some cases, utterly destroying a world when there was any resistance. They had the viciousness of trolls combined with the seeming strength of the Gods.

"We met in Council and argued for long hours as to what course to take. It was our Grand Master of the game of

Jannisaries, Chiang, who finally suggested a most desperate plan to try and save our world."

Murdoch stopped reading at this point and glanced over to his own three layer board for the game of Jannisaries. Although he had never formally entered competition, Murdoch had played some of the most adept players of the game, when they had chanced to pay a visit to Xanadu. He had dreamed of the chance to play a Grand Master someday. The game of Jannisaries combined the elements of combat, diplomacy, and intrigue with the random element of a third player who assumed the role of "dragon" and was empowered to actually change the rules of the game during the play.

So Chaing was a Grand Master. It was an intriguing thought and Murdoch began thinking about ways to bring the subject up and ask for a game when he was reminded by his own inner discipline that there was serious work to be done. He returned to The Chronicles.

"Chiang quoted some ancient scholar to the effect that trying to oppose force with more force was simple-minded, and in this case, at least, doomed to fail. A better strategy was to oppose force with guile. This led to what came to be known as the 'Great Plan', which is still being carried out, even as I write this.

"The Great Plan was in…three parts. First, when the Outsiders arrived, we would resist and bring about an attack on our world. Second, we would have to somehow survive that attack. Third, and most difficult of all, we would create a massive illusion that the attack succeeded and try to convince the Outsiders that our world was actually destroyed, in the hope they would then move on.

"It was a desperate plan, offering small hope and enormous risk. Any number of things could go wrong. The slightest misstep would end in the destruction of all. It was a forlorn reed for a drowning man to clutch.

"And yet, it worked. Beyond all hope, it worked. The illusion of a destroyed and burned out world was maintained long enough to deceive the Outsiders and they left us."

Murdoch put the heavy book down. He dropped one hand beside his chair to absently scratch the ears of the cat, and chewed on a licorice morsel while he thought. His reaction was obvious and simple; an illusion once created could be created again. It deceived them the first time and might well continue the deception, when they came again.

Murdoch was troubled by this thought being so obvious. Both his master, and their guest seemed too disturbed for the solution to be this simple. Although Murdoch did not belong to one of the religious temples, he was attracted to the teachings of the Temple of Chardain, with their emphasis on orderly thought and the search for ultimate truth. The teachings of the Temple of Chardain would indicate if something seemed too simple, look deeper. Murdoch drew a long breath and got up to get more books.

Several hours later, he joined Sahm-el and Chiang in the Grand Salon. The sorcerer was smoking a long-stemmed pipe whose bowl had been carved out of a single large emerald. Chiang was hefting a drinking horn full of dwarven mead. Murdoch silently took his place and prepared to respectfully listen to these near legendary beings. Murdoch was mildly surprised when the cat leaped into his lap and made himself comfortable.

Chiang was speaking. "I agree with you. The King of the Wazuli Empire, on the veldts of Carpathia, is wise, strong, and dependable. Once informed, he will assist. We need not be concerned about that one. We must concentrate our efforts on the other two."

Sahm-el drew from his pipe and blew three perfect smoke rings. They were impressive in their perfection but Murdoch knew this was a very modest feat for one of Sahm-el's talents. Then, with a wink, the sorcerer turned all three of the smoke rings into butterflies of dazzling color that cheerfully flitted around the room. Then with just a hint of a chuckle, the sorcerer turned to the scholar. "Well, God Sage. What have your studies found for us?"

"I believe, Sire, that I am missing some critical facts, for

I am sure I found nothing you do not already know."

There was a bark of a laugh from Chiang, enough to wake up the dozing cat who merely looked at him and went back to napping. Sahm-el smiled and continued. "That is as it may be. But come now, share your observations with us."

Murdoch, who had been afraid he would look foolish telling these two of history that they had personally made, now eased in his chair, and began in the pedantic tones of lecturer. "Upon the occasion of their first visit to this world, the Outsiders were observed to be immensely powerful. Far too powerful to be opposed militarily. In the intervening thousand years, they must have traveled widely. I submit that we have no reason to believe they are any weaker now than they were then. That would be a matter for you to investigate through the Art."

Sahm-el nodded, and Murdoch continued. "As Master Chiang has said on an earlier occasion, force cannot be met with force, it must be met with guile. That would suggest that the attempt should be made to continue the illusion that this is a destroyed world."

Murdoch hesitated, unsure about offering speculation based on his inner feeling that it could not be that simple. He thought he saw Chiang direct a slow wink at Sahm-el. Sahm-el looked at his resident sage expectantly, obviously waiting for him to continue. With some disquiet, Murdoch took the plunge.

"And yet, I feel there must be something missing, some additional fact or circumstance not known to me. I can offer no reliable evidence for this, but I am struck with the sense that there must be some difficulty in recreating the illusion, or that I have somehow overlooked some obvious bit of information." Murdoch stopped, thinking he had probably just spoiled a simple report with these wanderings of feelings, and chided himself for a lack of discipline.

Sahm-el quietly held out his hand toward Chaing, palm up. Chiang slapped his hand in the ritual of conceding a wager lost, and in a voice tinged with just the faintest hint of a deep rumble murmured, "As you said, he is competent." Murdoch relaxed.

Chiang then grinned, a sight more fearsome than warm, and spoke again, now in a light and teasing tone. "I do believe, O Mighty Deathwind, Savior of Worlds, that this explanation falls more within your province that in mine."

Murdoch turned back to his Master who was drawing smoke from his pipe.

When three more brilliantly colored butterflies were flitting about the room, Sahm-el explained. "Good Sage, while you have been studying the past, that is upstream on the River of Time; Master Chiang and I have been searching the future, that is looking downstream to what might be.

"Now the River of Time has eddies and crosscurrents that are caused by obstructions that are hidden below the surface. We have found three such ripples downstream that may affect an attempt to recreate the illusion. You may think of these as possible turning points in the course of the stream, each of which may bring failure to our enterprise.

"One of these is located in the Wazuli Empire on the continent of Carpathia. One is located in the Empire of the Khan, and one is located in the Kingdom of Telluria, specifically in its capitol city, Caprice.

We must find a way to deal with each of these problems if we are to be successful in re-creating and sustaining the illusion for the Outsiders when they come some years hence."

Murdoch nodded his understanding but refused to interrupt. Chiang picked up the explanation. "It is a matter of stability and cooperation. A worldwide illusion requires the assistance of all of the major powers. If even one clack-brained twit withholds his help and seeks personal gain, the illusion could collapse and the plan fail. Each of these three locations radiates dangerous instability during the critical time."

The cat rolled over on his lap, for his tummy to be rubbed and Murdoch absently stroked him. "But that time is not yet. You said ten years, at least. Cannot something be done to stabilize these places?"

Chiang looked at Sahm-el and arched one dark eyebrow.

Sahm-el put the long-stemmed pipe down and frowned. "There is the rub. The answer to your question is both yes and no." He leaned back in his chair and laced his fingers together in a manner that Murdoch had often seen his Master use when he was seriously troubled.

Sahm-el continued, "The King of the Wazuli is a strong man and a man of honor. Forewarned, he should be able to keep things stable on the Carpathian continent.

"It is Suliman the Dread who is stirring up trouble in the Empire of the Khan. But with my own Beloved to pose as a harem girl and keep a watchful eye on him over there, I think we can handle anything he might do.

"Thus two of the three regions are reasonably safe. It is Telluria that is the worry. Elric the Dark cannot be trusted."

A soft chuckle from Chaing drew Murdoch's attention away from his Master's troubled face. Chiang rumbled, "'Tis no real problem. As I said earlier, Kings can be replaced." Just the faintest wisp of sulphur seemed to come from Chiang's direction.

"And I have said nay to that, repeatedly. I will not overthrow another kingdom. Twice now, I have disposed of a tyrant, only to have him replaced by something worse. It is a simple-minded solution that just does not serve. For a government to be stable, it must arise from the people and have their support. No puppet that I put on the Dragonthrone would have that."

Chiang responded in kind, and Murdoch felt the room actually get noticeably warmer and knew what was meant by the phrase: heat of an argument. Chiang's reply was, "You quibble at trifles with a world at stake! This is a torch you must carry."

"Nay! I have been burned by that torch before. I will not be responsible. Besides, it simply will not work."

The two of them glared at each other for a moment, and Murdoch was sure the room grew warmer still. Then both of them relaxed and Murdoch let out a breath he had not realized he had been holding. The room became silent for several long moments as all three thought and no-one spoke.

Suddenly, Chiang turned to Murdoch. "Scholar, tell us the legend of the Dragonthrone." The command was peremptory and Murdoch found himself trying to collect his wits and search his mind for the tale almost before he knew he was doing it.

With a quick glance at Sahm-el, who nodded, Murdoch began. "The throne of the Kingdom of Telluria is called the Dragonthrone because it is said in an age long past, a Great and Golden Dragon asked a young girl, who was Queen of Telluria at that time, for help in being freed from the enslavement of a sorcerer. This heroic Queen did just that, with the result that not just that dragon, but a number of dragons were freed from bondage.

"In gratitude, the Dragon promised great reward to this Queen of Telluria. She asked instead, for help for her kingdom in a time of crisis. The Dragon, and all of others of his kind, then swore an oath, that when a time came that the Throne of Telluria had no illigitimate heir, they, the Dragons, would choose a new ruler and insure the safety of the Kingdom."

Murdoch, of course, instantly grasped the implications, but Sahm-el was clearly puzzled. Murdoch answered his Master's question before it was asked, in his excitement forgetting to wait to be called upon by his bettors. "I see it! It must be the time of the Prophecy. Elric the Dark has no legitimate claim on the Throne of Telluria. He ascended to the throne after murdering Charles the Meek and forging some documents. He is not the rightful ruler of Telluria."

Sahm-el looked suspicious. "Are you certain of this? You have not been primed by Chiang the Inscrutable with a tale to tell me, have you?"

Murdoch gaped, speechless at the question. Sahm-el waved his hand and apologized. "Nay, do not bother to answer that. I know your work. Even this one could not make you give false information to me. I am sorry. I spoke hastily."

Murdoch swallowed a lump in his throat but before he could speak, his Master had turned to Chiang. "You knew of this, of course? I mean about Elric not being the rightful King?"

Chiang nodded lazily, clearly pleased with himself.

Sahm-el continued. "Serves me right for not paying attention to local politicians. I presume you are suggesting that the time has come for the Prophecy of the Dragonthrone to be fulfilled. Is that it?"

"I believe it quite likely is so. It will require confirmation, of course, but I expect it to be confirmed, even to your satisfaction."

There was silence in the room again, as each of them turned this idea over in his mind. Sahm-el broke the silence. "Very well! If this proves to be the time of this prophecy, I will help in the changing of kings in Telluria. But I insist on certain conditions.

"First, there must be evidence that this new ruler is the genuine article and not simply another false face or puppet. Agreed?"

"That would be part of the prophecy. Agreed."

"Second, this change of rulers has to be done slowly and in an orderly way so as to avoid bringing shock to the people. The long term stability of the Kingdom is our goal. Agreed?"

"Most certainly!"

"Third. You Chaing, and such others as are appropriate, shall have the responsibility of finding and testing this new King. I will have nothing to do with it, and do not wish to even know who he is. Agreed?"

"Agreed. That is in keeping with the prophecy itself. No other could do it." Murdoch thought Chiang seemed amused.

"Finally, since we have the time we might as well use it. Elric must be exposed for what he is so the people of Telluria will acknowledge the prophecy and accept the new King. I think that task shall fall to our good scholar here."

Murdoch was stunned. "Me? Why me? I am but a scholar. I know nothing of politics and intrigue!"

Chiang and Sahm-el both laughed together, much to Murdoch's discomfort. The cat jumped from his lap at the noise and scampered across the room. Chiang directed another slow wink at Sahm-el and said, "Good Scholar, I understand you play Jannisaries with some skill. It is fitting preparation for this task. Regard this as simply a larger form of the game."

Murdoch was not amused. He did not have the faintest idea as to how to expose an evil King.

Seven

"Greed Kills."

—The Red Book of Roland,
Book of meditation for the Paladin order
known as The Companions.

Twila awoke with the mind befogged sensation of not remembering where she was or how she got there. Her first glance caused her to cling white-knuckled to the fishnet hammock she was sleeping in. It was bound to tree limbs about six meters above the ground in a large elm tree. The hammock swayed gently with the movement of the tree in the light breeze and Twila was sure it was going to turn over and she would fall to her death.

She closed her eyes and willed her self to relax with the three long breaths of the Ritual of Calming. Although the hammock was swaying slightly, it appeared to be even and stable. Twila opened her eyes and forced herself to look around. She immediately saw her Healer's bag hung on another small limb, within easy reach. Next to it was a shoulder bag, of the kind used by travelers.

Twila carefully turned to her other side and found a nice broad heavy tree branch running along the side of the swinging hammock, just a handspan away. A glance toward her feet reminded her she was fully dressed in her hunting leathers and wrapped in her own travel cloak, as she lay in the hammock. Then the memories of the previous night came flooding in on her.

She and her bodyguard, whose name she couldn't remember at the moment, had departed the hidden escape tunnel entrance before sunrise, and then quietly walked away while the castle fell to the royal forces. Twila had looked back, only once, to see Lyestehr Keep in flames and to know her father, mother and sister, and many good friends were gone, and hope gone with them.

The escape itself, had been relatively easy. Good Oscar Wyndham, now dead, had carefully planned the route and it had been practiced recently, although Twila had treated such training sessions as something of a joke, at the time, never dreaming that her life could be shattered so easily. Once away from the castle, it was quiet, and her bodyguard seemed very sure-footed in the dark. They had walked for several hours, until well after the rising of the Three Suns. Twila had been led like a young child, obediently doing exactly what the guard said, her mind mercifully numb.

She now remembered that it was he who had told her there would be patrols of light cavalry roaming the countryside soon and they must hide during the day and move only at dark. They traveled through a rather dense forest of large old trees and Twila could not see anyplace to really hide where one could sleep safely. She had been astonished at his suggestion of sleeping in the trees, but after he had strung the fishnet hammock and helped her into it, she now remembered thinking it quite safe and a rather clever idea that would never had occurred to her.

Judging by the triple shadows cast by the light of the Three Suns it must be late afternoon. An awareness of hunger and other bodily needs forced Twila to decide it was time to get up and make her way to the ground. She was tempted to simply lie there and wait for her guard to help her, but she was also a bit embarrassed at the amount of help she had required from him last night. Twila would feel better if she could demonstrate a bit of competency to him and stop being the burden she felt she must have been up to now.

It proved to be surprisingly easy to roll out of the hammock and onto the tree limb beside it, ending up astride the limb. There had been a brief moment when she had feared her boots would become entangled with the hem of her cloak and bring about her fall, but a slight breeze flared her cloak just enough for her to move cleanly onto the limb.

In just a few minutes, she had managed to untie the hammock and roll it up in a ball, then put it into her bag. With her own bag over one shoulder and the guard's bag over the other one, she then very carefully climbed down the tree to the ground.

Once on the ground, Twila remembered Oscar's training and stood silently next to the tree, counting to a thousand before she moved. She appeared to be alone in the forest. Twila thought it likely that her guard was probably foraging for food and should be back shortly. He obviously had not abandoned her for he had not taken his own bag. She tended to her personal needs, then moved to a spot where she could keep her "sleeping tree" in sight and sat down under a bush to try and wait patiently. She had no food, but did have a small water bottle which she sipped from. Naturally, she didn't even consider opening the guard's bag to look for food. Such an invasion of privacy would be an unforgivable insult.

Twila had waited for nearly an hour when she heard movement through the forest. Her first impulse was to jump up and call for the guard, for she was very hungry and was sure it was he. But something about the sound caused her to pause. Last night, her bodyguard had walked in near silence, like a cat. This was a bit too loud, a thrashing through the under-brush, and she wasn't sure, but she thought there might be more than one. She waited silently and tried to remain very still.

When she did see movement, a chill went down Twila's spine. She had caught a clear glimpse of the green and gold of the Royal Tellurian Legions. Twila glanced about wildly but it was too late to move to another hiding place. She tried to make herself small and remain very still, hoping they might go on past.

There were three men, all wearing the green tunics and gold tinted armor of the Legions. Each carried a large oval shield and a javelin and wore a short sword on his belt. They had plain helmets which indicated they were simple foot soldiers and not officers. They had not seen her because they were too busy cursing the underbrush and complaining to each other.

The one in the lead said over his shoulder, "This is bloody worse than Fangorn Woods. Probably full of pixies. I doubt not that we meet a goblin or even a troll or two before we're out of this."

The second one prodded him in the back with his javelin. "You been whinin' and complainin' since we left. I'm gettin' sick of it. Shaddup and march."

There was a guffaw from the third one who then added, "'Twas your idea to throw off the patrols. You think anyone'd come through here looking for a few deserters? They've got too much to think about back at the castle."

The first one stopped and fetched a water bottle from his belt. The others followed suit. After a generous pull on something Twila suspected was not water, he said, "There's truth in that. God-cursed place! What a fight!"

The others nodded agreement, as they too drank. He continued, "The entire Fourth wiped out to the last man. I thought the Great Black Bird had come for me for sure outside the Citadel, when they made that stand. Whoever trained that bunch is one bloody Hell of a soldier."

"Was, you mean. He's bloody well dead now. And we're not."

"Aye. To hell with the bloody legion! To Hell with Elric the Nasty!" They toasted each other and then started to move on.

They were about ten meters from where Twila crouched, trying not to shiver. She thought they were going to go on by, but it was not to be. Twila felt some small crawly creature land on her cheek and start crawling toward her ear. She tried to very slowly bring her hand up to brush it off, but even that slight motion was enough to betray her.

One of the men turned and looked directly at her. With a wordless shout, he pointed with his javelin, and the other two saw her as well.

"What's this? Stand up! Show yourself! I can nail a rat at seventy paces with this, I can certainly put it through you. Now stand up!'"

They quickly encircled her and pressed in close. As soon as they could see her figure in the tight fitting hunting leathers, and note that the only weapon she had was a small dagger in her boot, grins broke out on all three.

"Well lookee here. 'Tis a pretty thing. Soft, too." Twila felt callused hands running all over her. She clenched her teeth and tried to think of something she could do. It did not require an Empath to know the intentions of these three. She looked about for her missing guard, in vain.

All three of them had discarded their shields and javelins and two were pinning her arms painfully behind her while the third began undoing the laces down the front of her leather tunic. Twila began to see a lot of old nightmares start to come true for her. She screamed. They laughed.

One of the soldiers, the one pinning her right arm, suddenly stopped laughing. Neither Twila nor the other two noticed until he suddenly let go of her and fell over. Just as suddenly, Twila saw a handspan of sharpened steel, which she dimly recognized as the point of a rapier, suddenly appear out the front of the neck of the other soldier holding her. It disappeared again, as he slumped to the ground.

Twila felt frozen, rooted to the spot and unable to move until a gloved hand rudely shoved her to the side. As she tumbled into the brush, she saw her guard, holding a bloody rapier, advancing on the third soldier, who had drawn his short sword and was backing up.

Although Twila had watched many a sword drill in the Castle courtyard, she found the intricate and subtle movements of parry and riposte to be simply incomprehensible and had usually regarded them as a kind of dance. She thought her guard probably had the advantage here due to the length of his slender rapier, but she wasn't sure.

As she watched, both men circled cautiously, swords pointing at each other and making small movements in the air. The blades sometimes touched, only to slide off of one another. She couldn't figure out why her guard simply didn't use his longer reach to stab the fellow.

There was a brief flurry and the clang of steel as the two blades came together like lightening in a storm. Then both men were backing away again and continuing their circling. It seemed to Twila that the soldier with the short sword was able to move every bit as fast as her guard with his long rapier. Moreover, her guard seemed anxious to avoid coming to close quarters with the soldier, over and over again, jerking back and jumping clear when it looked to her like he could move right in.

It ended with a flash of blades too quick for her to follow and the guard's rapier suddenly slashing through the soldier's throat. Twila found she had been holding her breath again and had not moved from where she stood. The guard cleaned his blade on the cloak of the dead soldier and then returned it to its scabbard and slowly walked back over to her.

"It seems, young Mistress, that I cannot leave ye even to forage for food without misfortune seeking ye out." He had just killed three men and he seemed unaffected by it, although the sight and smell of death, once again had driven Twila's appetite away.

"Will there be any more of them…looking for us. I mean?"

"Nay good Lady. I should think these were not looking for us. Legion patrols do not travel through a forest such as this one in groups of three. No. These were deserters who lost their stomachs for a fight and went to looting. 'Tis a pity. If they had done their duty and remained with their comrades, they would still be alive."

"You seemed afraid of that last one." She stopped, suddenly aware that her words had not come out as she had wished. The guard's eyes narrowed in a slight frown at the implied insult.

He spoke curtly. "Ye speak from ignorance, Lady. Would you draw the short sword from that body please?"

Embarrassed, Twila leaned over and took the short sword from the belt scabbard of the nearest dead soldier. It was heavier than she had expected and felt awkward to hold. The sword was made entirely of metal, with a straight double-edged blade and wire wrapped handle. It was about as long as her arm, much shorter than the nearly meter long rapier.

He spoke in the teaching tones one would use in explaining things to a child. "If ye will observe the hilt, that is the crosspiece between the blade and the handle. Mark ye well these heavy lugs on each end of the cross-piece that point down toward the blade like teeth."

When Twila nodded, he picked up a small stick. "This stick is the blade of my rapier, much thinner than the heavy blade of the short sword." He ran the stick down the length of the short sword blade until it came to rest against the crosspiece. "Now lady, twist the sword you are holding, fast."

Twila twisted the heavy sword and the stick caught on one of the lugs and snapped of cleanly. She understood his little lesson.

"'Tis called a swordbreaker hilt. All of the Legion swords have them. Caution was needed."

Twila felt like a silly fool. Once again, she was conscious of her own ineptitude and of being a burden on this good soldier of her father's house. It would seem that Oscar had chosen well when he made him one of the family bodyguards.

"Good sir...my manners seem gone with my wits. I meant no insult to your courage and have misspoke myself."

Twila saw him relax a bit at that, and noticed for the first time that this bodyguard was somewhat older than she had thought. Rather than being close to her age, he had the tiny wrinkles about the eyes and even a few flecks of gray in his hair that suggested ten to fifteen more years than she had.

"Come Lady. We should leave this place. Land crabs will be drawn to these bodies."

"Where...where are we going?"

"I am told there is a branch of your family in Ruritania. It would seem to be the safest place for ye."

Twila allowed her elbow to be taken and herself to be guided across the small clearing as she thought about it. "I have cousins in the City of Troyes, in Ruritania." Looking down at the dead soldier as they passed him, she shivered. "That will be a long journey, good Sir. And I am not feeling much like a Lady just now." She brushed leaves off her hunting leathers and in quick embarrassment remembered to relace her tunic.

Pretending to ignore her embarrassment and what she was doing, the bodyguard replied. "Fear not, young mistress. No harm shall come to thee while under my protection."

"Please...my name is Twila, and I would be pleased if you would address me so."

"As you wish. Twila. I am called Finnegin. I shall stand in for your family as a substitute for the older brother you lost, until I deliver you to your relatives in Troyes."

They walked on through the forest.

Eight

"A leaf, blowing in the wind, may deflect a falling raindrop from its original path, causing it to land in a brimming puddle, causing that puddle to overflow into another, and eventually leading to a flooded river which destroys a city which causes the downfall of a kingdom. It can thus be said that the fall of the kingdom was brought about by a leaf blowing in the wind. All things are related."

—Book of the Vehdahs
Sacred Text for the Temple of Isis.

The sage who had named himself Murdoch, looked at his image in an obsidian mirror. He did not find himself to be an impressive sight. The man looking back at him was clearly in his forties, balding, and somewhat chubby. An unkind girl had once told him that he resembled a lizard, and he had believed her.

Today he was dressed for "the great adventure", as Sahmel kept calling it. He wore boots and breeches, full cut flowing shirt with puffed sleeve pockets, leather tunic, belted with a wide leather belt holding two belt pouches, and over all that, a hooded weather cloak. He also carried a large shoulder bag. He wore no sword because the one time he had worn a sword to a costume ball, he kept whacking people in the back of the knee with it every time he turned around. He didn't know how to use a sword anyway. Like all men, however, he carried a dagger in his right boot and pipe and pipeweed in a pocket inside his left boot.

Murdoch frowned. He felt silly. In the safety and comfort of the library at Xanadu, he found reading about heroes slaying monsters and righting wrongs very enjoyable indeed. But reading and doing are very different. Murdoch did not feel like a great warrior and he certainly didn't look like one.

When he had hesitantly raised this subject, both Sahm-el and Chiang had laughed and chided him for a lack of faith. Sahm-el had then lectured him on the benefits of "field study" and insisted this was an opportunity for personal growth, a phrase Murdoch had come to dread when used by the sorcerer.

Both Sahm-el and Chiang wore irritating grins when he entered the Salon and Murdoch was conscious of how really ridiculous he looked. With as much dignity as he could muster, Murdoch bowed formally to them both and then sat in one of the stuffed chairs.

Master Sahm-el spoke. "Well Murdoch, you look well prepared. Is there anything you need before I send you off to Caprice?"

Murdoch struggled and found his voice just as the cat leaped into his lap and made itself comfortable. "By your leave, Master, there is a great deal that I need."

He thought he heard a low chuckle from Chiang, as Sahm-el replied, "Pray tell us of your needs."

"In sooth, my Lord, the more I examine this the worse it does appear. I have no plan of action, nor do I have the knowledge or skills to create a plan of action. What steps do I take to prepare the people of Telluria for a rightful King? How do I chart my course? You must give me complete instructions if I am to succeed."

Sahm-el appeared to pause in thought, then spoke. "You would like a step-by-step plan to follow, one that says do this first, then do that and success will be guaranteed."

At Murdoch's nod of the head, Sahm-el turned to Chiang. "I do believe our scholar feels ill-prepared for this task. What say you? Shall we plan his campaign for him, minute by minute?"

Chiang gave a snort, and there was just the faintest whiff

of sulfur in the room. "I believe what he really needs is the key to success to all difficult ventures."

Murdoch leaned forward slightly in his chair. Was it possible that these two great and powerful beings were going to tell him one of the universal truths?

Sahm-el thought for a painfully long moment, then looking deeply into Murdoch's eyes said in a tone of absolute seriousness, "We are about to share with you one of the great secrets understood by all who must plan and carry out great deeds."

Murdoch gave his full attention, prepared to commit these words to memory.

Sahm-el looked at Chiang, and Chiang looked at Sahm-el. Then they both sang in unison, "We makes it up as we goes along." Then both of them broke up in roaring laughter. It was a line from a Halfling song.

Murdoch muttered an obscenity under his breath and sat back in the chair, red in the face. Secret of the Universe indeed!

Chiang finally stilled his rumble of laughter and attempted to placate the angry scholar. "We jest with you only a little, Master Scholar. Plans exist only in books. Real events must be played with the give and take of a dance."

Sahm-el agreed. "'Tis an unfortunate truth. While I believe your scholarly skills will be of real help to you, they will not tell you what to do. Each decision is a conscious choice that books or lists on parchment cannot make for you."

Murdoch no longer tried to hide his bewilderment. "Then what am I to do, Master? I know not where to begin."

"As to that, you speak truly. I never intended to send you off without help. We have gifts for you, to aid you in your task." He drew a black cloth, like an ordinary kerchief out of his sleeve, and shook it out so all could see a large hole in the cloth that somehow did not go all the way through it. "You know what this is?"

Murdoch did indeed know what it was. "It is one of the transdimensional magic sacks that have no bulk or weight yet can hold and carry a barrel's worth of goods."

"So it is. You may regard it as your bag of tricks. I have placed a number of enchanted objects inside it that you will find useful. There is also a parchment explaining the uses of each item."

Chiang spoke up. "I, too, have gifts for you, Scholar." He produced two books, leather-bound and old. Murdoch noticed with some eagerness that each book had the traditional notch cut in the side of the pages. These were genuine Dragonbooks, intended for dragons to read. The notch was for the single tooth that was used to open them.

"This one," he said as he handed it to Sahm-el who promptly put it in the hole in the black cloth, causing it to disappear into the sack, "is Drury's Primer for Princes, a book on the acquisition and uses of political power that has some helpful chapters on the nature of intrigue.

"And this one," also handed to Sahm-el to be put in the sack, "is the Silken Veil, a virtual manual on assassination and intrigue. It comes from the Tauhng Society, a world-wide sisterhood of very competent assassins."

Sahm-el handed him the flimsy looking black cloth. "I suggest you tuck it up your sleeve like an ordinary kerchief."

Murdoch stood up, carefully put the magic sack into his sleeve and moved to sit again. The cat, who had been dumped on the floor looked at him blinking, then looked at Sahm-el, and crouched for a leap.

Momentarily distracted by the cat, Murdoch didn't see Sahm-el point the short black staff he always carried with him. Murdoch looked up again when he heard Chiang mutter something about good luck.

Two things happened at once. The cat jumped to Murdoch's shoulder, and the whole world twitched violently around him.

Murdoch found himself out of doors, in what appeared to be an alley in a city, with the cat on his shoulder. He had a sinking feeling that he was already in the City of Caprice, without time to collect his thoughts or even say good-bye.

The Master's cat jumped from his shoulder to the ground and went scampering, tail high, down the alley. Murdoch watched it turn the corner. He was still frozen to the spot where he had appeared. After a moment of mental groping, he managed to collect his wits and quietly eased against the building, putting his back to the stones.

The alleys and darker streets of Caprice were notorious for being inhabited by footpads and predatory creatures of every kind. For the first of perhaps hundreds of times to come, Murdoch asked himself, "What am I doing here?"

He detected no movement in the shadow, could hear no footsteps, or, even worse, claws clicking on the stones approaching him out of the dark. He drew the small dagger from his boot, here-to-for used mainly for peeling oranges, and held it tightly.

He looked both ways down the alley. In one direction, there was light and street noises. The other direction, the one taken by the cat, was darker and quieter. Layered on top of his own feelings of peril and incompetence was the knowledge that he had just lost the Master's favorite cat and he wasn't about to go into the darkness to find it.

Murdoch stood there for several minutes, clutching the dagger, and when nothing horrible happened to him, he began to breathe again. He began easing toward the street, holding his dagger against his leg to half conceal it.

As he cautiously peeked around the corner into the street he confirmed that he was indeed in the City of Caprice, capitol of Telluria. The streets were lit with oil lamps on poles and there was a lot of traffic. Coaches went by, accompanied sometimes by men at arms. There were caravans composed of sedan chairs and their escorts, city guardsmen in their green and gold livery, and the occasional individual boldly walking alone.

Murdoch found he was standing next to a rather popular building and a hesitant step out of the alley showed him it was an inn. The sign had a blue star painted on it. It stirred something in his memory. A Blue Star Inn had been mentioned in several of the Master's Chronicles as a place he frequently visited.

With what he thought of as considerable courage in the

circumstances, Murdoch slipped his small dagger back into his boot and straightened up, to walk into the inn. He could not, after all, stand foolishly in the street without attracting exactly the kind of trouble he feared. The common room of an inn should be somewhat safer than a dark street corner.

Murdoch tried to assume the bold swaggering look he had seen manifested by the young nobles in the streets, with their long cloaks, plumed hats, and ever-present swords swinging from their hips. Unfortunately, his short stature, chubby figure, and simple scholar's clothes didn't quite achieve the noble bearing he wished for. As he pushed through the double doors and entered the noisy taproom he feared he looked far too harmless to be impressive.

The room was crowded. There was a huge stone fireplace at one end, stairs going up at the other, and a bar across the back. The middle area was crammed with heavy wooden tables and oak chairs. Most of these were occupied. Murdoch saw a noisy table surrounded by Halflings and piled high with food. As far away from them as possible, there was a table with five Dwarves. And there was some kind of dark shape at the table in the corner by the stairs. The rest of the occupants were human-looking to him and most wore swords.

To his immediate right there was a table with three strikingly attractive women, wrapped in light blue cloaks. One of them looked up at him and frowned. Unsure of what he might have done to give offense, Murdoch awkwardly bowed to her. The frown faded on her otherwise pretty face and she then ignored him. He hastily moved through the crowd of tables to the bar, feeling that all eyes were probably on him. An innkeeper greeted him with a smile.

"What is your pleasure, sir?"

Murdoch glanced around, aware that he was nervous, and answered. "A room to meself, if you have such," and produced a gold coin.

The innkeeper raised an eyebrow at the gold and Murdoch sensed he had made an error. He shouldn't have shown gold in a place like this, but should have paid in silver. He thought he had probably just made himself a target for six or seven thieves that he was sure must be watching him.

The innkeeper picked up the coin and said, "If you will follow me, sir?" He came out from behind the bar and led Murdoch across the room to the stairs. Murdoch was trying to look in all directions at once, and had one hand firmly on his belt pouch to guard against pickpockets as they threaded through the tables.

Just as they reached the stairs, Murdoch caught a glimpse of the person, that is creature, at the corner table that he hadn't been able to make out before. It was large and furry, had several eyes, and seemed to have tentacles of some kind. It was pulling apart something on a platter in front of it and paid him no attention. The innkeeper went on up the stairs and Murdoch hurried to follow.

The room proved to be small but quite comfortable. It had a rope and tick bed, a small table and chairs, an oil lamp, a chamber pot under the bed, and the traditional three pegs in the wall. These were normally for hat, weather cloak, and sword belt. Murdoch needed only two of them.

As soon as the innkeeper was gone, Murdoch took the only precaution for his safety that he knew by getting a wedge of wood out of his meager belongings and wedging the door tight from the inside. Then he sat at the table and drew forth the magic sack.

His first impulse was to simply spill the contents out onto the table, but he reminded himself of tales he had read of mighty heroes who had done just that only to discover the contents included several glass vials with magic potions. When dumped from the bag, the vials sometimes break causing an unexpected and unwished for sudden mixing of magic potions with startling results.

Murdoch reached gently into the bag and felt several bits of parchment. He carefully drew each one forth and found he had small objects wrapped in parchment, along with an ordinary scroll and small leather bound book of the type used to keep journals. There were also the two large heavy books.

His scholarly training suggested he read the scroll before touching anything. It was written in the tiny and precise hand of Sahm-el.

Faithful Friend, here is the 'bag of tricks' to aid you in your task. Guard their secrets well for they are beyond price and would attract much danger to you if their existence were to be known.

In the packet marked with the number '1', you will find a plain ring. Put it on. It will keep you healthy and whole of body.

In the packet marked with the numeral '2', you will find another ring. Wear it on your other hand. It will free you from any kind of bondage. If you are now wearing both these rings, be not concerned when they disappear. Their presence is supposed to be a secret. Like all of this magic, they will show no magic aura until actually in use. Even a Sorcerer will not know they are there.

In the packet marked with the numeral '3', you will find a gold medallion on a chain. Wear it about your neck under your clothes. It will defend you from physical attack and attack by magic spell.

In the packet marked with the numeral '4', you will find an earring, of the type worn by young lords and landed gentry. It is to be worn in your right ear. It will allow you to listen to any conversation that you can see.

You will also have found a small journal book. Please keep a daily journal for me of your doings. Have no fear, none but you will be able to read what you write there.

There are, of course, the two books from Master Chiang. I call your attention to the traditional notch cut into pages. I am sure you know the significance of this.

Finally, good Murdoch, knowing that you are not a warrior and yet may find yourself in combat before this is over, I have included a weapon for you. It will come to you if you whisper, or even think about pronouncing the name 'Miranda.'

Fear not! You are quite able to do this task. I know you would rather be in your study here, for it has the warmth and comfort of a Halfling home. However, I perceive depths in you that cannot be discovered in a library. Experience in the field, as it were, will be character building for you.

With kindest regards, Sahm-el

Murdoch had immediately put on the rings and medallion as he read. He examined his hands now and could see no ring on either hand. He checked with a mirror and found the Medallion had also disappeared. The earring was visible but looked very ordinary in his ear. He sat back in thought.

A kind of excitement wholly foreign to his experience began to rise within him. These were powerful tools. They changed his perspective. With these, he was no longer the weakling and foolish scholar that he had been feeling. Perhaps he could act the hero after all.

He went over the parchment again and his attention turned to the two books given him by Master Chiang. Sure enough, his eyes had not deceived him. There was a notch cut out of the edge of the pages on each book. Murdoch found himself breathing faster as he examined each book. Such a notch was only made on books meant to be read by dragons. The notch was so the young dragon could use the so-called scholar's tooth in the very front of his mouth to open the book and turn pages. For a scholar like Murdoch, having two such books was worth almost any risk and his remaining fears faded away in his excitement. This was going to fun.

Like most scholars, he gave no thought at all to the weapon, confident that it would be there if he ever really needed it. The dragon books came first, and he settled in for a night of pleasurable reading.

Nine

"The best of plans, greatest care, and layer upon layer of precautions cannot insure protection from everything. There are forces loose in the universe that are simply overwhelming. When meeting such, all that may remain is to hold to the belief that death and defeat are not one. Death comes to all, but defeat only comes to those who admit it."

—The Decree of Salamanca,
Sacred Text for the Temple of Leto.

On the same day that Murdoch arrived in Caprice. Twila and Finnegin reached the banks of the Dire River. They had been forced to hide numerous times to avoid patrols of lancers, and had slipped across the King's Highway just before dawn.

Finnegin had hoped to find a fisherman to take them across the mighty river. But the first three they found, all pointed to posted proclamations grounding all boats and issued by the Royal Wizard of Telluria. None would oppose Fairchilde the Feared.

They were left with trying to make the best of ill choices. Unless one could fly, and neither of them could, the Dire River could only be crossed in three ways. Along with ordinary fisherboats, there was by bridge, or by ferryboat.

After much discussion, they decided it would likely be easier to mix with the farmers who crossed the High Bridge rather than the ferryboat. Both would be guarded, and the wizard's proclamation was ominous, but it seemed the only way.

As Twila drifted to sleep in her hammock that night, she

was unaware that a portion of her future was being selected for her by that same Fairchilde the Feared, in the Wizard's Tower at Caprice.

Like all great sorcerers, Master Fairchilde had a long memory. While it was true that such minor things as the face of a girl could be pushed from his mind by more weighty affairs, it was also true that even the most minor of things would surface once again in his attention.

This having occurred, Fairchilde was reminded that one of the Lyestehr family may have survived and he had neglected to mention that to the King. Minor research quickly showed that the face he had seen in his spell belonged to the youngest daughter, named Twila. She was known to be a Healer and thus no possible threat to anyone. Still, Fairchilde was meticulous in attending to just such minor details.

He therefore prepared a search spell for the girl Twila.

Fairchilde stood in the middle of the pentagram inlaid with tiles on the floor of the laboratory. With a negligent wave of his hand he summoned into existence the protective globe of energy provided by the pentagram. He never took chances on being vulnerable while concentrating on a spell.

He then drew power from his own life force, transmuting it into a ball of magic that only he could see. He poured more and more force into the glimmering ball of light, causing it to grow in size and brightness until he was satisfied it was sufficient to his need.

Next he carefully formed in his mind the clearest image of the girl Twila that he could manage. This was not just a picture of her face, but rather a series of mind images of everything he knew about the girl, her name, family, birth order, studying to be a healer, color of hair, last known position, and so forth, all woven together into a kind of tapestry that clearly identified the girl Twila and no other.

This done, Fairchilde moved smoothly to the next step in the creation of his spell. He connected the rune for "sensing" with two principles of magic drawn from the Minor Arcana, that of "Knowledge" and "Locus." When these were all in balance with the image of the girl's identity, he added direction and range and then released the spell with a shouted command word.

The swirling and twinkling ball of light that was his spell began to expand, rapidly growing larger and larger, until its surface filled the room and expanded outward from the Royal Tower. Completely invisible to anyone but a sorcerer of equal rank to Master Fairchilde, it continued to grow like some giant soap bubble until it included the entire city, and still it continued to grow.

In the Royal Tower, Fairchilde composed himself in an old leather chair, closed his eyes, and began watching a growing map in his mind's eye. A colorful circle first showed him the Tower, then the palace grounds, then the City of Caprice and then more and more of the surrounding countryside as his searching spell spread further and further.

In a very short time, a point of light, like a diamond lying on a blanket, came into existence on this inner map. It marked a spot on the bank of the Dire River, some thirty leagues from the city. This was the present location of the girl Twila.

With just the faintest of sighs, Master Fairchilde allowed his magic spell to unravel and disappear harmlessly like a cloud on a summer day. He now knew certainly that one member of the Lyestehr family stilled lived and where she was. This minor problem was all too easy to solve.

He got up from his chair and strode to the main worktable, with its various beakers and scalpels, parchment scrolls, and jars of powder. On the shelf above the table there was a curious little wooden box. It was curious because in addition to having a normal lid, it also had a tiny door on one side. Fairchilde gently placed the little box on the table and made a chirping sound with his lips. In a moment, the tiny door opened.

Emerging from the small opening, he saw, as he expected, a glossy black wasp with golden eyes. It was about twice the length of his own thumbnail and one of his trusted servants.

The Shadow Wasp, for that was what it was, walked nimbly out onto the table and stood facing him, waiting.

Fairchilde gave it instructions in the same light chirping sounds he had used to call it forth. The black wasp rubbed two hind legs together, making a chirp of its own, then launched itself into the air, flying straight up with a buzzing sound until it was at eye level with the sorcerer. Then with a spark of light, it blinked out of sight and was gone. Master Fairchilde turned his mind to more important matters.

Sleeping comfortably in her hammock, Twila never saw the tiny wasp suddenly flash into existence a few meters above her, then lightly fly down to land on her shoulder. It waited a moment to insure she remained asleep, then carefully crawled underneath the collar of her leather jerkin where it could ride unseen on her, all the while, keeping its master informed of her whereabouts and doings.

The next morning, Twila and her guard walked along the bank of the Dire River, unaware of the tiny spy hitching a ride on her clothing. They bought food from fisherfolk and walked all day in the direction of the City of Caprice. They camped that night and continued on the next day, finally coming in sight of the walled city toward dusk.

Finnegin suggested that they join in the crowd of farmers leaving the city by way of the bridge and get across it and out of the dangerous city as quickly as possible. The risks were great, but Twila could see no other course of action. Once across the bridge, they would be in the country of Ruritania and reasonably safe from Elric the Dark.

They made their way past the Navy Yard, where a row of war galleys were docked, all bearing the green standard of Telluria. No one stopped them as they joined in the stream of traffic approaching the High Bridge.

It was called the High Bridge because its center span was high enough for a sailing ship to pass under. The long spans on either side of the center span curved upward in a graceful but easy slope to the center. High Bridge was said to have been built, or rather created, by an unknown sorcerer in the distant past. To the dismay of many of the long line of Tellurian Kings, there was an accepted legend that said the bridge would fall if ever a toll was charged for its use. Thus passage across High Bridge was free to all.

This evening, High Bridge was crowded with farm carts pulled by oxen, most of them empty from having sold their crops within the city. Twila and Finnegin had no trouble joining the traffic and slowly walking up the curve of the first span.

There had been guards posted at the entrance to the bridge, but their attention seemed to be in the opposite direction, watching the small amount of traffic that was coming into the city from Ruritania. Twila and Finnegin simply walked right past these guards and up onto the bridge.

As they approached the battlement towers that supported the center span, Twila was beginning to breathe easier and was hopeful that the main danger was past. Then she heard a rough voice call out "Hold!"

Twila froze, stumbling on the stones of the bridge and looking wildly about. Her bodyguard, Finnegin, was smoothly drawing his rapier. She saw four men step out, wearing soft leather and the embroidered livery of Fairchilde the Feared, Royal Sorcerer. All four had drawn swords and were blocking their way. She looked back and was appalled to see the Royal Guards had closed the bridge road behind them and taken up positions. She and Finnegin were trapped.

Twila found she couldn't move, but her guard danced lightly forward, holding his thin rapier out and making small circling moves with it. She thought he was actually going to engage all four men, and wondered if he was simply desperate or had lost his reason.

She watched Finnegin move forward and she thought he sort of invited the first man to attack him. Number one made a thrust and had it parried with a feathery soft deflection by Finnegin's blade, then before he could withdraw from the thrust, Finnegin made a twisting movement with his wrist and slashed the tendons of the man's arm, just above his sword handle.

Number one screamed, dropping his sword, but he was already being ignored as Finnegin advanced to the second man and made a double feint, disengage and then a strait thrust through the chest. Two were out of the fight in barely as many seconds. Twila began to think they might make it.

The third man backed up and he and number four tried to cooperate and attack at the same time. As she had suspected earlier, her guard now proved himself to be a superb swordsman, handling the rapier with the delicate moves of a painter making a portrait. His blade flicked and danced, slithering off the opponent blades, and pushing them just far enough aside so their thrusts missed target.

Twila could see strain on the two men's faces as they discovered they did not have an advantage against this level of skill. He was playing them off against each other so when one moved he got in the way of the other. Indeed, Finnegin seemed to have a slight but grim smile on his face.

Twila turned around and found the Royal Guards were advancing up the slope of the bridge toward them, halberds at the ready. She turned back to warn Finnegin when there was a clap of thunder and cloud of smoke. Out of the smoke stepped an elderly man in black robes with a hornet embroidered on his chest. Her heart sank.

Fairchilde the Feared, paused after his dramatic appearance and surveyed the trap he had set. It had been child's play to track the foolish girl and her guard once the wasp traveled with them. He had recalled the wasp and set his own minions to take them on the bridge.

The swordsman was proving to be a bit of a surprise, but it gave him no concern. Raising one hand, Fairchilde pointed a ring he was wearing at Finnegin and uttered the release command. Visible only to the Mage, a ball of force came forth from the ring and struck the swordsman.

Finnegin suddenly found himself being pushed by some kind of force, almost as though there was a heavy galewind, but there was no wind. He felt himself shoved across the bridge to the railing by something he couldn't see. Twila's last view of her faithful guard was that of seeing him topple over the railing and fall from the bridge.

She stood there numb at the loss of the man who had saved her life. She really did not notice the Royal Guards come up or the sorcerer give them instructions then leave in a flurry of smoke. She came to herself when she felt chains put on her wrists and herself being led back down the bridge and into the City of Caprice. Twila had no doubt as to what was coming next and in very short time found herself in a dungeon cell in the palace.

Ten

"The successful intrigue is best planned backwards; beginning with the result that is desired, then progressing through who should accomplish that desired action, and thence to what would make them want to do that desired action."

—The Silken Veil,
Sourcebook for the Tauhng Society assassins.

Murdoch the sage, was making his first entry in the journal he had been ordered to keep.

"Thus, I have spent the past five days in study of the two books given to me by Our Friend. In doing so, I have made some interesting discoveries about myself. Is it not strange that a quiet man of letters, such as myself, should find the wielding of political power to be fascinating? The subtle thrust and parry of intrigue begins to interest me greatly. I was surprised to recognize gambits from the game of Jannisaries being described as basic strategies used in government.

"I confess, that at first this task given to me seemed impossible. Now I begin to see the faint whisper of a plan.

"Elric the Dark is widely feared but is actually popular with only the very wealthy and the more ambitious nobility. They number about two in ten of all the peoples of Telluria. The common people hold no love for him. He holds them in his grip through fear. Should something happen to reduce their fear of him, I believe the people would welcome a change in ruler.

"Hence, the first step is to find a way to show Elric is

vulnerable and thus lessen the fear of him. I have begun to give thought to ways and means of accomplishing just that.

"Finally, I regret to report that I have managed to lose your favorite cat, the one known as Fang. He jumped to my shoulder just as you sent me to Caprice, and upon arrival here, scampered off before I could quite collect my wits. I have searched for him each day, but to no avail. I know not what can be done about it, and do sincerely apologize for this misfortune."

Murdoch laid aside his quill and capped the small vial of ink. He read over his words, then closed the journal and returned once more to his studies. He had spent nearly all of his time in his room, having meals brought up by the innkeeper whom he had learned was called Tweedy. There was a communal privy down the hall and a covered chamber pot under the bed so he had simply bolted his door and buried himself in study.

The only real exception had been his brief trips out during the day looking for the cat. He had discovered that there was a large stable behind the inn and thought it likely that the cat was probably somewhere about the barn, but he never saw it, and did not want to attract attention by calling for it. So each afternoon, he would pretend to take a bit of afternoon air, enjoying the light of the Three Suns, and then would return to his room and his books.

By viewing his main task as a game of Jannisaries, Murdoch found a well-spring of ideas began to surface in his mind. He examined each, turning it over, making notes and carefully filing it away for possible future use. It soon became apparent that he was going to need help to try out most of these ideas, as he personally lacked the training and skill to do them.

This study took several hours and late in the afternoon, he decided to stretch his legs with another walk about the stables looking for the lost cat. Upon returning to his room, without the cat again, he opened the journal to continue his entries.

There was additional writing in his journal. Following his last entry, there was now handwriting in bright green ink. It looked like the Master's hand.

"It would seem you have made a good beginning. Well done! Do not concern yourself over the cat. He is well able to take care of himself. He travels widely and will find you when it suits his nature.

"The Blue Star Inn is a reputable place and as safe as any such place can be. That is to say, be wary, and carry yourself alertly. The innkeeper, Tweedy, can be trusted. He is an old friend. However, he should not be told of our business at this time.

"I have arranged for an assistant to join you. He is an interesting chap, friend of my Beloved, and quite useful. He will meet you in the common room of the Inn at the seventh hour. Keep the Faith!"

Murdoch leaned back and smiled. So the journal was a means of sending messages. He had not been cast up here all alone after all. Equally cheering was the news that he was to have help, and he could stop worrying about the cat. The day looked much brighter to him.

At half past the sixth hour, Murdoch took one of the small tables in the common room and ordered his evening meal, consisting of stew with large chunks of bread on the side and hot tea. He had tried to find a place where he could sit with his back to the wall since that had been advised in many of the adventure sagas he had read. Unfortunately, there were no such places in the common room, since any seating near a wall was also near a window.

He therefore took a table close to the bar and waited for his new assistant. Meanwhile he cautiously looked about the room trying to guess who might be a friend of the wife of Sahm-el the Sorcerer. As usual, the place was full of customers.

He saw a group of Lyranian Amazons at one table in their blue cloaks, and having finally remembered the significance of the blue cloaks, made a mental note to try to avoid that part of the room. The large corner table was occupied by something or someone who had draped the entire corner in darkness and might be anything. Two man-sized, cat-looking creatures were sharing a table nearby. He didn't know what they were, but they wore a leather harness with curved sword at what would be called their waists. There was a lone lizardman at the bar, noisily munching something from a large wooden tub placed in front of him. He too wore a large curved sword and Murdoch noticed the other patrons gave him wide berth. He decided to do the same, if possible.

Finally, there was an assortment of humans in the room, drinking, eating or sometimes gambling. With an eye sharpened by his recent study, he began sorting them into likely groups according to the clues presented by their appearance. There were young richly dressed men wearing cup-hilt rapiers. Their fine clothes and the fact that the customary dagger that each wore was in the right boot proclaimed them as members of the nobility rather than serious fighting men. Murdoch had just learned that fighting men usually carried their dagger in the left boot to have it at hand while holding a sword. There were three such gaming at dice at one of the tables. They wore plain leather, with wool travel cloaks and each had a very ordinary rapier and plain dagger within easy reach. Murdoch marked them down as being another potential threat and vowed to try to stay away from them as well.

He nearly overlooked one small fellow at a table by the stairs. He wore a hooded cloak with the hood pulled far forward, completely hiding his face. Even the sleeves of his clothing were extra long and covered his hands so it was impossible to tell exactly what he was. He might be dwarf, Halfling, or any one of the many smaller beings that exist here. He obviously wanted his privacy. Murdoch was very suspicious of him once he noticed him.

At that moment, the double doors swung wide and Murdoch eagerly turned to the front, expecting some powerful ally to enter and come to his table. Instead, he saw four men in chain mail and surcoat, wearing an emblem of a red hornet on their chests. It took him a moment to remember that was the device of the royal sorcerer, Fairchilde the Feared, who was in service to Elric the Dark. Clearly these could not be allies.

The four soldiers started pushing their way toward the bar. Two young nobles hastened to get out of their way as they shoved chairs aside. Murdoch was amazed at their arrogance in assuming everyone would naturally give way before them.

Their path would bring them to the bar right next to his table, and he was beginning to regret his choice of tables. Wendy, the pretty brown-haired barmaid, was clearing a table of tankards and didn't notice them until the first one, a very large and heavy set fellow casually shoved her aside, causing her to fall.

Murdoch reacted automatically. He rose from his chair and said, "Have a care there sir, you tread heavily on other people." Almost before it was out of his mouth, he was regretting the impulsive act. The big one turned and Murdoch found himself staring directly into the red hornet on the soldier's chest, with the brute hulking over him.

He felt himself being grabbed and lifted clear off the floor until his face was even with the soldier's face. "Did you speak to me, little man?" said a very nasty voice. The soldier had both the strength and the manners of a troll, and his breath reeked of garlic.

Murdoch thought of his magic bag of tricks and tried to think of the release command for the ring that was supposed to protect him. He could not recall it so he thought "Work Ring!" as hard as he could. Nothing happened.

When he did not answer the soldier's question, he was shaken hard and then tossed over a table, landing hard against the edge of a chair. Murdoch's vision blurred momentarily and he was afraid he had broken bones. Even at this moment, his mind remained orderly and he was stuck with two observations.

The first one was, "This kind of thing never happens to the heroes the bards sing about." That thought was followed by another, "What of all this magical protection I am supposed to have?"

He heard a loud guffaw and was dimly aware of the soldiers going on past him to the bar. One of the soldiers started to kick him as he went by but somehow managed to get his leg tangled in the legs of a chair and stumbled into the next, causing him to utter a string of oaths.

At that moment, Murdoch felt the needle and pins tingling of magic in the ring on his left had. A wave of warmth swept over him, spreading from his hand and arm to his chest, and then throughout his body. Suddenly all of the pain ceased and he was feeling perfectly fine.

Murdoch carefully got to his feet, causing looks of surprise by nearly everyone. Some had thought him killed.

One of Fairchild's guards said to the first one who had tossed Murdoch aside, "Look Miggs, the little man has gotten up and is asking for more."

Before Murdoch could protest and deny he had any further interest in being thrown around the room, they were interrupted by a high-pitched singsong voice saying, "I have business to conduct with this man and you are interfering with it. Please mind your manners or leave."

The voice belonged to the short little creature in the hooded robe. How he got in the midst of them without being noticed was only one of several mysteries. He was still completely shrouded and the face of his hood barely reached the knee of the angry guard. The one called Miggs looked down and gaped at him in surprise. Then his natural temper returned. "What's it to ya?"

But the little guy had already turned to Murdoch and was ignoring the guard towering over him. "Please precede me to your room where we can talk without these oafish interruptions." A hand extended from one of the long sleeves, pointing to the stairs, but it was bright blue in color and the fingers looked more like tentacles as they didn't seem to have any bones.

Murdoch took one look at the four guards and decided he was out of his depth. He hastily backed up and made for the stairs. He heard a snarling curse from Miggs and turned as he reached the bottom step just in time see an incredible sight.

The little guy was right behind him, but facing the guards. His face was still shrouded by the deep hood. Apparently Miggs had drawn his sword, but in doing so had nicked one of the other guards in the hip. In reaction, this guard had turned angrily and seemingly accidentally bumped a third guard as he was raising a tankard of beer to his lips. This caused the beer to slosh in his face and with an oath he swung a wild punch that connected, by chance with the fourth guard, knocking him backwards several feet into the table being used by the Lyranian Amazons.

There was a sudden hush in the room as his flailing body overturned the women's table. Miggs was clearly heard to say "Damn!" The guard with beer in his face was about to swing wildly again. Murdoch noticed that virtually everyone else in the room, including the innkeeper, were diving for the floor.

Murdoch watched in fascination, heedless of whatever the risk was. The three women in blue cloaks leaped to their feet in fury. Instead of drawing weapons, which is what Murdoch had expected, their leader glanced down at the fallen guard and then around at the three other guards wearing the same livery.

What looked to Murdoch like brilliant blue lightning flashed from her eyes, first to Miggs, then rapidly to the other three. When struck, each of them went perfectly stiff and then crashed to the floor. None of them moved after that.

A second woman in blue nimbly bent over and snapped a collar around the neck of the guard nearest to her. As Murdoch watched, collars were fastened on all four guards. The other patrons were getting up now and resuming their seats at tables. The innkeeper went over and bowed respectfully to the Amazon leader, and arranged for the four bodies to be dragged out to the stable.

The little guy passed Murdoch on the stairs with a follow me gesture. As Murdoch turned to follow him, he heard that same singsong voice say, "Always bad business to trifle with a Lyranian Amazon, especially for a male human." It was said casually, and Murdoch was forced to silently agree.

He recalled now, as he climbed the stairs, that the women in blue, were from an island kingdom totally ruled by women, and they believed males were semi-intelligent animals suitable only for breeding stock and physical labor. These guards were now slaves to the women.

As he looked at the small figure climbing the stairs ahead of him, apparently his expected ally, Murdoch thought that he was certainly meeting some interesting people.

Eleven

"Simple things are never simple. They only have the appearance of being simple on the surface. Beneath the surface there is always layer upon layer of complexity."

—The Korakorahm,
Sacred Text of the Temple of Dhao.

Across the Dire River, which separates Telluria and Ruritania, the King's highway goes through deep forest for many a league before coming to the city of Troyes. It then goes further south through grassland and prairie until it finally comes to the capital of Ruritania, Schalim.

Schalim is a walled city about twice the size of Caprice. The palace is protected by an inner citadel and is widely regarded as one of the most formidable castles on the continent.

Inside that old gray structure there are over one thousand rooms. One of them is the Private Council Chamber of the Grand Patriarch and Priest King, Machis the Omnipotent and His council of Cardinals.

The King of Ruritania, who is also the head of the state religion known as the Temple of Dominic, and his advisors met around a diamond shaped table. They felt completely secure in this safest of chambers, with its walls lined with Peace Enforcers, in this safest of castles. In this, as well as other things, their faith would be misplaced.

The previous evening, just after the last of the three suns

had set, a large bird, a condor, had soared quietly over the city and come to an ungraceful but soft landing on the battlements of that same great castle. It had taken three silent steps to the edge of one of the upper battlements, and then in the briefest of shimmerings had altered its form to that of a stone gargoyle, matching hundreds of such all over the castle.

It perched upon the castle walls, calmly watching the changing of the guards until well into the middle of the night. In every way, to every sense, it was one with the stone of the castle. If someone should happen to touch it, they would have felt cold stone. Once changed into its new form, it could not be detected from the original, even by magic, for it actually became what it was mimicking, and yet remained alive and thoughtful and able to move.

As the changing of the guard trooped past it in the dark, it shimmered again, and took on the form of a Holy Peace Keeper, complete with Badge of Blessedness and simply fell into step at the back of the line, apparently carrying a spear, like the rest of the guards. At the next guard station, the guard going off duty fell into step behind it, without ever thinking of counting the number of guards in the detail.

The intruder followed the group, marching in step, into the barracks, where it paused to study a duty roster posted in parchment on the wall. It then followed all of the motions it saw of a guard getting ready to sleep, casually shifting its positions within the guard barracks so no one would notice it was an extra without an assigned bunk. When it was certain no one was looking its way, it flattened against one wall and took on the form of the wall itself, waiting until all were asleep.

When the room was full of snores, it resumed the form of a Peace Keeper and moved silently to a bunk it had noted after reading the duty roster. It quietly leaned over and touched its forehead to that of the sleeping guard, holding the contact for nearly a minute, absorbing memories and knowledge from the sleeping man. Then it turned and left the room.

In the morning, the Peace Keeper Guards at the Private Council Chamber watched alertly as servants cleaned the room, rearranged the chairs, and bustled in and out bringing the usual bowl of fresh fruit and carafe of wine for the middle of the diamond shaped table. They failed to notice an extra servant who was shifting the chairs around the table. They did not see one of the chairs swiftly tipped over on its back and then slid underneath the middle of the broad table, for the simple reason that a moment later, there was a chair in its place and all was in order.

Thus, the room was declared safe when Machis the Omnipotent and his Cardinals entered it an hour later. No one had reason to suspect the presence of a spy in their midst.

The Grand Patriarch took his seat, arranging the folds of his flowing golden robe carefully and then glancing up to see his Cardinals all standing silently in the attitude of submission awaiting his pleasure. With a negligent wave of one hand, he gestured to them to sit. The Peace Keepers lining the walls stepped back into their niches where they could see but not hear what was being said.

Machis formally intoned, "Let there be no magic among us!"

The Cardinals replied by ritual, "May the Evil Power be gone!"

Then all relaxed around the table. Some helped themselves to wine or fruit and all waited to hear their Lord and Master's words.

"The GOD has spoken to me. The time for the glorious crusade is finally at hand." There were exclamations of utter bliss all around the diamond shaped table.

"Dominic, blessings be upon his name, has decreed that we shall set loose our Blessed Legions upon the profane who would usurp GOD's Holy power and use it for themselves."

In unison, those at the table chanted, "Magic is reserved for the GODS alone! Suffer not its use among mere mortals!" It was the central teaching of their state religion.

The Patriarch continued, "Dominic, may his name always be spoken with reverence, has warned that major sorcery is about to be attempted in the country to the north of us. Such blasphemy must be prevented." The men around the table nodded their agreement joyfully. The long awaited day had come and they were selected to lead the holiest of crusades to rid the world of magic and restore it to its rightful place among the GODS alone. Each felt truly blessed.

Machis the Omnipotent turned to the man seated at his left, the only one at the table wearing the white leather armor of the Peace Keepers rather than clerical robes. "Tiggelenus, what is the status of the Heavenly Host?"

"Holy One, we have twenty-five full legions of heavy infantry and five legions of the cataphract mounted troops. In addition we have seven full legions of the enslaved troll auxiliaries to use as spearhead troops. This amounts to well over 250,000. All are equipped with the Blessed armor that is proof against magic." He gestured toward the glossy white hard leather armor he was wearing, whose composition and manufacture was Ruritania's most closely guarded secret.

The Patriarch nodded pleasantly and went on. "How long will it take to mobilize these troops and have them ready to cross the Dire River and conquer Telluria?"

"Holy One, the cataphract mounted troops could be there in less than a week, but the legions are in the camps throughout the middle of the kingdom. I would say they could not be moved into position in less than three weeks, four would be better."

"Order them to march then. We will attack Telluria in four weeks. The Crusade begins." There were cheers and applause around the table.

Marshal Tiggelenus raised his hand and waited for permission to speak once more. When he got it he raised a question. "Holy One, the small kingdom of Sardonicus that lies next to Telluria has been a stone in our boot for a very long time. Might this be an opportunity to rid ourselves of that stone as well? We have more than enough troops They don't believe in armies."

Machis the Omnipotent thought for a moment, carefully noting the nods of agreement and smiles on his Cardinals.

"Although Dominic did not specifically mention Sardonicus to me, I feel sure he would be pleased to have this land of blaspheming jokesters cleansed as well. So be it." With that casual comment, Sardonicus, the country devoted to humor that produced all of the best jesters, also came under threat from the Ruritanian Crusade.

The meeting ended pleasantly, with each of the cardinals well aware of the historical significance of the moment. The room cleared, and the guards came out of their niches along the walls, and after a routine search of the room left. No one noticed that there was an extra chair under the table.

Likewise, no one saw a large bird, a condor, awkwardly leap from the battlements in the middle of the night and with occasional laborious flaps of its wings begin soaring northward toward Telluria. The spy was a free agent and he knew of sorcerers in the city of Caprice who would pay well for this information.

One that he had in mind was at that time leaving the city of Caprice and walking eastward along the bank of the Dire River. He walked slowly, swinging a black staff that was topped by a large emerald, his rust colored robes swishing as he moved.

He had come out of the city to get away from the noise and distraction of the mob and sought the peace and tranquility of solitude and the soft noises of the river. He also wanted to be away from prying eyes of his colleagues, especially the Guildmaster, Fairchilde the Feared.

He wanted to think and had learned the hard way that the usual practice of using the Art to isolate himself only drew the attention of other wizards. So he quietly sought solitude without drawing upon the forces of magic.

This had brought him out of the city about three leagues to the east. He wanted to think, really think. Strange and worrisome images had been appearing unbidden in his visions during the routine practice of the Art. They appeared to be portents of approaching violence, but their meaning was not clear. Thus he had come to meditate upon them.

Having stepped off the King's Highway and followed a well-remembered path through the forest toward the river, he now cleared his mind of the drab and routine and prepared to bring these images to the front, singly, for examination while his dusty boots carried him along the path to the river.

Just as he was prepared to concentrate on the first image, the river came into sight and his concentration was broken by what he saw.

On the riverbank, where it had washed up like some drifting log, there was a mud encrusted body. He stopped and carefully looked around, without moving. He sent a small spark of light from the staff firmly gripped by his left hand, to move at great speed first over the body and then in ever widening circles through the trees.

He waited patiently, completing his search and insuring there was no one about, then returned his attention to the body. It was a man, rather tall with mustache and neatly trimmed beard. The man was dressed in leather doublet and breeches. An empty scabbard for a rapier hung limply from a baldric. That and the empty dagger scabbard in the man's left boot proclaimed him to be a man experienced in fighting.

Taking a few steps closer, he sorted out more details through the thick river mud and decided the man probably wore a sweeping cloak and plumed hat before misfortune struck him.

Another spark of light leaped from the staff and flew back and forth over the body, sparkling as it went, then flashed in the forehead of the wizard. This man was still alive, just barely. He had broken bones and injuries inside and was slipping deeper and deeper towards the final sleep, but he did live.

The wizard kneeled next to the muddy body and drew forth from his sleeve a flimsy black piece of cloth, like a kerchief. He spread it on the ground and it formed a circle about as wide as his boot was long. Then he reached his hand inside it, as though the cloth were an actual hole in the ground, reaching deep, well past the elbow and feeling around among its contents.

His fingers groped familiar objects until he came to a small leather case with raised lettering on its lid. He drew this forth and opened the little case and removed one of the three glass vials it contained. It was small, about the size of his little finger and had a glass stopper. The liquid it contained was colorless as water but to his eyes it glowed with the energies of magic.

He set the potion case down and carefully opened the vial, moving with a practiced gentility so as to avoid spilling even one precious drop of the magic potion. Then he poured it between the lips of the unconscious man.

He replaced the empty vial in its leather case and returned the case to the black circle of cloth, then folded the cloth and put it back in his sleeve pocket while he waited for the potion to take effect.

Within a few moments, he could perceive the golden glow of magic spreading all over the man's body. Flares of light erupted around the ribs and knees as bones straightened and rejoined and injuries began to close. There was a palpable feeling of heat and steam rose from the mud-soaked clothes. The precious healing potion did its work, restoring the half dead man to perfect health in a matter of minutes.

His benefactor watched as he opened his eyes and quickly glanced around, trying to get his bearings. With a smile, the wizard drew his own dagger from his boot and casually tossed it to the ground next to the awakening man. He then said, "These days, no man should be without a weapon."

The man raised himself up on his elbows, and picked up the dagger, putting it into his boot with a nod that acknowledged the trust it implied. Then he spoke, "Where is it I find meself, and who might ye be to be helping me?"

The wizard leaned on his staff and announced, "I am known as Develon, and am a member of the Fourth Circle of the Masters of the Art. As to where we are, we are on the bank of the Dire River just a few leagues east of Caprice. Do you not remember how you got here?"

The man got up, feeling himself all over and looking surprised to find himself whole. He looked at the wizard and apparently coming to a decision gave the formal bow of respect that is the due of all those who have mastered the Art, then spoke. "I am known as Finnegin and I last remember escorting a girl who was trying to get to her kinfolk. I do no know what brought me here."

"Tis a common reaction when one has been as near to death as you were when I found you. Escorting a girl, you say. Hmmmmmmmmm." He looked at the river mud on Finnegin's clothes and the swiftly flowing river. "Could it be that you are the one from the High Bridge that is all the talk in the taverns?"

"I do but dimly remember something about a bridge. Tell me about it, if ye would."

The local bards are even now singing songs of a girl who somehow earned the enmity of Fairchilde the Feared, and of the bodyguard who tried to defend her until he was thrown off High Bridge by the powers of Fairchilde himself. Be you that bodyguard?"

He watched as Finnegin thought long and hard before finally admitting "I am he. Does that make us friend or foe?"

Master Develon laughed, a full rich easy laugh. "Clear your wits, man. I believe our friendship is already established. It is not often I give away one of my prized potions to a stranger. And I am no friend of Fairchilde or his master Elric the Nasty."

"What of the girl? Know you of what has happened to her? I am responsible for her safety."

"'Tis said she is unharmed and now resides in the Royal Dungeon, upon orders from Fairchilde, though no one seems to know or be willing to say why."

"I think I can at least partially answer that, but it may serve you ill to know such things."

With an easy nod, the wizard said, "As you wish, I shall not pry into your secrets. But what now, where are you bound?"

Finnegin looked as if it were a foolish question. "Why to help the girl, of course, where else would I be bound?"

Develon laughed again. "Now here's a man of heart. Just fished out of the river, no sword, probably no money either I'll warrant, and yet he is ready to rescue a girl from the royal dungeons and oppose His Majesty's personal sorcerer." He laughed again.

Finnegin looked down at his muddy clothes, empty scabbard and absent coin purse and smiled ruefully. "Humble as I am, I must try."

"Well said! Allow me to put forth a suggestion. I came out here to ponder certain matters that also relate to Elric and Fairchilde, and now I think it was not chance that led to our meeting. Let us join forces and marry our two concerns together. I think I shall have need of a man of heart to protect my back in the coming day, and you shall certainly need aid in your quest. What say you?"

Finnegin thrust his left arm forward and they gripped each others forearms in trust and friendship. "Done! And I too say well-met."

The wizard turned and started up the path that led back to the King's Highway. "Come then, we shall get you cleaned up so you can pass the muster of the city guards at the gate, and then we shall see to getting you a sword and other necessaries. I am to meet a friend of mine at the Blue Star Inn this evening and I do believe you will find the meeting interesting. He is a strange little chap with blue skin. I'll say no more and let you judge for yourself." The two of them began walking toward Caprice.

Twelve

"Each thread in a tapestry is but a bit of colored cloth. It is the weaving of these bits that creates the beauty."

—The Book of Vehdahs,
Sacred Text for the Temple of Isis.

Murdoch was upset. He liked a nice quiet orderly existence and he was now feeling that events were rushing ahead a bit faster than he could comprehend. It was like being in a runaway coach lurching down a mountain road with the scenery flashing past and having no control over what was about to happen. It was very distressing.

He was now sitting in the common room of the Blue Star Inn with the strange little blue skinned creature he had met just an hour ago, and they were waiting to meet a "friend" of this creature. Murdoch had not yet composed himself to the first stranger and now he was expected to meet another.

He closed his eyes and took a sip of tea and reviewed the past hour in an effort to bring some order to his thoughts.

The encounter with the sorcerer's guards had been anything but calm. Upon following the little creature up the stairs, Murdoch had noticed that he was being led directly to his own room, which had not been a comforting discovery.

Once inside, the creature had put its hood back, revealing a very inhuman appearance. It had an elongated bulbous bald head, no ears, no nose, no mouth, just two beady little black eyes set low down on the front slope of its skull. It was entirely blue in color and its fingers really were small tentacles. Murdoch had no idea what it was and instantly backed up against the door.

The creature had turned to Murdoch and in that same whining sing-song voice had informed him it was known as an Ort and was here to help him not frighten him. It then went on, answering his questions before he could voice them by informing him its name was Flettcher and it had once traveled with the Lady Crickett, Beloved of Sahm-el the Sorcerer.

Flettcher had gone on to say that he thought Murdoch's preliminary plans were sound and that they were to meet someone downstairs in the common room who would prove useful to the cause. All of this before Murdoch had said a word.

The little creature, Murdoch had never heard of an Ort, then stood there blinking at him exuding great patience by his manner.

Murdoch had collected his wits sufficiently to ask if he was in the presence of some kind of wizard and had been informed in tutoring tones that an Ort does no magic but does have some small skill in the realm of thought.

Murdoch had privately doubted that anyone who traveled with Lady Crickett had "small skill" in anything, but he spent a fruitless half hour trying to elicit what exactly was meant by "The realm of thought." He then found himself being led back downstairs by his new found ally, still feeling very confused.

At table, he carefully examined the Common Room, noting who was present. The amazons were still there, richer by four new slaves. The lizardman still slurped unmentionable things from his wooden tub. Whatever had spread the darkness in the corner was gone, replaced by a quiet party of dwarves. The cat-like creatures that he now remembered were called Mriss were gone. There was the usual mix of humans in the room including one new fellow, a large muscular warrior in barbaric brightly colored clothes, who had a heavy two-handed sword slung across his back. He was drinking from a truly huge drinking horn and Murdoch marked him down as the likely new ally they were to meet because he fit the bardic descriptions of "brave companion to the hero" in many of the sagas. His manner of dress proclaimed him to be a Trosian freebooter, who was likely traveling to hire his sword out.

Murdoch's attention was drawn away from the warrior when he felt something softly touch his leg. He looked down with some trepidation only to see the Master's missing cat, the one known as Fang, looking up at him. The cat's coat was glossy, his eyes bright, and his tail up in the air. Whatever he had been doing, it had obviously not harmed him. The cat gave a silent meow and hopped into Murdoch's lap, making himself comfortable and promptly dozing off with a loud purr. Murdoch stroked the warm soft cat and wondered what would happen next.

The steady drone of talk suddenly stopped and everyone was looking at the double doors of the main entrance to the inn. A dark-haired woman in a truly regal wine colored gown was standing there with a slight frown on her face. At first look, Murdoch would have said she was wondrously beautiful, but something in the frown and a certain hardness in her eyes made him hesitate in that judgment and finally decide that there was an element of coldness about her that modified her beauty.

Murdoch threw an inquiring glance at Flettcher, who sat across the table from him shrouded in his hooded cloak like some kind of Halfling sorcerer. Flettcher made a slight motion with his tentacled hand and whispered, "Nay, that is not our friend. That is the King's Spymaster, Miriam."

For the very first time, Murdoch felt a special kind of thrill flow through his body. If he had any hair on his head he was sure it would have stood up at that moment. Here he was, engaged in plotting against the King and face-to-face, so to speak with the King's Spymaster. In later years, he would recall that first sense of danger and describe it as "the whisper of the ax." It was not altogether unpleasant.

The Spymaster had hesitated just inside the doorway, surveying the room. Her gaze passed over Murdoch but paused upon the heavily cloaked little figure sitting at his table, before moving on. Apparently, she did not see whatever it was she was looking for.

She surveyed the room a second time. As she left the doorway and began moving on into the room, the drone of talk resumed, only to halt a moment later. She had gone over to the only table in the common room that would give her a view of the entire room and its occupants. It happened to be the table where the big warrior was having his meal.

The warrior was slurping down a large bowl of beebee, a kind of spiced bean soup with meat, and he didn't seem to mind that some of the soup was getting into his beard. Miriam walked up to him and stated flatly, "I would have this table. Move to another." She spoke in tones that suggested she was quite accustomed to having people leap at her command. The room got quiet.

The warrior put down his wooden spoon and wiped his mouth with the back of his hand. With an appraising eye to her slender figure he said, "Well now, what have we here? Are you looking for a good time little girl? I might oblige thee. Otherwise, run along and leave the menfolks to enjoy their supper."

Murdoch, who had read many of the sagas from the Temple of Leto that preach chivalry, automatically started to rise to assist the lady, but was restrained by Flettcher, who whispered, "'Tis the warrior that is in danger."

Miriam calmly reached over and with a cold smile dumped his bowl of steaming soup in his lap. The warrior roared and leaped to his feet, reaching over his shoulder for the great sword he carried.

Instantly, there was movement throughout the room. Some were abandoning their tables to stand against the wall. Others sat still but put various hands on various weapons, just in case. The innkeeper and serving wench, disappeared behind the bar.

Murdoch felt the cat jump to the floor from his lap and saw

it start walking toward the conflict, ears forward and tail high. He started after it, but was again restrained by Flettcher's "hand" on his arm. To Murdoch, who was witnessing his first actual combat, events then seemed to move as if each motion was greatly slowed.

The warrior was drawing his great sword. Miriam seemed to move much faster than he and took two quick steps, approaching him at an angle. Patrons were leaping up or falling over in their chairs trying to get out of the way, especially of the large sword. The cat was calmly trotting through the middle of this toward the spilled bean soup.

The sword came free of its scabbard and the warrior started a mighty swing with it. Miriam flattened her hand and put her fingers all together and with a quick rap, struck the warrior across the nose with the edge of her hand. The cat skipped between them and reached the bean soup which it began lapping up.

The warrior's swing went wild and he staggered back shaking his head, as though to clear it. With a decidedly predatory grin, Miriam raised her hand to strike again. Murdoch, fearful that the Master's cat was about to get stepped on while its attention was on the soup, rose to his feet and shouted "No!"

Miriam hesitated for the briefest of moments, but it allowed the warrior to nick her in the arm with a backswing of his heavy sword. Her face went gray with the pain and she reacted to it with an almost animal growl and a strike across the warrior's throat that dropped him like a tree felled by a woodsman.

She turned angrily to see who had shouted. Murdoch was the only other person in the room standing up. Blood was dripping onto her fine gown. It looked to Murdoch like it was really just a scratch and not anything serious, but she didn't seem to be taking it that way.

Barely controlling her fury, she hissed at him, "Thy name, wretch! So I may place it on my death list."

Murdoch glanced around the room and down at Flettcher, who sat quiet offering no help. Then he stammered, "I am

Murdoch, a sage. I meant no harm to thee. I..."

"Silence fool! Thy insignificant life has run its course." She moved to step around a turned over chair but somehow got her gown tangled in it. In anger she tried to kick the chair aside and tore her gown. This infuriated her even more and her temper was not helped when she stepped in some spilled soup and slipped falling down amid barely concealed chuckles.

With her arm and dress bloody, her dress torn, and her hair now unkempt and bedraggled she was in danger of becoming a figure of jest. Miriam got to her feet and took one slow look around the room, causing men to cringe and put on mask-like expressions of great respect. Then with what dignity she could manage, Miriam stalked out of the room, only to scream an obscenity outside as a passing coach splashed her with mud.

Murdoch sat down, feeling all jittery inside and tried to calmly sip his tea, which now seemed cold and tasteless to him. He looked at Flettcher, across the table whose only comment was to voice a scholar's question. "Those now known as Spymasters used to be called by another name. Do you recall it?"

Murdoch closed his eyes for a moment, grateful for the orderly exercise of his mind to calm him. When he found the answer he stated it and then, hearing himself say the words suddenly realized their meaning. "I believe they used to be called Masters of Assassins...Oh!"

"Just so. And this one does not seem to be very fond of you."

Murdoch looked glum.

Later that night, alone in his room, with the cat sleeping on his bed, Murdoch wrote in his journal.

> *...After managing to give my name to the King's Spymaster, I thought nothing else could possibly add to the events of this day. Alas! There is more news, none of it good.*

Our little group of rebels has grown in numbers by three new members met this evening. Flettcher says he can vouchsafe all of them as true and loyal friends and that you would understand that. They bring ill news.

We are joined by a Wizard named Develon, his bodyguard, and a man who talks like a thief and calls himself Rheilly. This last is an associate of Develon.

Develon reports some of the same kinds of visions that you and Master Chiang experienced, and also feels there is some connection between the threat of the Outsiders and Telluria. It is another confirmation, although none were needed.

This man Rheilly reports he has recently spied upon the King of Ruritania and that Ruritania is launching some kind of religious crusade against Telluria, probably within the month. Ruritanian Legions are even now marching toward the Dire River. It would seem to me that this greatly complicates our plans.

If Elric engages in a war and wins it, he will be that much harder to reveal to the public. If he loses the war, we then have to start with the new conqueror, whom I have been told is just as unstable as Elric, though in a different way.

It has been a long and full day. We have agreed to meet in the morning to explore our opportunities. Now that I have had a chance to pause and reflect, I believe I rather like Develon, and Flettcher seems quite useful in a mysterious way. He seems to know things he shouldn't. I'm not as certain about this Rheilly. There is something about him that reeks of the exotic, although Flettcher trusts him.

There are two other matters that I wish to mention. First, the cat, Fang, has returned and seems in good health. Second, twice today, events occurred that struck me as strange. When the wizard's guards were here, they seemed to suddenly have an attack of the clumsies at a most opportune time. By that I mean there was a string of rather innocuous actions, missteps, minor accidents, that when put together seem to me to be a little strange. The second time was during the unfortunate encounter with the King's Spymaster, Miriam. Here too, an individual who clearly has had advanced physical training suddenly became most awkward and at a moment when it was useful for that to happen. I do not have an explanation for this, but I can think of no application of the Art that I have read about that would explain it. I do not believe in fortuitous coincidences. I would appreciate your comments.

Even with the news from Ruritania, I must report a certain feeling of confidence that I did not have when I arrived. There are allies to assist and the objective becomes clearer even if the means to accomplish it remain murky at the moment.

Signed, M.

Thirteen

"Loyalty has to be mutual or it is not loyalty.
It becomes mere servitude disguised."

—The Red Book of Roland,
Book of meditations for the Paladin order
known as The Companions.

Miriam the Spymaster, and Fairchilde the Sorcerer arrived at the door of His Majesty's private chamber at the same moment, in response to his summons. Like two hungry jungle cats, they eyed each other warily, hoping the other would give way and acknowledge precedence. After a long tense moment, Miriam stepped back and inclined her head in the slightest of bows, allowing the sorcerer to enter first. He did not notice the hint of a cold smile that flickered across her face as she entered behind him and it did not occur to him that in winning this petty point he had positioned the King's assassin at his unprotected back. Miriam was content to let him have precedence since it did not make him any harder to kill should she wish to do so.

These trifling matters vanished as they beheld their king and master, Elric the Dark. He was holding the black-bladed DemonSword unsheathed, resting across his knees and stroked it the way one might stroke a purring cat. There was an audible hum in the air that seemed to come from the sword itself.

Elric had a wide but strangely hard grin on his face and his eyes glinted like ice. He clearly was flushed in the face and neither of them liked the eager way he stroked the sword, nor the way it was humming.

Both quietly took their seats at the table and awaited his pleasure with growing apprehension. When the King finally spoke, Miriam discovered she had been holding her breath, a measure of the tension in the room.

"You are aware that Ruritania is moving against us?" At their silent nods, Elric continued. "We have decided that this affords an opportunity to give a demonstration of our true powers."

Miriam and Fairchilde flicked glances at each other. Glances that eloquently demanded to know what in the world he was talking about. Neither dared to speak.

The King did not seem to notice and continued. "Montrose tells us that if used with cleverness, our legions are sufficient to check Ruritania and drive them back. In this, We agree. However, We have decided not to use our legions in opposing this invasion."

The King's Sorcerer and Spymaster both looked blank. Each had similar thoughts. Not use the legions? What manner of madness was this? But again, neither dared to speak. The sword was humming louder than before.

Elric paused dramatically and then announced. "We have no need of legions. We, ourselves, in our own person, are sufficient to oppose this invasion alone." The sword hummed even louder and Miriam thought she could glimpse flames flickering behind Elric's eyes. Fairchilde was certain of it.

"We are gratified to see that you are both surprised at our decision. This is good. If the secret of our awesome powers have not reached even Our loyal Spymaster and Sorcerer, then they are indeed safe. Ruritania will have no warning until that day when we, ourselves, face their entire army with naught but our own sword to show." He laughed a cackling wild laugh.

Miriam steeled herself to show not the slightest hint of expression on her face, and noted Fairchilde was gripping the arm of his chair with a white knuckled hand while presenting a most calm and loyal face to the King. At the same moment, they both bowed formal acknowledgment of a King's decision, then took turns praising his wisdom and cleverness at creating such a plan.

Once released from the King's presence, outside the chamber in the corridor with the door safely shut behind them, both Spymaster and Sorcerer paused looking at each other in calculating ways. Fairchilde spoke first.

"It is the cursed sword! It has finally claimed him and now leads him on to bloodshed and folly."

Glancing around to insure they were indeed alone, Miriam agreed. "Of course it is the damned sword. It brings ruin to us all."

Each of these people had reached their current exalted positions of power through cunning, cleverness, and ruthless treachery. Neither of them needed to pick the bones of a carcass to reach the heart of the matter. It was Miriam who voiced the thought both were having.

"Perhaps it is time to launch lifeboats before the ship goes down. Much better to change captains than lose the whole crew."

With a thin smile, Fairchilde agreed. "I like that thought and would add another to it. Why not replace a king with a puppet under our control? It would solve many problems."

Miriam nodded. "It would do that, providing a way can be found past this cursed sword itself. It will protect him until it is finished with him."

With a low chuckle, Fairchilde took Miriam's arm in his and started escorting her down the hallway. "And have you not often told me that no one is proof against the assassins blade if the assassin be sufficiently clever? And are we not clever? Even more so as partners?"

Miriam joined in his laughter. "That we are," she said.

Just as the King was making his dreadful announcement to the Spymaster and Sorcerer, another meeting was taking place in the manor home of the Earl of Lancaster. In a room protected from all forms of intrusion, including spells, the Earl was meeting with two other nobles. They too were discussing the future of Telluria.

Present were the Earl, dressed as always in yellow velvet, Baron Simsohms who favored the color red, the Baron Ahrlehn who always dressed in silk of a stone gray shade. Baron Simsohms was a portly man, wide of girth, with a full dark beard that covered his many chins. Baron Ahrlehn had the lean figure of a fencer, pale complexion and white hair. He was the oldest man present, and in fact not a particularly good swordsman. His talents lay elsewhere.

They were seated around a heavy oaken table that had roses carved into its surface in a twisting chain that circled the edge of the table. There was the usual bowl of fruit and decanter of wine with goblets in front of each. Baron Ahrlehn puffed a long stemmed pipe. When the Earl was certain that the protective seals were in place, he began the discussion.

"My Lords, our venture moves toward fruition. The many seeds we have been planting are blossoming into war. I have received a report from our bankers in Schalim. The Ruritanian Legions are on the march. We can expect hostilities in about two weeks. May fortune favor our profits." They all drank to that happy thought.

Baron Simsohms laughed outright and slapped the table with his hand. "Upon my soul I wasn't sure we could do it. Success and fortune to us all."

Baron Ahrlehn puffed his pipe and with a smirk of satisfaction said, "Surely you had no real doubts. Machis is very predictable and so rigid in his thoughts that he is easily maneuvered from afar." All three nodded agreement to that, but it was the Earl who finally spoke of the real risk they had run.

"Machis was not the worry, as you well know. The dangers all lie in the Other." He would not say the name. Each of them paused in sober thought, pondering the enormous risks and savoring the special victory that comes only after having dared everything and won.

It had been a year filled with enormous tension for all of them. This business of creating a war where none existed had been very delicate. The ground had been prepared by the usual methods of spreading false rumors through the bankers in both countries. This was a simple matter, accomplished with the judicious use of gold. The real challenge had been in insuring that Machis the Omnipotent received the right message from the God he worshipped.

It was believed correctly that the fanatical Machis would only act on a commandment from his God, Dominic. Therefore the hazardous business of manipulating one of the Gods had to be undertaken. Being no fools, they had enlisted another of the Gods in their endeavor by appealing to the Temple of Baalsha, knowing that Baalsha would lend a friendly ear to any project that might involve domination.

Spells of great power had been cast by the Wizard's Guild in Telluria, flaunting the power that Dominic's Temples had forbidden, until the wrath of Dominic was stirred. Thus the commandment was given to Machis and all was in order for what they had been calling their Great Enterprise.

In truth, the dangers did not all lie in their daring to play power games with the Gods. But it was heartening to see the first round turn out as they had predicted.

Baron Ahrlehn allowed a smile to spread across his face. "Fortune and glory, gentlemen! Fortune and Glory!" He raised his goblet in a toast and they drank with him.

The Earl set his wine aside and returned to business. "How stands the Tellurian Legions?"

He was answered by Baron Simsohms. "Ideal for our purposes. They are well able to hold the Ruritanians at bay but not of sufficient strength to destroy them. We can look forward to a long war." It was a gratifying thought to him. His family owned shipyards and the rights to the major caravan routes of trading. A war meant huge profits for as long as it lasted.

The Earl was equally gratified from the same reason. His family had a virtual monopoly on the making of arms and armor, with control of iron mines and smithys. Baron Ahrlehn had similar motives for the huge risks they had jointly run.

He puffed his pipe and casually asked, "And what of our dear King Elric? Can he be counted upon to act in the proper fashion?"

Lancaster responded, "The good Baron here speaks wisely. Elric is our chief concern now that events are in motion. He is hot tempered. But I think this very fact makes it likely he will unwittingly fall into our plan and assist the Enterprise. After all, he has little real choice. He cannot stand by and refuse to defend the country from invasion. He has to order the Legions to fight, and once he does, events will be effectively out of his control."

With another puff of the pipe, the Baron replied, "True. True. Yet he is unstable, and there is always the cursed sword. Some have suggested it drives him mad. I think a close watch on Elric is in order over the next few weeks. What think you?"

They all three exchanged glances. Baron Simsohms declared, "It would do no harm to be prudent after having taken such risks. I have a thought. The Spymaster Miriam is three quarters ours all ready. Why not enlist her to keep the King on his proper leash until such time as the Tellurian Legions are marching? We have planned to include her in the long run, why not now?"

The Earl slapped the table with his hand. "Good thought! Good thought! The time is ripe to bring her in. We can offer her wealth beyond her dreams. And I think she prefers the winning side for herself. I shall meet with her."

On that positive note, the meeting ended.

Murdoch was writing in his journal.

Sire, I am pleased to report that our plans are coming together. With the able help of Flettcher, we have recruited a goodly band of rebels and each has been apportioned his task.

I am to remain at the center of the web, like a spider and organize and control events so we do not work at cross purposes. It will permit me to have the larger view of the whole tapestry while others work on individual threads.

That strange fellow, Rheilly, has volunteered to become a spy in the palace for us, claiming special skill in such matters. He will keep us apprised of doings there.

Flettcher is to recruit new rebels, with a particular eye toward military skill since we will need some kind of military force and someone experienced in such matters to train and command them. It would appear that there are very few likely recruits in the current Tellurian Army as most of the officer followed the tradition of buying their commissions, and thus are loyal to those who sold them.

The sorcerer Develon will use his art to protect us from discovery and keep watch for potential threats. In like manner, a swordsman companion of his has been given the dubious task of bodyguard for myself. This man, Finnegin, seems concerned about some of Elric's most recent victims. A good chap, I think.

Develon tells me the rumors about Ruritania are true, but he is confident he can provide us with a month, perhaps two, of delay before this stupid little war reaches us and interrupts the more important matters we are concerned with. Events proceed apace.

One more thing. A stable hand was struck by lightening behind the inn yesterday. There is some mystery, as it was not a rain day by the calendar and the sky was fair. Flettcher made some comment about it having something to do with your cat, but would not elaborate. I begin to think there are things about this cat that I really do not comprehend.

Fourteen

"One who truly wishes to master the Art must pay attention to the small things for all great things are but compositions of small things."

—The Khambrellian Grimoire,
Master sourcebook for all sorcery.

Master Develon once again made his way outside the city of Caprice. As was his usual practice, he wore the clothing and manner of a harmless old man, hobbling along with the aid of a walking staff. The huge emerald that surmounted his staff was covered with leather wrapping so as to avoid attention.

Indeed, it was the need to avoid attention that had brought him outside the eastern gate of the city once more. Shuffling along, nodding amiably to all he met, he retraced his earlier steps to the same small opening by the river where he had met Finnegin but a few days before, completely unnoticed.

There, after setting certain wards and insuring he was indeed alone, Master Develon removed the leather wrapping from his staff and let the deep green jewel catch the light of the Three Suns so it glowed with green fire. He then prepared the spell that he did not want the Guild, in particular the Guildmaster, to take note of.

Planting the staff firmly in the ground in front of him and holding it with both hands, his arms outstretched, Develon took the ritual three breaths of calming and sought the power of the staff with his mind. He felt the warm glow of contact with power at rest and under control.

Drawing upon years of training and skill, he drew forth a small portion of that power, forming it into a kind of small stream flowing out of the staff and into him. He added some of his own life force to this morsel of energy and then, with the sureness of a true wizard, used this combined energy to make contact with a plane of existence beyond the normal reality. This crossing of dimensions required use of the principles *transdimension* and *time* from the *Major Arcana*. This permitted him to use the ancient staff to draw forth a virtually unlimited amount of energy from across the planes and use that energy in major spells.

Having obtained the power he needed, Master Develon now focused in his mind an image of the Ruritanian fleet that would be needed to bring their invading army across the Dire River. He then created a sphere of magic, hundreds of leagues in diameter and added the activator *Seek*, along with the principles *knowledge* and *locus* from the *Minor Arcana*.

Upon his release, an ever expanding circle of magic, perceptible only to him, spread forth from his position on the river bank. When that expanding circle touched the designated target, the enemy fleet, Develon saw a point of light in his mind imposed upon a map. The Ruritanian Fleet was anchored in Salt Bay, awaiting the arrival of the troops. It was the information he sought. With a simple tap of the staff against the ground, he allowed the entire spell to simply dissipate like a cloud on a warm day.

Salt Bay was a former seaport located on the estuary of the Dire River, on the Ruritanian side. Sometime during the ancient Sorcery Wars, the entire seaport had been destroyed, leaving only rubble and mounds of natural salt. Hence its name, Salt Bay. The bay itself was unchanged and still provided excellent anchorage for the type of coastal galleys favored by the Ruritanians.

Develon knew that the galleys would have the well-known white Armor of God supplied by the Temple of Dominic, which would protect the ship against attack by magic. This meant he could not do something simple and direct like raining down splashes of magic fire on them. There was nothing to prevent the summoning of a storm though. In such a case, the ships would be damaged by wind and water rather than magic. The Armor of God would be useless.

A violent storm could be summoned in two ways. There existed spirits and elemental forces that could be commanded to create such a storm. These, however, were tricky and difficult to control. Much easier, but requiring much more power was to create the storm itself.

Like all sorcerers who had achieved the Fourth Circle of power, Develon knew that the universe was orderly rather than randomly chaotic. There were rules that remained true everywhere and could only be broken at enormous expense. Yet these same rules could be put to use by one of clever and subtle wit.

One example of such a rule was the experience well known to teamsters, that of a wagon rolling down a long hill which will appear to get heavier and roll faster and faster as it goes down the hill. Another such simple rule explained weather. It was well-known to sorcerers, and to some sages, that if an adequate amount of warm and moist air could be suddenly mixed with the right amount of cold air, and it was done in the right way, a storm would be naturally created. Thus a storm could be summoned by applying magic to the known rules of the universe. This Develon prepared to do.

With deft control and keen concentration, the sorcerer drew upon his own life force and, as he had earlier, used it and the power within his staff to touch the Continuum, called by some the Ethereal Plane, another dimension of reality. From there, he drew huge amounts of energy and set about weaving them into a pattern.

He used the activators: *move, control, heat,* and *speed* and combined them with the principles: *polarity, causation,* and *synchronicity* from the *Minor Arcana*. He then added the truly powerful principles from the *Major Arcana* of: *Synergy,*

Perversity, and *Disruption.*

When all of these elements were balanced together in a woven pattern of energy, he added the activator *designate* and identified it as the mass of air he wished to influence. Then, with a sharp command, he released his spell.

Develon then watched in his mind's eye as the entire pattern of glowing energy streaked off to the west, out over the ocean and surrounded a mass of warm moist air, then began moving it, like herding an invisible cloud, up the estuary to Salt Bay.

As this mass struck the cooler air over the river, it formed very dark clouds that began to roll as the natural law of cold meeting warm began to take effect.

♜ ♜ ♜

That very same morning, the admiral of the Ruritanian fleet anchored in Salt Bay consulted the calendar very carefully before issuing orders to his captains. Having satisfied himself that it was not a rain day, according to the calendar, he then ordered major work done in preparing the fleet for invasion. The first Ruritanian troops were scheduled to arrive in about a week and he wished to be ready.

Throughout the 140 galleys, sailors began to work. Some were using pitch to seal seams between timbers. Others were brushing fresh linseed oil onto sail canvas to stiffen and strengthen it. Still others were painting some of the upper works. Fresh tar was being applied to ropes. Oars were inspected for cracks or wear. The galley slaves were fed, given a day of rest, but of course left chained to their oars.

All was proceeding as expected when a sailor in the crow's nest of the flagship called attention to signal flags begin waved from a high look-out post on shore. The ship's captain informed the admiral and they both read the flag signal together. The lookouts were warning of an approaching dark cloud bank that looked like a storm.

The breeze was picking up and the cloud bank became

visible to all as the admiral and flagship captain hurried below to check the calendar again. There had been no mistake, it was not supposed to rain today. The captain of the ship was frankly astonished. In all his experience, the calendar had never been wrong in listing days that brought rain. The admiral was fearful.

He had complete faith in a calendar that had served for a thousand years without error. Therefore the approaching storm was not a natural one, but a storm created by someone. The Armor of God that protected his ships against attack by magic would have no affect against this indirect use of magic. He rushed back on deck.

Already there were waves in the bay. The storm was growing larger and darker and could be seen to be rotating as it bore directly down on the bay. The admiral began shrieking orders. Sailors began hurriedly putting lids on barrels of tar and pitch. Additional anchors were deployed into the bay from those ships who reacted quickly enough to get it done. Hatches were closed. Canvas was stretched over the open air grates that admitted the air and sunlight into the slave gallery, then tied down tight. Sailors began stringing lifelines the length of the decks. The storm continued to grow in fury and was approaching at a terrifying speed.

It roared into the bay, tightly packed with anchored ships. Rain, sleet, horrendous lightening with thunder, and then cyclonic winds struck the puny wooden ships like a giant swinging some colossal battle-ax. The hurried precautions taken by the fleet proved pathetic when the storm finally hit. Whole ships were lifted into the air before crashing to the bottom of the bay. Ships who were double anchored were pulled from their moorings, in some cases crashing into each other. The rotating winds stirred up waves that capsized ships and flooded the small camp on land that had been created for the expected army.

In less than twenty minutes, 127 ships were destroyed with most of their crews, including the helpless chained up slaves. The handful of ships that survived were those who ignored the admiral's orders and immediately put out to sea upon the first warning of the approaching storm. Not all of the ships were sunk by wind or water. Indeed, seventeen of the ships, including the flagship, burned when paint, tar, pitch and other such things caught fire in the opening minutes of the storm. Whether sunk or burned, the plain fact was the Ruritanian fleet was effectively destroyed and the invasion delayed for at least two months, perhaps more.

Standing on the broad balcony of Xanadu, Sahm-el was satisfied. He had taken the liberty of subtly increasing the force of Develon's storm by taking the energy being generated by the storm itself and folding it back into the storm creating a multiplier effect, so that the storm, as it grew, fed itself and continued to grow stronger. Develon would be offended if he knew, but this had been accomplished without Develon becoming aware of it.

♜♜♜

Just as the last of the Ruritanian galleys were sinking in Salt Bay, a hurried and whispered conference was taking place at the Palace in Caprice. Master Fairchilde had encountered the Earl of Lancaster on one of the broad stairways and pulled him aside into a window alcove to inform him of what they had witnessed with the King. The Earl found this to be disturbing news indeed and agreed to meet in the Royal Library in two hours with all parties to the "Enterprise". This now included Miriam the Spymaster. The library was chosen because it could be sealed for privacy without exciting comment, as scholars wishing to work undisturbed often set the Glyphs and Wards.

At the appointed time, all gathered in the library around one of the round stone tables. It was a pleasant setting for such a meeting. Rack upon rack of scroll cases, holding scrolls with their tags hanging out the ends to be read, and shelf upon shelf of leather bound books, many with locks and seals on them. There was a large stone fireplace on one wall, and one of the many old hounds given run of the place was dozing fitfully in front of the warm fire on a fur rug. They had the library to themselves, and Miriam quickly sealed it from intrusion.

Baron Simsohms heaved his heavy body into a chair with a grunt and asked petulantly, "What is the meaning of this most dangerous meeting? I thought all our plans were set."

Baron Ahrlehn echoed the thought. "Surely it is not seemly for us to be seen together, especially here in the palace."

The Earl, always composed, spoke in his usual quiet voice. "We meet at need. As to this place, I am satisfied as to its proof against spies. Events have occurred that alter our plans."

Both nobles flashed quick glances at the Spymaster and the Sorcerer. Tension was easily readable on their faces.

The Earl continue. "Our good king Elric has been captured by the cursed sword. He means to oppose the invasion alone, by the strength of his sword, rather than use the Legions. The meaning of this should be obvious."

Baron Ahrlehn recovered from the shock of this announcement first. "If true, this would mean disaster to us. Even the DemonSword could not be victorious over a whole invasion force. They will simply overrun him, and having done so, will easily conquer Telluria. There will be no protracted war, with its attendant profits."

Baron Simsohms could not contain himself. "Bloody Gods! It's worse than that. The Cursed Ruritanians will ban all magic in the name of their Dominic. This is calamitous."

Ahrlehn nodded. "Aye, all that is certain if this be true. How do you know the sword has finally captured him?"

At a nod from Lancaster, first Fairchilde and then Miriam described their meeting with the King. There could be no doubt.

There was a momentary pause as this news was digested. The solution was obvious and had already been discussed among Lancaster, Fairchilde, and Miriam; but it took a few minutes for the other two nobles to play catch-up ball and reach the same conclusion.

It was Ahrlehn who spoke the thought they all knew to be waiting to be spoken. "Elric must be replaced. Our success, indeed our very lives demand a Sovereign that we can depend upon." There. It was out in the open. To kill the King! It was a thought so large as to take one's breath away.

Simsohms, speaking in tones of either fear or awe, said, "'Tis a great thing to kill a king. Can it be done?"

Miriam laughed, a peculiar laugh devoid of mirth. "Anyone can be killed. Oh yes, my good Baron. It can be done. The only real problem is the cursed sword." Her tone carried a warning of her own power, implying that anyone of them could also be easily killed.

Master Fairchilde, Royal Sorcerer, spoke up in a similar tone. "The sword can be dealt with, by those of special knowledge. I can counter the effects of the sword." Fairchilde deemed it unnecessary to mention his soul held in bondage. If someone else killed the King, someone other than he, his soul would be released and his private little problem solved.

Simsohms pressed him. "Are you certain? 'Tis said this sword contains a most powerful demon."

Fairchilde gave him a withering look of disdain. "I have bound demons before. I can bind this one. Consider it a solved problem." He was successful in keeping his inner doubts and fears from appearing on his face.

Miriam smiled at Fairchilde. "What each of us could not do singly before, we can now do together."

Lancaster coughed nervously and then proceeded with business. "With the King...er...removed, who should hold the throne? It should not be one of us, of course."

Simsohms looked surprised. "Why not? Each of us is more fit than Elric. Why not you, or even me?"

With an engaging, yet superior smile, Fairchilde replied. "Subtlety, my good Baron, subtlety. Even though Elric is mightily feared and many will not weep to see him go, yet the matter of his replacement will rouse strong passions. Would you place yourself in the path of a dagger? No! What we need is a puppet to take the public glory, and danger, while we control all from behind the throne." The others found his argument persuasive, and quickly nodded their agreement.

Baron Ahrlehn voiced their consensus. "You speak wisely. But what puppet? Who would be so foolish as to take on the role, even unwittingly? You do not suggest Elric's son, do you?"

"Nay, I think we need not count the boy in our plans at all. Even the commoners know that he is a mean-spirited child who devotes his time to playing at swords and pulling wings off flies. He is a coward and will run at the first threat. There is no-one who will agree to his ascending to the throne. I think we must look elsewhere for our puppet. Perhaps one of the minor nobles can be found with large conceit and small caution."

Baron Ahrlehn agreed. "There is much advantage in your suggestion. Let us all search our minds for such a person. 'Tis certain that one will present himself in response to careful thought. Meanwhile, let the preparations for the removal of Elric proceed. All must be in place before the Ruritanians attack."

Lancaster pointedly looked at each one, and each one slapped a hand flat on the table in the ritual gesture of agreement. It was settled.

They left the library singly and quietly, with considerable caution to avoid being seen together.

When the room was empty, the old hound dog, that had been dozing by the fire, ignored by the entire group, suddenly blurred in the outline of his form and quickly took on the appearance of a household servant, complete with the proper livery. This servant got up off the rug, assumed a docile air, and left the room.

After making his way through the palace to the huge kitchen on the ground floor, he assisted in carrying out the garbage to the garbage pit. When no one was about, he resumed the shape of the hound dog and walked across the palace courtyard to a wagon that had just been unloaded at the woodpile.

Again, when an opportunity presented itself and no one was looking, he hopped up into the firewood wagon. There, safely unseen, he assumed the shape of one of the large hampers used to carry firewood. He then patiently waited until the driver returned to take his wagon of empty hampers out for another load of wood.

The guards at the main gate, dutifully searched the wood wagon as it left the palace, finding nothing but empty hampers, as they expected, they waved it on through. The wagon crossed the bridge that connected the palace isle with the main part of the city.

Once into the main part of the city, the hamper again changed to the hound dog form. As the wagon lurched around a corner, the dog nimbly jumped out and scampered up an alley. A few moments later, a man who was known to some as Rheilly emerged from that alley and began walking in the direction of the Blue Star Inn.

♜♜♜

The following morning, Murdoch eagerly checked his journal. He had written a full report of the news brought by Rheilly, and the news brought by Develon last night. He then had spent the rest of the evening trying to divine what these events might do to alter their plan. Develon had bought them precious time, as it would take the Ruritanians at least two months to replace the destroyed fleet. This other thing, though, was a wild card in the deck.

He had pictured two different assassination plots unfolding at the same time and two different assassins suddenly meeting each other with drawn daggers, behind the throne. It was ridiculous. An alteration in their plan was obviously needed.

When he opened his journal, that morning, he was relieved to see a message written there in the Master's hand.

"Now as to plans. We will allow the nobles the honor of removing Elric. Take no steps to interfere with their conspiracy. Their interference forces upon us steps that we would not choose on our own. I have searched the timelines and can provide you with some guidance.

"Within a few days, a week at most, you will be approached by a noble who will introduce himself as Lord Christopher. He will seek to engage your services as a scholar. In spite of his appearance and your certain judgment of him, I wish you to agree and to serve him loyally, as he will bring about your entry into the palace itself, where you can be much more effective.

"Keep the faith. We shall yet bring this endeavor to success."

Murdoch closed the book and sat in thought. The cat jumped to his lap and began purring. He absently stroked it and found himself saying, "Well Fang, it would seem that we are to go to the palace."

Fifteen

"Opponents arise from the natural differences individuals have in viewing the world. Enemies are created in one's own mind."

—The Divine Thesis,
Sacred Text for the Temple of Chardain.

Murdoch had gotten into the habit of taking an afternoon break, by accompanying the cat, Fang, out to the Inn's stable yard. The cat had been following him around and staying close, of late. The excursions behind the Inn were a pleasure to them both. The cat would scamper on into the stable to cheerfully reek havoc on the rat population, and Murdoch would enjoy the sunshine and rich odors of horse and hay while smoking his pipe.

He regarded the stable yard as being safer than a stroll on the city streets and was a bit scornful of the bodyguard, Finnegin's, concern for his safety. After all, who would bother with him, and who would think to make trouble here?

He leaned against the stone wall of the stable and drew deeply on his pipe. All of a sudden, Murdoch began to feel a tingling inside him and seemed to be hearing a voice crying "Danger! Danger! Danger!"

He couldn't tell where it was coming from but in looking about he saw two men emerge from the broad alley to one side of the Inn and another step out of the shadows of the narrow alley on the other side. They all wore cloaks that covered their clothing, and all had drawn rapiers.

Murdoch tried to think what to do. He kept hearing "Danger! Danger! Danger!" His feet seemed rooted to the ground and unwilling to move. The three men were approaching with drawn swords and their intent seemed obvious.

There was no one to help and he had only the dagger in his boot and no real training with it. He remembered the Bag of Tricks and sharply called out "Weapon!" but nothing happened. They were moving across the courtyard in what seemed like very slow movements, but Murdoch knew that was illusion caused by his fear and they would be on him in seconds.

He reached behind him and fumbled with the latch of the stable door. His fingers couldn't seem to operate it, thick and clumsy with fear. He tried to think of the word that would call up the dreaded secret weapon he was suppose to have, but his mind seemed to be swimming in molasses, except for the sharp screaming of "Danger!" that he kept hearing.

The first of the swordsmen reached him and with a sneering laugh tapped Murdoch on the shoulder with the point of his blade, neatly slicing into his sleeve. "Would ye be known as Murdoch the Sage, perchance?" The words were polite, but the tone was ice.

Murdoch found he couldn't speak as with a sickening dread he began to picture steel violating his body with burning pain and his own lifeblood pouring out onto the ground.

A second swordsman added in a drawl, "Why, we have here a speechless sage, what a find."

The third one laughed and cut a neat circle out of the front of Murdoch's doublet, just barely scratching his skin. They were playing with him and even in his terror, he hated them. Yet he could think of nothing he could do. So much for the mighty and clever hero.

The first one sneered again. "What could a little mouse like this have done to so anger our mistress?"

The third said, "Who cares? Get on with it." Murdoch closed his eyes and prepared for death.

In answer to his unspoken prayers a fourth voice sounded.

"Surely a little mouse is no fitting match for three such dangerous cats as ye be. I should think ye would prefer the dog behind ye."

Murdoch opened his eyes and there stood Finnegin, a grim smile on his face and his sword in hand. The three whirled around, taken completely by surprise. They beheld a tall thin man dressed as they were in leathers, cloak and plumed hat. He was holding a well-worn rapier, but their confidence increased when they noticed the few gray hairs at his temple and in his mustache and beard.

Without further words, the three assassins spread out, trying to form a ring around the lone swordsman, the prey momentarily forgotten. Finnegin drew the long heavy dagger that he carried in his left boot and with a cat-like grace began the dance of death with them.

Three blades flashed at once, to be evaded and parried with a slithering ease as he turned counter to their circling movement and moved sword and dagger with small but very precise and controlled motions. He was very quick, and over and over again, thwarted their attacks. The assassins found that they were bumping into each other and sometimes blocking each others attacks in their efforts to catch him off guard.

The swords flashed faster than Murdoch could follow as he waited breathless, still rooted to the spot to see the outcome of each engagement. There would be dizzying circles, then a sudden flash of blades, then a pause as all four caught their breaths and tried a new attack.

Suddenly one of the three was down, clutching at his throat with a bloody hand after a passage of blades too quick for Murdoch to understand. Instantly the fight changed.

The assassins could no longer encircle Finnegin, and he had proved to be a much better swordsman than they had even remotely expected. He now maneuvered them to one side of the stable yard, casually flicking his needle sharp rapier between both of theirs, applying just enough pressure with rolling parries to prevent them from touching him in any way with their blades.

One of them tried to fish a throwing dagger out of his belt and lost a hand to Finnegin's flashing blade. He stumbled back, dropping his sword and clutching the bloody stump as his severed hand fell to the ground.

The third one tried a combination of feints, parries and disengages only to find his sword seemingly tangled up in Finnegin's rapier blade long enough to get it out of the way and allow Finnegin to thrust him straight through the chest.

Seeing this, the assassin with one hand summoned the strength to run out of the stable yard, still trying to stop the flow of blood on his stump.

Finnegin let him go, turning to Murdoch who hadn't moved throughout the brief fight, and who now discovered he had been holding his breath.

Murdoch let it out in a long sigh. He looked at his bodyguard and savior and it was all he could do to keep from crying in heartfelt gratitude.

Finnegin wiped his blade on the clothes of the fallen and returned both sword and dagger to scabbards. He then put one hand gently on the quivering shoulder of Murdoch and said, "Perhaps now ye will listen to yer bodyguard's suggestions." He smiled, and Murdoch found he could move again, finally released from the terror.

Murdoch gripped Finnegin's hand in silence, and then jumped as something plopped at his feet. He was saved from appearing the complete fool by Finnegin's strong grip on his shoulder. Looking down, he saw Fang, looking up at him and awaiting his praise for the large dead rat he had just presented.

Finnegin laughed and Fang got a good back scratching. Murdoch was not amused.

While Finnegin dealt with the city guard, Murdoch went straight to his room. Locking the door he sat at his desk. His hands were trembling so much he couldn't fill his pipe. He could still see those three coming inexorably closer and closer, feel the sharp steel scratch his skin, hear it as it cut through his doublet. He had never been more terrified.

He put aside the still empty pipe, and pressing his hands

flat on the desk to stop their shaking, took the ritual three deep breaths of calming, breathing in through his nose and out through his mouth.

Feeling a little steadier, Murdoch turned to his notes and papers. There was something he must do before anything else. It took only a moment, thanks to his orderly ways, to find the scroll he had been given with the bag of tricks. He eagerly reread the part about a weapon:

> *Finally, good Murdoch, knowing that you are not a warrior and yet may find yourself in combat before this is over, I have included a weapon for you. It will come to you if you whisper, or even think about pronouncing the name 'Miranda.'*

"Miranda."

Upon voicing the name, Murdoch heard the same voice in his head that had been screaming "Danger" earlier, say to him, "I am here, Master."

Appearing in the air, just above his resting hands, he saw a glossy black dagger, floating steadily, its blade pointed to the ceiling and its handle down within easy reach.

Feeling a little silly, he spoke to the floating dagger. "What art thou, and what is thy function?"

Again he heard a reply inside his head. "I am a dagger of Xanthium, here to protect you. Call me at need. Release me onto thy enemies, and send me away when there is no need of my presence. I am bound to thee."

Murdoch pursed his lips and thought for a moment, in silence. The dagger hung motionless. "Will you always come at your name?"

"Always!"

"Begone then." And the dagger vanished.

Murdoch thought for a moment at how foolish he must have looked, yelling "Weapon! Weapon!" in the stable yard. He must never again panic and fail to remember this name. He considered getting quill and ink and actually writing it on the palm of his hand, but decided that would also look very foolish, and the ink would rub off just when he needed it most. His hands always got sweaty when he was nervous.

After considering several other equally ridiculous ideas, he finally reached the conclusion that the terror of this event had likely burned the name indelibly into his memory and he was worrying about nothing.

That evening, he sat at ease with the wizard Develon in the common room of the inn, having stew for supper.

The Blue Star Inn had its usual complement of exotic and mundane customers. There were three Dwarves at one table, and what looked like an alchemist and his assistant at another. There were several merchant types, a party of boisterous Halflings, and three members of the City Guard, in green and gold livery, their halberds leaning against the bar where they were drinking.

Of interest to many in the bar was the lone elf, sitting quietly by himself near the fireplace. Elves rarely ventured into the city at all, and the sight of one here was rare enough to cause quick glances in his direction from several of the Inn's patrons.

Like all elves, he was very thin, slightly shorter than a human, with blonde hair, very fair complexion, pointed ears, and gray eyes. He was dressed in gray leathers, with soft boots. There was a fully recurved Elven bow and quiver full of white arrows on the table. He was sipping something from a mug, and apparently ignoring everyone, although Murdoch thought it must be a real effort for him to shut out the mixture of feelings radiating from all the people in the room.

Watching the elf, Murdoch missed the entrance of another stranger, until Develon snickered and said, "Now there is an apparition to behold."

Standing just inside the double doors, and wrinkling his nose as if he smelled something unpleasant, there was a man dressed in blue velvet. He appeared to be a noble, and to Murdoch's mind one of the worst sort. His clothes were rich to the point of being gaudy, with sapphires sewn all over his doublet, rare furs trimming his sweeping blue cloak, and he even had diamonds on his hat. He wore a bejeweled sword that hung from his waist more like an ornament than a weapon, and had a matching glittering dagger in his right boot.

He appeared to be in his late thirties, was fair of skin and dark of hair, and clean shaven. He made his way through the crowded inn toward the bar, walking so as to suggest he was a thoroughbred racehorse among donkeys. Upon reaching the bar, he dramatically drew forth a silk kerchief and dusted off the bar before leaning his elbow on it.

Tweedy, the Innkeeper, hurried over to serve him. "What is your pleasure, Milord?"

The voice had a faint whiny twang to it. "I can assure you sirrah, that My pleasure does not extend to such unseemly establishments as this except in need. Burn me if this be not full of cutthroats and knaves." He made a negligent gesture toward the common room. "It would be too much to hope that you might have a decent wine with which I might wash this choking dust from my throat, I suppose?"

Tweedy had dealt with this type before. He put on his most pleasant smile and in very respectful tones said, "We are fortunate to have a most excellent array of fine wines to offer to our customers, that have been imported from as far away as Terice. May I suggest some for your approval?"

There followed a lengthy discourse on wines and vintages, with the stranger holding forth at length on the exact color, bouquet, and body of the wine that he must have, and of course, that he would accept no less.

Murdoch was musing as to how such a richly dressed and empty headed idiot came to be still alive in the streets of Caprice, when Develon pointed out the window to the waiting sedan chair and full platoon of guards in matching blue livery that were lined up outside, awaiting their master's pleasure. The bodyguard was sizable enough to deter most troublemakers, even in Caprice. One of the guards, Murdoch assumed the captain, entered and took up position just inside the main entrance, watching over the safety of his Master.

Tweedy went into the back and came out with a dusty bottle that evoked gasps of envy from a number of patrons when it was opened. Out of it Tweedy carefully poured a pale blue luminescent wine immediately recognized by those who know of such things, to be the rare Wildflower Wine, most expensive of all vintages.

The stranger sniffed it, sipped it, and acknowledged it was adequate to his needs. He paid over a sizable stack of gold coins for the single glass of wine, then an even larger stack of coins for the bottle. Having refreshed himself, he then leaned over and whispered something to the innkeeper.

Murdoch and Develon watched, amused, until this strutting bubblehead caught their eye, and picking up the wine bottle and his glass, came straight over to their table and sat down, without waiting for an invitation, as though it was his right to sit wherever he pleased and others would cheerfully accommodate him.

Suddenly tense, Murdoch eased back away from the table, preparing to say the name of his magic weapon. Develon absently stroked the staff he cradled against his elbow. The stranger smiled and offered them both wine. Murdoch and Develon watched carefully as he poured the blue wine into their glasses. He poured himself another glass and spoke.

"The innkeeper tells me you are a trained sage. I have need of one in my service." His remarks were addressed to Develon.

Murdoch gritted his teeth, wondering how to get rid of this fop without causing a scene. "I am the sage he spoke of. However, I am not seeking a position at this time." He sat more easily in his chair, feeling certain that this featherbrain could not pose a threat to him.

The fop turned from Develon and looked at Murdoch. "Really? You are the sage? I would have thought you were assistant to this one." He indicated Develon again, with his rich beard and flowing robes.

Murdoch smothered his own indignation while noticing the briefest of smiles flicker across Develon. He tried once more to find a polite way to dismiss the idiot. "I assure you good sir, I am the sage good Tweedy was speaking of, and I must repeat that I am not seeking a position at this time."

"Hah! A man of spirit. I like that. Surely for the right price you would accept the honor of being in my service? I mean to say, all of you tradespeople are willing to do anything for gold, and I assure you I have gold in more than adequate quantities. My family traces its lineage back to the original royal families of Telluria."

Again, Murdoch found speech difficult. He started to give the only possible excuse the fellow was likely to accept, that of already being in service to someone else, when he was interrupted by the featherbrain who went on talking.

"I see that you do not realize to whom you are talking." He stood up and with a perfect courtly bow announced in a regal tone, "I am Duke Christopher de Reayses, Lord of Whitehall, Holder of the sacred White Feather, Keeper of the golden Shield of Telluria, and master of the finest stable of racing horses in the land."

It required only a few seconds for Murdoch to register the name Christopher, and when he did, his jaw dropped in astonishment.

Sixteen

"To live, is to do more than merely exist day-to-day. Real living involves an on-going inquiry and dialogue with the universe at large."

—Attributed to an imperial dragon named Jasmine

Ginseng had set one portion of his mind on watch when he retired to sleep and it was that which brought him awake. He needed no water-clock to tell him it was nearly morning and the other two would be arriving soon.

With a simple guttural sound, he brought light to his sleeping chamber, then proceeded to carefully stretch his serpentine body, unfolding the great leather wings and holding them out stiff for a brief moment before carefully tucking them back against his dorsal scales. He stretched each clawed foot, raking long troughs in the pile of coins he was lying on, then climbed to his feet.

A gold coin had lodged itself between scales on his left hip and he used a claw from his left hind foot to flick it out. For the ten millionth time he thought with envy of humans and other ephemerals who could sleep on something beside dense metal without becoming infected with the dreaded Khatarh that the metal protected against.

His own bed was a pile of mixed gold and platinum coins some one hundred meters across and heaped a full three meters high. Like all dragons, except those afflicted with the Khatarh or dragon sickness, he gave no thought at all to the monetary value of these coins, but only their medicinal value.

Ginseng nibbled a little bit of anthracite from the pile kept at hand, in order to settle his digestion, then proceeded from his cave sleeping chamber through a large tunnel to the bath.

He emerged into another large cave that was nearly filled with a lake. There was no need for him to command light in this chamber for the lake itself was composed of a mixture of water and fire that could not occur naturally. Huge flames roared upward from the surface of the lake, suddenly winking out only to appear at another location on the lake. There was a constant dull roar and very pleasant aroma of brimstone that he found quite refreshing.

He plunged into the lake of fire, with gusto, completely submerging his great body and head, then bursting upward, clear out of the water before plunging back into it again.

Like his bed of coins, the lake of fire provided vital aid in maintaining his health and sanity. There were tiny little creatures called Mindmites, no bigger than a dust mote, that lived on gold coins when they were heaped together in large amounts. These Mindmites were parasites that would crawl into the ear and proceed to devour the brain of any sentient being that came in contact with them. They lived, undetected on the gold.

Mindmites made excellent guardians of his bedchamber, but it took a dip in the lake of fire to cleanse them from himself.

He emerged from the pool, his scales glistening in clean obsidian and gold colors, and proceeded to preen himself before flapping his huge wings to dry. Then, in the sheer joy of the moment, Ginseng raised his head up and with a roar breathed a tongue of flame straight up toward the center of the cave. It was exhilarating.

With a stop at the ice cave that served as his meat locker, for a quick breakfast, a whole ox and three sheep, he proceeded to the meditation chamber. Preparations must be made for the Ceremony of Schamoohze.

The Chamber of Meditation was a natural cave roughly a hundred meters in diameter, with a high vaulting rock ceiling that appeared to be supported by natural columns of limestone that had grown drip by drip over the centuries. The floor had been smoothed of all stalagmites and had one large circle inscribed on it, that contained three smaller circles within it. In the center of each of the smaller circles there was a sloping stone shelf mounted firmly on stone pedestals. Beside each of these, there was a small round table, also within the small circle.

Ginseng arranged for self-refilling crystal decanters of pure cold water and a tray of assorted meat snacks to be placed on each small table. Then, with a wave of one small foreclaw, he dimmed the light in the chamber and moved to the sloping shelf in the nearest small circle.

He approached the resting shelf from behind, where it sloped to meet the floor, and smoothly slid his mighty chest and ventral scales along its well polished surface until it was comfortably supporting nearly his whole weight. Tucking his wings in tight, and carefully curling his tail around so it was entirely within the circle, he then performed the ritual three breaths of calming and breathed the incantation that created a circle of blue light around the large circle that enclosed his and the other two small circles. An energy barrier had just been created that not only protected against outside intrusion, but also protected his home from any threat that might appear from other dimensions.

With the perfect punctuality possible only to those who are masters of time and space, his two colleagues suddenly appeared within the field and mounted their own resting benches. One of them, known by his shortname of Chiang, was completely gold all over, with no black markings of any kind. The other, Jadefire, had beautiful stripes of obsidian angling over his body in parallel patterns, like that of a tiger. Ginseng himself was spotted like a leopard.

Ginseng began the ceremony with a greeting. "Welcome, my Brothers from Across the Void. Let us commence." There was no need for polite chat or explanations as to why they were there. All three knew that with a clarity of thought that made formal statements quite unnecessary. Having all the time in the world, they wasted none of it on the superficial.

Each took just a twinkling of a second to prepare a protective field that would enclose his own personal circle at need, leaving it ready but inactive. It was a minor but standard precaution.

Jadefire then reached out with his mind and lightly touched the powerful minds of his two colleagues. There was a slight bit of shifting about as the three strong minds fitted themselves together into a unity or fusion. When they were harmonized as one, Chiang gave direction while Ginseng provided raw power and their collective mind began searching outward through the universe.

Although each was quite capable of doing this by himself, by joining together, they greatly increased both their range and their accuracy, due to the Multiplier Effect.

Each saw within his mind's eye the same scene from the focus point of their collective mind. It was a scene that began in the Chamber of Meditation and swiftly passed through the rock of the mountain and up into the air until it reached a height where the air turned black and cold and the stars appeared to be diamond points of light.

It flashed on out beyond the paths traveled by the Three Suns of Eridani and began questing across the universe, seeking the Outsiders.

The three of them had done this sort of thing on many occasions and they were not surprised to see the multitude of stars arrange themselves into a blue-white whirlpool pattern. Many of these stars had worlds tied to them with the invisible strings of gravity. Some of these worlds were dead, just floating rock. Others were frozen balls of gas. But some of them were living worlds.

Among these living worlds, each of them recognized places they had visited in the past, traveling there in an instant by folding time and distance with the power of their minds.

Indeed, each of them knew of others of their kind living on some of those distant worlds, as well as friends of other species. On this occasion, though, they were not seeking friends.

The focus of their collective mind swept onward, across the whirlpool pattern of stars to the far side. There, the three found what they sought.

Humans fought the Outsiders in grim battles to the death, in a desperate effort to slow the inexorable conquest by these reptilian monsters. The collective three watched silently as humans enclosed in round flying ships sent spears of light at the bulky wedge-shaped metal ships of the Outsiders and received the same from them.

The collective three carefully charted the progress made by the Outsider fleets since last they looked upon them, noted so many worlds destroyed or enslaved, measured the speed of advance of the border that separated the territory of the Outsiders from all else.

When they had seen enough, the collective mind of the three withdrew as silently as it had advanced, its presence undiscovered by Outsider and human alike. With a soft sigh, each allowed the fusion of their minds to dissolve and they were once more in the Chamber of Meditation.

There was a long pause as each digested this experience in his own fashion. Their individual reactions differed in minor degrees. Ginseng was impressed with the power and scope of the invasion by the Outsiders, likening it to the remorseless advance of an endless horde of army ants. Jadefire took note of the lack of success of the human defenders and was reminded of what an unevolved species humans were. Chiang, who of the three had spent more time among humans voiced his reaction aloud.

"They show spiritual strength, these humans. They die bravely and refuse to submit to slavery."

Jadefire was not impressed. "To what end? They are a suicidal specie who have blocked their own growth by traveling a dead-end path. They remain beneath our notice."

Ginseng joined in. "True, they are most self-limiting, yet

I do sense a potential there for something greater. They seem to have an abundance of raw spirit."

Jadefire narrowed the pupils of his eyes to more slits and turned to Ginseng. "You have evidence of this potential?"

"I have!", interrupted Chiang. "I have known a few rare humans who have managed to transcend their dependency bonds and fully develop their spiritual powers. Sahm-el is such a one. His abilities match our own."

"You would not suggest that this and other humans will be able to defend this world from the Outsiders, would you? Even if what you say is true and there are these rare exceptions, why should they do better than the humans we have just observed?" A bit of steam curled up from Jadefire's nostrils.

"I say only that there are some of these humans who have backed away from their self enslavement to artificial machines and have actually developed their own powers. And I agree that the specie has large untapped potential. If a large group of them ever managed to realize that potential, I suspect they could equal us in every way."

"Master Chiang, I know better than to doubt your wisdom. But I have seen no evidence of this. Furthermore, to return to the need for this meeting, my visualization of the time lines of the Cosmos indicates there is little chance these Outsiders can be prevented from destroying this world, regardless of what the humans may do."

Ginseng, who had been watching the discourse of his colleagues in silence, now offered his thoughts. "I too, have reluctantly reached the same conclusion. This world is lost. It is the reason I invoked the Schamoohze. I believe we must arrange for our brethren to migrate to other worlds." Jadefire nodded his agreement. There was a long pause as each gave thought to this.

Finally, Chiang spoke. "I have no evidence to offer that would alter that conclusion. However, a handful of these 'rare exceptions' of humans are pursuing a plan of desperation that has some slight possibilities. I shall continue to assist their efforts."

Ginseng looked almost startled. "Assist? You know the First Law!"

"I do indeed. Allow me to quote.

'Lend not the help of a single claw, for the very act of assistance weakens those thee would help. Rather, provide opportunities for growth by creating tests and challenges, so that those thee would help will find their own strengths and earn spiritual rewards.'

"Be assured, I shall observe First Law. Their plan involves the fulfillment of prophecy by finding the true heir to the Dragonthrone of Telluria. I have agreed to find this heir and provide the tests that will confirm prophecy. I have located a likely candidate."

Jadefire took a sip of clear cold water. "A true heir to the Dragonthrone? Where?"

"In a most unlikely place, believe me."

Ginseng voiced the obvious. "A true heir to the Dragonthrone would change everything. We would be obligated to remain, even to our death."

With what could only be described as a smile, even for his kind, Chiang replied, "Just so."

Seventeen

"In politics, the reason given to the public for an action taken, and the real reason it was taken are never the same."

—Drury's Primer for Princes,
An ancient text about the acquisition and uses of power.

The man casually turned into the alley, reasonably certain that no one took notice of him, or at least those that did would be such that would keep silent about his actions. He was cloaked and hooded, and the scabbard of a rapier peeked out from under his cloak. He looked much like many another in this part of Caprice, the east end near Temple Court.

Moving quietly down the alley, he came to a small open courtyard framed by the backs of several buildings. In the center of the courtyard was a well, with winch and bucket. He glanced about and saw no one, which was what he expected. Nevertheless, he made the appropriate sign with the fingers of his left hand, bringing comfort to the unseen watchers that he knew were there, waiting silently with cocked crossbows, to pass only those who knew the signal.

He walked straight to the well, and after leaning over to look down it, awkwardly swung his legs over the stone retaining wall. He felt for the iron rungs that he knew to be mounted inside the well, and cursed to himself as his sword scabbard tangled with his cloak and nearly precipitated a fall.

Having finally gotten all straightened out, he descended into the well. About halfway down, a certain rock pushed in a certain way, opened a small hidden door in the side of the well. He eased himself through this cramped door and found himself in a tunnel. It took him twenty more minutes to carefully make his way past a plethora of traps and hidden guards until he finally arrived at his destination, a very comfortable meeting room with a table of food and drink, and the people he had come to meet so secretly. He was the last to arrive.

Baron Ahrlehn seated himself next to the heavy Simsohms and across the table from the Earl of Lancaster. The sorcerer Fairchilde sat to Lancaster's right and the Spymaster Miriam to his left. They were in good humor, which was more than he could say, given their surroundings.

"Madam, is it really necessary for us to meet in this hole in the ground? I could have been injured climbing down that accursed well."

Miriam gave him a smile completely devoid of any warmth. "My Lord, you should be honored. It is not everyone who is permitted to enter the secret chambers of my Guild. Far fewer are permitted to leave."

Baron Ahrlehn felt himself brought up by a chill realization he had overstepped himself, having forgotten in his exertions of climbing that they were meeting in the Assassins Guild underground chambers. He blushed and sputtered his apology. "Good lady, I humbly seek your pardon. I meant no aspersion on your craft or this…er…noble place. A man of my years cannot easily scale castle walls as I might have done in my youth."

Lancaster, noting that Miriam seemed to be mollified by the Baron's obvious fear, interceded. "Well spoken, Baron. And yet I warrant there may be a thrust and parry or two left in those old bones, even yet." He chuckled in what might be taken for a friendly manner, then drew their attention to the purpose of the meeting.

"Baron Simsohms, I understand you have a candidate to propose for the role of puppet in our enterprise. Please, enlighten us."

Attention turned to the portly Baron who had just bitten into an apple and was caught with mouth full. He choked down the bite then composed himself and announced with a wide grin. "I have found the perfect gull, fitting in every particular. He comes from a noble line, actually does have a tie to the ruling family, is pleasing in appearance and acceptable to the people, and best of all, is a hopeless fool that will be easily molded to our design."

He paused dramatically, then announced, "He is Duke Christopher De Reayses, Lord of Whitehall, Holder of the White Feather, and Keeper of the golden Shield of Telluria." He waited for applause.

None came. From blank expressions he could tell that the name was unfamiliar. "The De Reayses family is one of the oldest in the land."

Lancaster sounded impatient. "Yes, yes, we have all heard of the family. But that line died out. Who is this Duke Christopher? What do you know of him?"

"The De Reayses Line did not die out. He is the last surviving one. He has spent his time away from court, raising horses. I tell you he is perfect for the part. Do you think I am such a fool as to propose a total stranger without some investigation. I have inquired into his background and found it to be as I have stated. Besides, I asked Master Fairchilde to examine him as well, to insure our safety."

At that, Lancaster relaxed a little and turned to Fairchilde. "What have you to say of this?"

"I will vouchsafe this Christopher. I made use of my Art to test his lineage and confirm his identity. Moreover, I set one of my servants to watch over him for a few days, from the shadows. He is a vain empty-headed fool, more concerned with his pretty face and appearance than of the content of his thoughts, of which he appears to have few.

"I have observed him lecturing a clerk he has hired, on the importance of fine dress and the cut of doublets and cloaks. He takes meals at a local inn and spends lavishly, seeking to buy admiration that he could not earn. He has no recognition of flattery and styles himself a man of the world, although in a conversation the other night, he confessed he did not know if Ruritania was to the south or to the west of Telluria and insisted it did not really matter since there were an abundance of clerks and scholars to keep track of such things. He is ideal for our enterprise."

Fairchilde took a sip of wine and leaned back in his chair. Lancaster thought for a moment then looked at each one around the table. Each member of the cabal slapped hand down on table in agreement. They had their puppet. Talk turned to how to recruit this brightly plumed bird and Baron Ahrlehn was selected to accomplish that delicate task. The meeting came to an end.

Each left this secret place separately, as they had come, save only Miriam, who had business to conduct. Fairchilde could not resist a touch of the dramatic and took his leave in a flash and a cloud of smoke.

The sorcerer appeared in the pentagram of his own laboratory, eager to return to another matter that had recently caught his attention.

Of late, he had been seeing the image of a crown in unlikely places. The first time had been when he chanced to catch his reflection in a wineglass and saw himself wearing a crown. This had occurred four days ago. At first he thought it but a trick of the flickering candlelight.

But the following day, while walking in Harmony Gardens, he had chanced to see his reflection once again, this time in the fish pond that contains the brilliant blue carp that flash as they turn in unison, like a naval fleet. Again, he saw himself with a crown, and not just any crown, but in fact the very crown of Telluria with its golden dragon emblem. This was no mere trick of light, but rather a portent of some kind. Its meaning remained unclear, for he did not dare to hope such an omen might presage what it seemed.

Then yesterday, it had happened again. The smoke from his circular fireplace had suddenly swirled and seemingly formed a hazy image of himself seated on a throne and wearing the Crown of Telluria. Three being known as the number of significance, this third vision could not be ignored.

Like all sorcerers who had mastered at least the Sixth Circle of Power, Master Fairchilde was knowledgeable of the nature and uses of the Infinite Scroll. Put simply, all beings who are capable of thought, shine forth with the radiance of those thoughts. This forms an endless and ever renewing pool of life-force energy in which the world is suspended. Since this pool is made up of the thoughts of living beings, it is visualized as an endless scroll of information that can be read by those with the wit and power to do it.

Of course, not everything written on this scroll could be read by everyone. There were masters of the Art, including Fairchilde himself, who could shroud certain subjects from all who were of less power than themselves. Then too, the various Temples were able to conceal certain matters under the cloak of the Holy Covenant, said to be an agreement made among the Gods themselves. Still, anyone with the ability to cross the dimensional planes with their mind could learn much from the Infinite Scroll.

This Master Fairchilde prepared to do.

He had several means at his disposal. The simplest, and cheapest in cost, was to summon one of the greater demons and force it to do his bidding by obtaining the information for him that he sought. This required the human sacrifice of an innocent soul, a cheap enough price and something he had done often. There was an uncounted number of serving girls, orphans, and the sons and daughters of enemies who were quite suited to the task.

There were two objections to the use of this method. First, if the Demon summoned understood that the information requested was really valuable, the Demon might lie about it for his own perverse pleasure. Secondly, and just as important, if the information was obtained by a Demon, then that Demon would know the information, itself, and the information could not be kept secret except by outright slaying of the Demon, a formidable task.

A second means of reading the Infinite Scroll was by use of an object of power, such as one of the great Staffs of Sorcery. Fairchilde had such a staff, but this too was a source of problems. Such objects of power as a Staff of Sorcery call attention to themselves each time they are used. Sorcerers all over the world would be aware that Master Fairchilde was wielding his staff. This could easily bring unwanted curiosity from the very ones who were actually capable of posing a threat to any of his plans.

The only safe way, was to personally prepare and cast a spell, drawing upon his own personal power. It was an arduous task and also contained some risk, for to succeed he had to send his mind across the dimensional planes of time and folded space. Loss of control during such a spell would bring devastating results. If he succeeded though, he would be in perfect control of the information he sought, and could prevent most others from learning it. The risks were well worth it, in this case.

Master Fairchilde began preparing himself for the spell. He stepped into the center of his pentagram and took the three deep breaths of the Ritual of Calming. He then began assembling the components, activators, and principles of magic, in his mind, that he would need to cross the dimensional planes and read the Infinite Scroll.

The sorcerer took a small amount of his own life force and shaped it with the activators: *join, control, sense,* and *open*. This allowed him to draw a large amount of energy from the continuum which he then molded by using the principles of: *knowledge, nexus,* and *association* from the *Minor Arcana.* Taking great care to keep the forces in balance, for a slip in concentration at this time would be disastrous, he then added the enormously powerful principles of: *transdimension, synergy,* and *time* from the *Major Arcana*. These last three allowed him to cross the dimensional planes from this level of reality without being disintegrated by the experience.

He then poured raw energy into the complicated matrix of the spell, building it higher and higher in power, yet keeping it in harmony with itself, so it would last long enough for him to read what he needed from the infinite Scroll. Then with a clap of his hands and a wordless command, he released the spell.

In his mind's eye, Fairchilde saw a stream of energy flowing from himself toward all points of the sailor's compass. There was the familiar tingle of magic washing through his mind, then a brilliant white flash of light and words began appearing before his eyes.

Now was the time of greatest care, requiring the greatest concentration. He allowed the words to flow past his perception, faster and faster until they started forming flashing images, pictures in his mind like shadows thrown from a large fire. As these pictures flickered through his consciousness, Fairchilde was unaware of his physical body being drenched in his own sweat, standing in the pentagram of his own laboratory, muscles tight from the strain, his eyes drying out from staring unblinking into nothingness.

He remained this way until the image he sought flashed before him, that of himself wearing the distinctive gold and emerald crown of Telluria. By pure force of will, he stopped the flow of images and watched them dissolve into words again. These words he read carefully and memorized.

"With the death of Elric, the crown passed to the Royal Sorcerer, Fairchilde, who imposed his will upon all his loyal subjects."

With a sigh, Fairchilde released his spell, allowing the forces to dissipate like a cloud on a warm day. He sank to the floor in relief. Yet, also in joy, for his wild guess had been confirmed.

Eighteen

"Never question a gift of Fate."

—The Korakorahm,
Sacred Text for the Temple of Dhao.

The next day, people on the streets of Caprice took no notice of a man stolidly plodding along toward the center of the city. He was dressed in simple clothes and if any of the early morning merchants took any note of him at all, they would have taken him for some common servant on a mundane errand. It was his intention that they do so.

Shapedancers use no permanent names to designate themselves. Unlike the Ghoneehmah, the fixed ones, their identity is too fluid to be confined within a single name. This particular shapedancer, for the moment a human servant, followed custom and used no name. He was known to the Royal Spymaster, Miriam, simply as "Number One," because he was her best assassin.

On this bright afternoon, he had a new task to perform, the killing of a meek little balding scholar who had incurred the displeasure of the King's Spymaster. As he maintained the dull vacant expression on the human face he was wearing, he thought about how different this day's work was compared to the recent challenge represented in the death of a wizard. The assassination of a competent sorcerer was the supreme challenge of his art, and brought a joy and zest that would surely be missing from this day's task.

A scholar. No danger, and thus no challenge there. He was still somewhat perplexed by the insistence of Miriam that he personally attend to such a minor task. True, there had been one attempt on this fellow that had failed. But who could have predicted that a swordsman of such skill would intervene and defend this nobody. No matter. Even assuming he is protected by a bodyguard, he should present no real challenge to a master assassin who had succeeded against really formidable targets. What good is a bodyguard when death can strike from a carpet, or desk, or literally anything else.

Still, for a human, Miriam was certainly no fool. There must be something unusual about this scholar. And, his own standard of professionalism demanded that he treat this killing with as much care as if the target really were dangerous. Hence, the anonymity of a common servant. During his hour long walk across the city he had changed his appearance four times, each time stepping out of public view only to re-emerge as a completely different person.

The scholar he was to kill lived at the Blue Star Inn, and recently entered in the employ of a duke. Miriam had explained that she wished to place her own person in that position so she would have an ear inside the Duke's camp. It was clear to "Number One," however, that she also had some personal animosity toward this luckless fellow.

He arrived at the inn shortly before the scholar's habitual afternoon walk in the stable yard. The plan was both simple and subtle. The inn had a small side door that opened into an alley on one side. This scholar, named Murdoch, had formed the habit of slipping out this side door every afternoon and simply walking down the alley to the stable yard behind the inn. Apparently the swordsman who thwarted the first attempt was still guarding the scholar and took care to survey the alley and accompany him on these excursions.

The alley was made up of large flat flagstones. It would be

a simple matter to pry up some flagstones and hide them in the barn, then take their place, in the shadowy alley. There would be only a brief time when a few stones would be missing, and this not likely to be even noticed should someone come down the alley at that precise moment.

Once in place as a flagstone, he had but to wait for his target and use the venomous sting all shapedancers have, striking right out of the stone like a phantom serpent. With great care, he had prepared his stinger with the devastating poison Bai Hara Chi. The scholar would have no warning and no chance at all. It would then be a matter of waiting in place as a cold stone until an opportune time to take on another shape, probably as a workman, replace the missing stones, and leave. While stone, the assassin could be harmed only by that which could damage natural stone.

It would be apparent that Murdoch had been poisoned, his skin would turn hard and black for one thing. But the means of the poisoning would remain a mystery. There was little real risk.

Upon arrival at the inn, it seemed all to easy. The side alley was deserted. The flagstones were easy to pry up but proved to be extremely heavy. He was forced to change his form to that of muscular stonemason in order to gain enough strength so he could move the stones, one at a time to clear a space large enough to hold his bulk, for although shapedancers can change their form, their overall size remains constant.

He was lugging the second stone down the alley when he became aware of a cat at his feet, intrigued by a loose bootlace. The bootlace was in keeping with the persona he had just created, that of a careless and somewhat slovenly worker. He had thought it a nice touch, along with dirty fingernails and bad breath. However, now he had a cat skipping and playing about his feet while he carried the heavy stone.

He stopped in the quiet alley, looked both ways to insure he was alone, then aimed a mighty kick at the damned cat.

Immediately, there was a blinding flash and roar of thunder and all went dark for "Number One." The Royal

Spymaster's chief assassin, with a record of 179 kills and no failures, never knew what it was that took his life in an instant of blinding pain.

Inside the building, Murdoch and Finnegin were coming down the staircase when they heard a bolt of lightening strike somewhere very near the building. Finnegin rested hand on sword pommel and halted Murdoch on the stairs, sweeping the room with his eyes. They were a few minutes later than usual, because Murdoch had forgotten his pipe and they had gone back for it. Otherwise, they would have completed their afternoon drink by now and been out in the stable yard, perhaps to be hit by this lightening.

The innkeeper, a portly man with a normally friendly smile and fussy nature came hurrying out of the kitchen. He was saying to no one in particular, "Not again. The third time this month. I shall have to raise the wages to keep stablehands, I am sure."

Finnegin kept Murdoch on the stair landing as the innkeeper hurried out the side door. Then the two men crossed the common room and took seats at a table, their backs safely to the wall and doors plainly in view. Each ordered a mug of hot tea and pretended to take only passing notice to the noise in the alley. Soon, Tweedy, the innkeeper, came back in, looking very disturbed. He poured himself a mug of strong black ale that was kept in the huge barrel at the end of the bar. Then his eye seemed to fall on Murdoch, and he hurried over to their table.

"Good sirs, may I join you for a moment? I confess I have just had an experience, oh my yes, an experience." He plopped down as soon as Finnegin gave him a smile and a nod.

Murdoch had come to like the portly little man, who not only served some of the best and most exotic food in the city, but was usually of a bubbly and jovial temperament, a friend to everybody. It was unusual to see him as he was now, clearly shaken.

It was Murdoch who gave Tweedy the opening he was clearly waiting for by asking, "Well Tweedy, you do look a sight. What has occurred in yon alley that causes such noise and excitement?"

Tweedy placed his mug carefully on the table and leaned forward, after glancing around the nearly empty common room. "Upon my soul, I do believe we have something of a mystery here. I do believe it. Mark you now, it was lightening that struck in the alley, and a monstrous bolt it must have been too. Imagine lightening striking right next to my inn, out of a clear sky."

He sipped his ale and went on. "Three times! Lightening has struck near this building three times in the past few weeks. Right out of the blue! First time killed a stablehand in the back. Not that he was any great loss, mind you. He was the type who would set a dog on fire just for sport.

"Second hit a thief as he was counting his coins in the loft of my stable. That almost set the stable on fire. Now this!" He leaned over and said very quietly, "Do you know, I do not even know what that thing is that is lying in the alley. Strange sort of creature, all muscle and tentacles, like some sea creature. But it has a hole blasted right through it, just like the others. Now what do you think of that?"

Murdoch added a bit of sugar to his tea, and in the same hushed tones leaned forward and asked Tweedy, "Truly? Not a man then? What do you think it is ...or was?"

Tweedy leaned back expansively, still talking in soft tones. Finnegin had the impression that the innkeeper was concerned about the affect this might have on his business, and was thus trying to be very discreet. If so, Finnegin thought he was failing miserably at it. Tweedy went on, "The very reason I have come to you, good scholar. I thought you might know the nature of this creature. I have heard that not all demons have wings. Is that true? For assuredly, this thing has no wings and I thought it might be some kind of demon, got loose from the Wizard's Guild."

Murdoch suppressed a smile. "I hardly think it could have been a demon. It is true, there are demons known who show no wings. But I can think of none that would be vulnerable to something as simple as a bolt of lightening, no matter how large the bolt. I believe you can rest assured it was not some kind of demon. As to what it was, at the moment I have not a thought."

The front doors of the inn were suddenly swung loudly open, banging against the walls, and a crowd of men came bustling in. Tweedy jumped up and ran to serve them; and Murdoch groaned when he saw who it was, Duke Christopher de Reayses, accompanied by Baron Ahrlehn and their combined bodyguards. In the few short days that he had been in service to Duke Christopher, on orders from his master, Murdoch had discovered that Duke Christopher was his least favorite person.

In public, the Duke had proved to be jovial, friendly, good humored, and a boon drinking companion to any who wanted a hearty good time. He spent lavishly, looked incredibly handsome, and wore the finest clothes. He was always accompanied by twelve members of his bodyguard, all dressed in his chosen colors, burgundy and green, and all well armed with spear, sword, and shield. Duke Christopher had instantly become a social sensation, even more so after meeting Baron Ahrlehn, who was in effect, introducing him to the rich and the powerful. In just four days time, the Duke and the Baron had been to three Balls at the homes of the nobility, attended the theater twice, been gambling at the Red Griffin, paraded their finest doublets through Harmony Gardens, and in general, become the talk of the city.

In private, Murdoch had quickly seen the Duke to be devoid of intellect, imperious and arrogant in manner, snobbish in the extreme, and much like molding clay in the hands of a skilled flatterer like Baron Ahrlehn. It had taken no time at all for the Duke to become a puppet to certain nobles that Murdoch had been keeping under his eye, since he started this business in Caprice.

They came in, now, taking the best tables as their due, and loudly ordering drinks. The Duke was dressed in a burgundy colored velvet doublet, dripping with so many pearls that any reasonable person would have thought it uncomfortable to wear. Instead of breeches, favored by many for their comfort and practicality, he wore hose of a green leaf pattern, with turned up soft shoes instead of boots. Each item of clothing was the absolute current height of fashion, but somehow, in combination, Murdoch thought they produced a slightly ridiculous image.

The Duke saw Murdoch, and with a curt gesture ordered the scholar to attend upon him. Murdoch and Finnegin immediately left their table and Murdoch went to stand respectfully, as the Duke had decreed he must, at the Duke's elbow, while Finnegin quietly took up a position behind Murdoch. The Duke and Baron were laughing at some drollery.

Finally turning to look at Murdoch, Duke Christopher issued orders in an imperious voice. "Scholar! I have a task for you. Henceforth you shall accompany me and record the words I speak. These shall then be bound into books and saved for the study of future scholars."

Murdoch gaped, took a deep breath, and asked, "Your words, Sire? Which words?"

With a twinkle in his eye and a very broad smile, Duke Christopher answered, "Why all of them, of course. Do you think you have the wit to sort them, some to be saved and some to be discarded. All of them. You shall be my witness to history."

Still floundering, at a loss as to the meaning of this, Murdoch managed to keep his wits and ask ever so politely, "Witness to what history, Sire? Has something occurred?"

The Duke laughed uproariously. Baron Ahrlehn condescended to explain. "We have discovered that Duke Christopher is not only of the Royal House, indeed he may be the heir to the throne itself. Something to celebrate! Eh—what?" Murdoch closed his eyes for the three breaths of the Ritual of Calming, while the two nobles clinked their glasses and laughed.

When he could find his voice again, Murdoch exercised immense self control and asked most respectfully, "The

Throne? You mean King? King of Telluria? Would you jest about such a thing? What of Elric?"

Duke Christopher smiled a very conspiratorial kind of smile and rudely pulling Murdoch to just a few inches of his lips, said in a loud stage whisper, "'Tis no jest. There is a prophecy that states I will become King, and soon. The good Baron came across it at the Sages Guild. Imagine, you serve the future King of Telluria." He giggled.

Murdoch, who thought in that moment that he might be seeing his life flash before his eyes, stood up, blinking, unable to utter a word. Duke Christopher was looking at him in complete sincerity, and Murdoch finally admitted to himself that at least this fool believed it, if no one else did. Prophecy indeed! Still, Sahm-el's bidding must be obeyed, even blindly.

With a most courtly bow, Murdoch said, "Your Grace, I shall instantly repair to my humble room and get my secretariat so I may record for all posterity the golden words, as you utter them." When he got the nod of dismissal, Murdoch backed away, then hurried upstairs, followed by Finnegin. They could hear laughter from the common room all the way up to the third floor.

Murdoch held his peace until they were safely in his room, with the door shut. Then he could contain himself no longer. "What in the names of all the Gods is happening here? Our entire carefully arranged plan is turned completely about by the sudden emergence of this idiot. What am I to do? This fop can no more lead a revolution than he can find his way to the privy without help."

Finnegin, as blown away as Murdoch by this event, had no advice to offer.

Nineteen

"Cloth of wool is composed of many separate threads, each twisted and bent at strange angles. Yet the resulting cloth is supple, smooth, strong, and beautiful."

—The Red Book of Roland,
a book of poetry, legends, and parables that is used
for meditation by the Paladin order known as The Companions.

The elf known as Sinueh glided effortlessly through the forest, disturbing not one leaf by his silent movement. This required no thought on his part, this silent unmarked passage through an upland forest of trees and thick underbrush, because, like all elves, his entire lifetime, a very long one, had been spent as being unified with nature, as part of the forest rather than a separate object trying to push through it.

He merged with the underbrush and sort of flowed through it, unconsciously shifting his weight and maintaining his balance without overturning a single pebble because he was fully aware of all of the pebbles, twigs, shrubs, trees, and everything living or not that was about him. Dressed in soft leather the same color as his gray eyes, he made no special effort to hide as he traveled, yet his passage went as unnoticed as the flight of a bee on a sunny afternoon.

All of this he did from automatic habit, because his thoughts were occupied in a very un-Elven way with human concerns. He had just left the Elven High Council, at Aehdelveiss, a meeting of very strong minds and vigorous debate. The words of Sahmutahr the elder still echoed in his mind.

"You have spent too much time with humans, Sinueh, and are losing yourself to their twisted thinking. What comes will come. The course of the River of Dreams cannot be reversed. We must follow the flow and not waste our strength in vain efforts to fight what cannot be fought.

"We believe the return of the Outsiders is inevitable and soon, as humans reckon time. However, this plan put forward by the Sorcerer is as ridiculous as the one that cost the life of my own mother the first time these Outsiders appeared here. We were wrong to join them then, as we would be wrong to help them now.

"Our interpretation of this event is different from that of the humans. As the Grand Cycle of Life continues to turn, some things end and others begin. The consensus of the Council is that these Outsiders bring a turning of the wheel. Our time on this world is coming to an end. We shall therefore begin making preparations for those of our people who wish to do so, to leave this world, crossing the dimensions and folding the vast distances to join our brethren on other worlds.

"If the humans can save themselves, so be it. If not, it is because it is the end of their cycle here and they have not the wit to see it. No one can tell another what to do. We are all free to choose our path. Know you now, Sinueh, if your path lies with the humans, it may no longer lie with us.

A decision of the Elven High Council is not an order but rather a reflection of the actual thinking of all elves. It would seem that very few elves, if any other than himself, saw more than one path to the future. As he traveled, Sinueh was struck with the thought that this might be a weakness of his specie. He dismissed Sahmutahr's implication that he might be aberrant in some way, thinking human-like rather than elf-like. Diversity, after all, was the very essence of the natural world.

He now journeyed to one of the few in Elven society who might have some understanding of this problem, and possibly offer some help.

There had been a few rare occasions when Elves mated

with humans. These nearly always ended tragically for the Elves due to the extreme difference in life span. Offspring of these matings tended to be outcasts of both kinds and lived very lonely lives. This repeated experience with humans was one of the reasons Elves tended to distance themselves from humans and avoid relationships that were sure to bring the pain and sorrow of leave-taking. Elves had learned, as a race, that they were simply too passionate to take such emotional risks.

One such offspring of an elf and human bond was Melissa Fey HalfElven, the person Sinueh was now seeking. Melissa was chief librarian of the Elven Archives at Lundunegal, widely respected for her brilliance and library skill. Her world was the world of books and scrolls, a relatively safe retreat for one such as she, tainted with the wild human blood.

Lundunegal was several hundred leagues to the south, in the mountains of Samos. Too far to walk, even for an Elf. Sinueh was, therefore, going to collect his mount.

To do this, he needed to make his way to Sweet Scent Valley, barely a league to the west. Coming down into the hidden mountain valley, Sinueh paused to inhale the perfumed fragrance drifting up from it. He could identify more than a hundred different scents, each distinctly individual, yet in combination not overpowering and cloying as one might expect, but rather a subtle blend of vapors that brought an exquisite pleasure to his delicate senses.

The elf made his way along a narrow defile and out into a clearing in the forest of the valley that was filled with waist high blooming shrubbery. The flowers were, for the most part larger than serving platters and there were many he could not reach around with both arms. They were of every describable color, including black and deep purple.

He waded into the middle of this sea of flowers and then clapped his hands in an intricate rhythmic pattern. Very quickly he heard the droning buzz and looked around to see the huge bumblebee flying toward him.

Sinueh knelt in the shrubbery until the flowers were up to his chin and watched cautiously, for bees, even giant bees, were notoriously clumsy in their landings, often bouncing and rolling over before ending up on their gripping claw-like feet. This time proved to be no exception as the burly giant insect came down, virtually dropping to the ground and falling on its side before standing up and shaking its wings.

Sinueh stood up and walked right up to its head, which was even with his own eyes, and patted the thick yellow fur on the top of its head, using the same drumming pattern he had used to call it. The giant bee immediately quieted down and stood with its wings fully outstretched from its sides. Sinueh held out a large sugarplum in his hand and felt the delicate touch of the long thin flexible tongue as the bee took this little treat from him.

He ducked under one outstretched wing and took hold of the four-cornered leather saddle that was strapped to the back of the yellow and black bee. With the aid of the stirrup, he swung himself into the saddle and carefully fastened the harness straps of the aerial saddle across both his shoulders. Then he was ready to fly.

The elf delicately tapped the top of the bee's head, just behind the bulbous eyes, and the giant bee lurched into the air with a mighty leap, then caught itself with its fanning wings and rose almost straight up with a loud buzz.

Sinueh liked riding the bee, controlling it by taps on its head, making it do dips and dives when he felt like it. Riding an Elven Bee is as safe as any other form of transportation on this danger filled world. Even with its rider, the bee was much faster than Samosian Flappers, creatures that resembled flying blankets, and was an even match with a griffin. Although these giant bees were considered to be food by some dragons, Sinueh had witnessed one instance when a bee successfully stung a dragon to death in mid-air combat. Unlike the normal bumblebees, the giant bee did not lose its stinger upon each use and could sting over and over again at need.

The flight was uneventful, a leisurely looping flight across a mountain range and then circling one mountain that looked no different from the others but was very different indeed. He guided the bee down to a bouncing landing on the side of a rocky escarpment, gave it another sugarplum, and released it. It would come to his call again when his business here was finished.

The mountain was actually no mountain but rather an extinct volcano known as Lundunegal. In times long past, Elven sorcerers had created an enormous illusion of a cap for the crater hiding its true nature from prying eyes. The illusion was permanent and perfect in every detail, down to matching the fine grain in the rock and individual trees and even tree leaves.

Lundunegal was the secret location of the Elven Archives. This contained the largest library on this world, for the entire mountain was one huge hollowed out cavern full of scrolls, and large leather bound books. Some two hundred elf scholars worked here under the firm but sweet guidance of Melissa Fey HalfElven. Here were enshrined the epic poems, ballads, and songs, composed by Elves since time began. Elven epics went on for several thousand stanzas, and some of their ballads required hours in the singing. There were also, of course, the great works of other races, including those of men. Here could be found books on the various theories of magic, including the Khambrellian Grimoire, as well as books on each of the main temples, and such varied things as alchemy, Dwarven law, and politics.

Sinueh had not come here to consult books, on this day. He climbed the narrow path to a certain point, and then turned and appeared to walk right into the mountain. Actually, he had just crossed the rim of the crater and he began descending the inner slope. From the inside, the mountain top was as clear as glass and let sunshine bathe the entire cavern from above. Huge trees had been planted here, when this mountain was first hollowed out. Over the thousands of years since then, complicated gardens had been created inside the crater. The great trees growing from the cavern floor had typical Elven treehouses in them, connected by rope walks. This is where the Elven Archives were actually housed, safely underground but still in a setting pleasing to elves.

He was not surprised to be met by Melissa Fey HalfElven when he reached the crater floor. She was known to be gifted in several ways and had no doubt felt his presence.

Melissa was a prim young lady, with the sharp features and slender form of an elf, but with raven black hair instead of the normal fair coloring. To a human, she would appear to be in her mid-twenties. On this day, she wore a lavender gown that went well with her dark hair. She stood, quietly waiting, with her hands clasped in front of her. Her emotions, like his, were decorously under control.

Sinueh stopped and made a courtly bow to her. "May the light of the Three Suns shine on your path. I give you greetings, Melissa Fey HalfElven."

She replied in the correct form. "A courteous guest is a welcome guest. I bid you welcome, Sinueh. What is it you seek at Lundunegal?" Melissa had a reputation for strict observance of elf custom.

Remembering this, Sinueh stood before her with his palms open, showing empty hands, in supplication. Ordinarily, custom required the granting of a favor that is sought in this manner, for it was clear the matter was an important one. However, he was not asking for an ordinary favor. "I seek a nexial vision at the crystal pool."

With a slight frown, Melissa reminded him, "Custom reserves the use of the crystal pool to the leaders of each clan. Have you become an elder, Sinueh?"

"Nay, good lady. I am still considered to be too green for such an honor. I do have great need, and so request an exception be made."

"Surely you know such a request should be made to your clan elder. Why come to me?"

"The matter concerns humans."

"Ah, I see. Your clan elder is Sahmutahr. Nearly all of our people agree with Sahmutahr when it comes to the humans. Why should you think I might grant such a favor?"

Sinueh paused, thinking of all he knew about this half-Elf maid, and that which he had guessed from her prim style of living, and how that would mix with the elf passion that simmered below the surface in all of them. "With favor, good lady, I thought to ask in the name of the love your mother once bore your human father."

A look of surprise flickered ever so quickly across Melissa's face and then was gone in an instant. She stood looking at him gravely for several minutes, showing nothing to him at all of whatever thoughts or feelings she might be having.

Then, with an almost wintry smile, she said, "Come." She turned and silently led him through the trees to a small glade in the forest. Although he had never seen it, Sinueh recognized the crystal pool so often described in sagas.

In times long past, even in Elven memory, cataclysmic forces had created from the remains of giant trees a single diamond, a huge crystal some four meters in diameter, and then broken it along a fracture line in half, crumbling the upper half into fist-sized gemstones. The lower half became embedded in the floor of a volcano crater which eventually became the location of the Elven archives. Each time it rained, this fractured crystal would fill with fresh water. An unknown elf sorcerer, thousands of years in the past had found it and discovered it made a perfect focus for certain mental and magical exercises. Hence, it was known as the crystal pool.

To answer Sinueh's request, Melissa Fey HalfElven now prepared to gaze into the depths of this pool and summon a vision. This was to be much more than a simple question put to the Infinite Scroll. Rather, a nexial vision had been requested, a summary of those events that were in some way related to the topic of inquiry. Aside from Elven weavers of magic, very few of even the most adept sorcerers were capable of this.

After the Ritual of Calming to purify the clarity of her thoughts, Melissa turned to Sinueh, as they both stood facing the pool and asked, "What is the subject?"

He had given careful thought to this and replied immediately, "The human response to the coming crisis brought by the Outsiders."

In the mind's eye of Melissa Fey HalfElven, images began

to form in the pool, shadows moving in the depths, shifting and reshaping and coming together. Sinueh, as he had expected, saw nothing but clear blue water and the natural facets of crystal that lined the pool. He stood quietly, with the proverbial patience of an Elf, as Melissa worked her magic.

The shapes began to resolve into understandable images. Melissa begin talking, describing the scenes as she saw them.

"There are creatures, reptiles, moving in great chambers of metal between the worlds, in vast numbers. A crude form of travel. They destroy or corrupt all that they touch. They are the Outsiders, and are returning to us. They bring the utter destruction of this world.

"Those few who would dare to oppose them seek to first balance the harmonies of this world, to strengthen it for defense. I see humans, great imperial dragons, and even elves.

"I see a castle over-run by an army bearing a green banner. The family of that place are all killed, except for a daughter that now lies in despair in a royal dungeon.

"I see a Demon pulling the puppet strings of a king, to bring about his doom and thus gain its freedom. This king is surrounded by jackals who claw for power. This king is doomed.

"I see an army under a white banner crossing a great river and threatening a walled city, and the death of the successor to that doomed king. The second king will die in battle.

"Above all, I see the gold and emerald Dragon Throne of Telluria. Whosoever shall become the third monarch of Telluria, shall determine the fate of this world.

"Finally, I see a be-robed sorcerer, a human of many faces, who holds the key to the throne."

Melissa let out a long sigh and looked at him with grave eyes. "That is all."

Sinueh nodded. "It is enough."

Twenty

"Killing is a simple thing. Animals kill. Subtlety lies in the ability to turn an opponent's very strengths against him and thus force him to bring about his own destruction."

—The Silken Veil,
Sourcebook for the elite guild of assassins
known as the Tauhng Society.

The body of King Elric was found by the chamberlain just after dawn. Lord Frawley had just come up the long flight of stairs from the Gallery, carrying the morning tea tray and carefully placed it on the small table by the door to the King's private chamber and quietly opened the door before turning to pick up the tray again.

He was trying to be very quiet because Elric was well-known for his black moods before he had his tea. Lord Frawley insisted on braving the King's early morning moods because having his tea usually put Elric the Dark into a receptive mood for any small suggestions Lord Frawley might have. More than one courtier had found himself banished to the frontiers of Telluria after Lord Frawley had brought tea to his Majesty.

This morning the King was sleeping late. Ordinarily, Elric was up before dawn for a round of practice with the great DemonSword that had brought him to power. The life-drinking magic sword had an aura about it that made everyone in its presence extremely uneasy, so Elric had adopted the practice of doing his sword exercises before most of the palace was awake. It was unlike him to sleep late like this, especially in a time of crisis when war threatened the country.

Lord Frawley entered the King's chamber bearing the tea tray and was surprised to see lamps still burning. He paused, looked around with growing unease and walked toward the curtain covered bed. He saw the scabbard for the great DeathSword in its usual place by the bed, but empty. The curtains were drawn on this side of the bed.

Lord Frawley paused, feeling slightly ridiculous as he stood there holding the tea tray, catching sight of himself in the huge gold trimmed mirror and seeing an elderly foolish looking man with short legs, round body, gray hair and silly looking sword hanging from his belt and unable to quite believe the suspicions that were seeping into his mind.

His image in the mirror convinced him he shouldn't just stand there so he moved around the curtained bed, intending to sit the tea tray on the sideboard and then awaken the king.

However as he came to the other side of the bed, he froze, this time out of shock, dropped the tea set on the stone floor and uttered an inarticulate cry. King Elric the Dark was lying dead across the foot of his bed, the Great DemonSword standing like a wooden stake pinning his body to the bed. There was blood all over the bed, most of it from the stump where Elric's hand had been severed and upon looking closely, Lord Frawley saw the severed hand stuffed into the dead king's mouth. The king was still wearing the court clothes he had been wearing the previous evening.

Lord Frawley regained his senses sufficiently to pull the bell cord hanging by the bed, jerking it hard three times so that on the third pull it broke and came down on him, unnoticed. He heard the great gong of the Palace alarm sounding, and then shouting and rushing boots but Lord Frawley just stood there blinking back tears and looking at his dead King.

Guards and servants rushed in the room and before he

could gather his wits to give warning, one of the guards grasped the DemonSword by the hilt, attempting to remove it from the body. The Chamberlain fully expected the guard to fall over dead from just touching the sword, for it had happened often in the past. Some careless servant, her mind on dust or the tray of food she was carrying, would absently brush against the DemonSword and it would instantly drink her life.

Lord Frawley found his voice and yelled, "Touch not the sword! It will drink your life!" The guard turned pale, staring at his own hand firmly gripping the sword's handle and let go of it with a shriek. He then stared wonderingly at his own hand, surprised to find himself still living.

The guards, including one shaking in fright, and servants stood back and Lord Frawley, unmindful of the dangling bell chord still draped about him began functioning as a chamberlain and giving orders.

The Bedchamber was sealed with the body left as it was found and a summons was sent for the King's chief minister, his Spymaster, and the Royal Wizard.

Upon closer examination, the DemonSword could be seen to lack the foreboding presence and sense of crackling energy it usually gave off. It looked dull and dead. Still no one else was ready to brave fate by touching it.

Miriam the Spymaster hurried in, understanding at a glance what had occurred and what the implications were. A servant reported that the Royal Wizard, Fairchilde was absent from his chambers and could not be found.

Miriam concealed a smile behind the mask of her set face. She thought, "So Fairchilde finally found a way to do it, after all these years. I wonder how he managed it." She spoke nothing, but let the chamberlain remain in charge.

News of the death of Elric, and of the missing wizard, spread through the city like a forest fire, touching here and there with the heat of fear, light of joy, and most often, smoke of confusion.

At the Blue Star Inn, Tweedy, the portly innkeeper, whispered with one of the cooks cautious relief at the removal of Elric and dark suspicions of the missing wizard. It proved to be a common theme throughout the city.

And although no one actually danced in the streets, many noted hesitant, half-hidden smiles on numerous faces that day. Elric the Dark would be missed with some pleasure. At the same time, the missing wizard suddenly gained in popularity among the masses. There was whispered talk at the Broken Tooth Inn of erecting a statue to him, this over many tankards of ale. Fortunately, cooler heads suggested there might be wisdom in waiting to see who next sat upon the Dragonthrone of Telluria before making such public displays.

That evening, the Cabal met at Lancaster Manor, as surprised as any in the city. For three hours, they poured over hundreds of questions as to what had happened, why Fairchilde had not given any warning of his plans, how he had done it, where did he get the power to overcome the sword, and most of all, what did all this mean for their plans? Had they known that Elric had years ago entrapped the soul of Fairchilde, they would have had many more questions.

As to their plans, when all was said and done, no reason could be given for changing them. Elric had a son named Roderic, but he was so obviously simple-minded that he was not likely to be accepted by the council as legitimate heir. Thus, it came about, that the Earl of Lancaster proposed they move with speed to propose their own candidate for the crown, the foolish Christopher de Reayses, Lord of Whitehall, Holder of the sacred White Feather, Keeper of the golden Shield of Telluria.

In the same section of the city, in a similar large manor house surrounded by luxurious lawn and wrought iron fence, heavily patrolled by newly hired guards, that same Duke Christopher was behaving strangely. Having purchased and staffed this place with what seemed like an endless stream of gold, and having this night, finally dismissed all servants and retired alone to his chambers, Christopher was staring intently into a small bowl of water and smiling.

But this was not the foolish simpering smile of the addle-witted idiot the public had come to know in the past few weeks. Nor was it the leering, arrogant smile that he used when making yet another outrageous demand upon the patience of his long-suffering cleric, Murdoch. This was a slight grim smile, a smile of satisfaction, a smile that Murdoch might have recognized, even on the face of this fop.

Within the strangely clouded depths of the small bowl of water, images flickered at his command. He had just watched a meeting at Lancaster Manor, and he was most please with the result.

On the morrow, they were going to propose that he become King of Telluria. He especially enjoyed the irony of that.

But now, he must rest. The struggle with the DemonSword of Elric had been a dangerous and tiring one. Only by making use of the higher sorcery of dimensional shifting and time-swimming had he been able to finally destroy the Demon after first forcing it to turn upon its own master. The look of shock on Elric's face when his own evil was turned inward upon him had been particularly pleasant to observe.

The irony had been multiplied when the Royal Sorcerer chose that moment to depart in pursuit of his own quest for glory, a delicious detail that had been arranged by a colleague and fortuitously timed to coincide with the removal of Elric.

Christopher withdrew his gaze from the bowl of water and prepared to retire. He would have a very busy day on the morrow, and even one such as he needed rest. Then too, this business of shape-shifting had its limits, and he didn't really like the too handsome appearance of the face he had created for this Christopher. At least not enough to be willing to wear it from now on, which was the risk if he didn't relax from it and resume his own appearance periodically.

After setting wards and alarms, he then retired to the canopy bed for some well deserved sleep. Slowly his features began to soften and relax into a completely different face. And Sahm-el the Sorcerer slept the sleep of the contented.

On that same dark night, streaking across the sky toward the east, the Wizard Fairchilde was full of glee. He was flying to his destiny. During the Sorcery Wars, all masters of the Art traveled this way, as a meteor-like ball of flame flying at enormous speeds. Although unsubtle, it was a demonstration of power and control that could be truly impressive. In those days, the sky would be lit at night by such slashes of fire, as the major sorcerers went to and fro about their business. In recent years, the practice had gone out of style and it was now an uncommon phenomena. Fairchilde gloried in it, as he did anything that reminded him of the mighty days when sorcerers ruled all on this world.

The research he had been conducting since the onset of these visions had led him to this journey across the world. His destination was an extinct volcano known among adepts as Enigma. It was one of the power nexial points of this world and originally a place where duels of sorcery were fought for supremacy. He now expected it to be a place of testing. Testing of himself.

The persistent visions of himself associated with the crown and throne of Telluria had started a chain of thought in his mind that had led him to the Sages Guild for historical information.

The chief scholar there, the Guildmaster, had dared to suggest he pay a fee, a very sizable fee, for the information he sought. Fairchilde thought that showed a lack of respect for his abilities and settled the matter by blasting to bloody splinters, three of the scholars and threatening to sink the entire Sages Guild and all its contents into the very depths of the fiery underworld. The information he sought was immediately forthcoming.

It concerned a legend about the Throne of Telluria. That there would come a time of crisis when the next king would be selected by a dragon rather than the High Council. That this dragon would make its selection on the basis of a test of strength that it would administer. That the strongest would succeed and become rightful king, displacing all other claimants.

Upon learning this, Fairchilde had repaired to his own chambers and had begun a search downstream in the River of Time, searching the future for confirmation.

Visions of himself, face to face with a gold and black dragon, followed by visions of himself standing alone on a tall pinnacle, holding a crown in his hands, had provided the confirmation he sought. A little further research had indicated the time and place for the Dragon Test.

Master Fairchilde had reason to be eager for such a contest in strength. For had he not engaged in a duel of magic with Olde Maude and overcome her, so that the very buckle he now wore on his belt was made of her golden scales? Had he not slain Imperial Dragons on two other occasions, each time growing in power from the combat? It could be fairly said, that he, Master Fairchilde the Feared, was the world's foremost dragonslayer, for certainly no other being was known to have defeated three Imperial Dragons.

Thus, he was streaking eagerly across the sky, impatient for the coming test and the leap to power it would bring.

Twenty-One

"A man of integrity is never understood by those without it. His actions will always seem mystical to them."

—Drury's Primer for Princes.

Christopher de Reayses was crowned King of Telluria one week later. In truth, not after much argument in the Privy Council, a few bribes of enormous size, two minor assassinations carried out by Miriam, and the hasty departure of Prince Roderic the Simple. The Earl of Lancaster backed Christopher as the only remaining heir, and the matter was settled.

Murdoch, once a slave who made mud bricks, suddenly found himself elevated to the position of private secretary to the King. Before he could adjust to this breathtaking leap, he found himself half drowning in a sea of crisply dictated orders on all manner of things. He spent his days, and some nights, madly scribbling on parchment as the new King, who seemed to not need sleep, let loose a deluge of commands. They came so fast that Murdoch seldom had time to even think about what he was writing, or to wonder at the change that had occurred in the silly fool he was pledged to serve.

Late at night, five hectic days after the coronation, Murdoch eased himself into his featherbed, hardly noticing the fine silk sheets, and absently dismissing the servant attending him, when he was suddenly struck by the thought that indeed here he was, actually in the Palace, where Deathwind had wanted him to be. It was something of a shock to him.

He had been so busy that this was the first chance to pause and reflect on the events. The realization led him to begin considering other things. For one thing, this Christopher his Master had chained him to was no longer the simpering, boring fool. Quite the contrary.

Murdoch sat up in the huge bed and uncovered a shielded lantern by his bed. He absently ran one hand over his bald pate as he began to review the orders he had written in the past few days. Like any trained sage, he had an excellent memory and could call each document up in his mind with no difficulty. As he did so, his amazement grew.

This new King was set upon massive changes for the country of Telluria. Not the minor changes one would expect of a new monarch, like a new color for the flag, but substantive changes that struck at the very heart of power. Moreover, these various changes began to fit together so neatly, each so reinforcing the others, that it was obvious that they were extremely carefully thought out. Such deep thoughts did not fit the idiotic Christopher of just a week ago.

The more Murdoch thought about it, the more worried he got. Sudden changes always make enemies. Everyone knew that. The new King, with Murdoch beside him, would quickly alienate virtually every center of power in the country. No matter that his reforms were beneficial. It suddenly hit Murdoch that this Christopher, whoever he was, might be inviting his own death, unwittingly.

At Lancaster Manor, the bellowing voice of General Montrose could be heard clear up on the third floor. "Five days! Only Five Bloody Days! We crowned him King just five bloody days ago! It's unbelievable!"

The Earl of Lancaster, who tended to find Montrose to be

something of a bore, continued his morning grooming before calmly descending the stairs to greet the general. Montrose continued to rant and rave until Lancaster met him in the salon.

My good General, you will steam your brain. What is the cause of your displeasure?" He filled a goblet with chilled fruit juice and turned, calm and smiling to the red-faced general.

"Displeasure? My displeasure? Do you know what your callow simpering puppet of a king has been doing?"

Lancaster sipped his juice. "In faith, I have given little attention to him since the coronation. I've been managing our affairs, as you well know. What could he have done in so short a time?"

"Hah! Turn the country upside down, that's what. Ruin everything, that's what. In just five bloody days! I'll kill him myself!"

"What are you talking about? This idiot can't harm us."

"This idiot is no idiot, I tell you! Now sit down and listen to me. First of all, I no longer command the army. I was dismissed this morning. Moreover, in the name of the Ruritanian emergency he has..."

The Earl of Lancaster listened for the next hour in absolute astonishment, then sent couriers to the other members of the cabal. In very short time, they were all around the heavy table in his private and shielded meeting chamber. The Earl was summarizing for his disbelieving conspirators.

"The King has declared an emergency, disbanded the Privy Council, dispersed the army throughout the country to keep the peace, replaced them with a brand new force called Dragoons, that no one knows anything about, announced an abolishment of slavery throughout the country, and lowered the taxes of the commoners. All in just the few days since the coronation. He has turned into a monster."

Miriam the Spymaster, was also grim. I too have been dismissed, and banned from the palace. He must be mad. How long does he think he can live, after making such announcements?"

At the mention of the abolishment of slavery, Baron

Simsohms had turned pale. The majority of his fortune rested upon the slave trade. Before he could speak to voice his own outrage, he was cut off by Baron Ahrlehn.

"Nay, Mistress Miriam. He has method in this madness, though I cannot see how he could hope to survive such a hazardous course."

General Montrose, still red in the face, asked, "Method. What method? I see only a fool who has suddenly gone mad with power and won't last out the week for it."

"Consider then, the results. By disbanding the Privy Council he removes the only legal body that can reclaim the crown from him, and concentrates political power in his own hands. By taking the army from our good general here, and dispersing it throughout the country, he removes any military threat to his rule. He then replaces the army with this mysterious force of Dragoons, all totally loyal to him, I'm sure, and thus holds the military whip in his own hands. The other measures are designed to placate the commoners. He has effectively isolated the nobility by mere proclamation."

The Earl of Lancaster leaned back in his chair, interested to hear another speak his own ideas and reach the same conclusions. Baron Simsohms could not quite see it.

"But how could such a fool come up with these things? Our own puppet turning against us! He has not the courage or the brains. You do not suggest he has gulled us from the start do you? I do not believe it!"

Lancaster slapped the table with open palm, for attention. "Good Baron, it would seem we have been gulled, but not, I think by Christopher. He is clearly a clack-brained twit who cannot find his own hind side with his own hand. Nay! I see another mind behind this."

His statement brought a moment of thoughtful silence. It was broken by Miriam. "The Sorcerer!" Light dawned on faces around the table.

"Yes, the Sorcerer. Where is our good Master Fairchilde? He hasn't been seen, to my knowledge, since the death of the King. Who else could have done this? Think for a moment.

Overcome the DemonSword, kill the King, then take over this fop and turn him into his own puppet?"

Montrose growled, "I never liked that bloody bastard. I'll roast his liver over a low fire! I swear I will!"

Lancaster relaxed in his chair, calm for the first time since the noisy arrival of Montrose, that morning. "It all fits." The others nodded their agreement.

Baron Simsohms drew forth a kerchief from his sleeve and mopped his sweaty brow. "But what is to be done now? The Ruritanian troops are marching. We have set in motion a war that cannot be stopped. Surely we cannot just kill the puppet now, with the army scattering all over the country and the city helpless."

Eyes turned to General Montrose. "With the army gone, the Ruritanians will be able to take the bridge and then the city. The war will be over and lost in a matter of days. No extended war of balanced forces, no arms shipments, no profits, and indeed our very lives and property in danger. We cannot allow that to happen."

Lancaster agreed. "Nay, we cannot allow that to happen, and yet we cannot simply kill the puppet either. At least not until we have a replacement for him."

Miriam glanced swiftly at him. "And who would that be? Yourself, perhaps?" There was menace in her voice.

The Earl laughed, as if to make light of her implied threat. "Not me, oh, no! I am not such a fool as to make a target of myself. Nay, I was thinking of the other legitimate heir."

Montrose, who was losing the thread of meaning once more, snorted. "What other heir? The only other real heir is ..., You can't mean Roderic!"

"Oh, but I do. What was unacceptable before will suddenly look very good to those dismissed members of the Privy Council. There are also members of the nobility who have just lost military commands. Others, many others, will be just as shocked by these sudden reforms as we. I think we can create a faction that would support young Prince Roderic as the King."

Montrose looked astonished. "But Roderic? Roderic the Simple? Even we felt he was unfit, and now you want to bring him back and make him King?"

"'Tis true, he is addle-witted, has a ferocious temper, and is overly fond of inflicting pain on others. His faults are well known. No one would have backed him before. But our good King Christopher has managed in just a few days to make enemies out of nearly everyone of importance in the Kingdom. I think Roderic can be turned into a suitable puppet, acceptable as a replacement to Christopher, now that he has turned on virtually everybody."

The Spymaster's eyes gleamed in such a way that Lancaster knew she favored this approach. Others, too, were beginning to nod. Miriam asked the practical question. "Can this be brought about before the attack? Is there time?"

The Earl turned to the General. "Can you get word to our friends with the Ruritanian Legions to delay for three days? I should think that would be enough."

Montrose nodded. "It can be done. But no more than three days!"

"Then Baron Ahrlehn, I suggest you leave immediately to bring back Roderic and offer to him the Throne of Telluria. Meanwhile, we shall approach various factions here and enlist them in our cause."

The Earl of Lancaster lifted his wine goblet. "Down with the Puppet King."

They all joined in.

Twenty-Two

"Many more problems are caused by a simple want of wits than are ever caused by cleverly executed malice."

—The Divine Thesis,
Sacred Text for the Temple of Chardain.

A short time later, General Montrose opened a cupboard and took out a small case made of wood and leather. He then sat at his desk, and placed the case next to the small cage holding a bat.

With quill and parchment, he wrote a short note, printing the letters boldly. Then he opened the cage and took out the small gray bat, stroking it. When it was relaxed in his hand, he rubbed the top of its head, between the upright ears until it started bobbing its head up and down.

At that, he placed the bat on the parchment and watched as it slowly traced each printed letter of the note with its foreclaw. When it was done, he opened the wooden case and took out a small vial of blood. He removed the stopper and daubed some of the blood on the bat's nose. It licked up the blood with its long tongue and uttered a squeak.

The general then picked up the bat, and tossed it into the air. It fluttered about for a moment, in circles, and then was abruptly gone, seemingly blinking out of existence.

Many leagues away, across the Dire River in Ruritania, the bat suddenly popped into the air and settled on the mail clad shoulder of a Ruritanian officer in camp with the legions. He was alone in a tent, so he quickly bared an arm and allowed the bat to slice through his skin with its razor like teeth and drink some of his blood. While it did so, he used one hand to spread a piece of parchment and open a small inkwell.

The bat slaked its thirst and hopped from his arm to the small camp table and thence to the inkwell. Dipping its foreclaw into the ink, it then commenced to trace printed letters onto the parchment for him. The trans-bat, for such it was called, knew not the meaning of these letters but simply copied designs from memory, giving him the note written shortly before by the general.

When he was sure the message was complete, he opened his camp chest and withdrew a small cage, gently easing the bat into it. He replaced it in his chest, next to a wooden case containing blood samples. Then he perused the note.

Safely alone, he muttered aloud to himself. "Bloody guts! He wants a delay of three days. We shall be lucky not to be delayed three weeks as things stand now. This message was unnecessary." He carefully burned the scrap of parchment.

Indeed, the Ruritanian Legions were many leagues further from the river boundary than they had expected. This was due to actions taken by their commander.

Machis the Omnipotent had ordered the army to advance in two columns, one bearing easterly to take ship and land in Sardonicus, and the other heading north. After the loss of an entire fleet due to a sudden and raging storm, he had altered his original plans and now ordered this northern column to assault the High Bridge and invade Telluria on foot.

It was this northern column that was now experiencing galling delays. Ruritanian Legions do not carry food, water, or firewood when on the march, relying on the locals to supply them. However, one small village had been unable to do so when demands were made, due to a recent epidemic. The village elders had humbly appealed to be excused from the burden since sickness had prevented crops from being harvested.

The commander, who by ill fate chanced to be a follower of Baalsha, ordered the village burned for defiance. This was now the cause of all the unexpected delays.

It seemed that village had been granted the status of elf-friend in times long past for favors done to the Elder Race. There was even an Elven shrine located on the edge of the forest clearing that contained the village. Unfortunately, when the village was burned, the shrine also burned, along with a section of the forest itself in a brief but fierce forest fire. It was an action intolerable to the local clan of elves.

Gray shafted arrows with white feathers began suddenly appearing in the backs of sentries and scouts. Horses began shying at nothing and throwing their riders. Huge trees began suddenly falling across the line of march. It was noted that only dead trees were falling, no live healthy ones. There was an increase in rats, fleas, lice and other vermin infecting the night camps and getting into everyone's armor. As the day passed, problems grew, causing more and more delays and eating away at the troops morale.

A road that looked like an inviting shortcut suddenly ended in a rock outcropping, revealing itself to have been an elaborate illusion. Illusory pits with spikes in the bottoms suddenly appeared under marching ranks. Even when they were recognized as illusions, they still slowed the march, for it takes a steady will to step out into what looks like a void.

Elven magic was known for its subtle use of misdirection and illusion. Indeed, this was the chief reason no one could locate Elves if they did not wish it, even by magic. Elven adepts were able to redirect the stream of magic around themselves so they were not detected.

Each delay added to the burdens, and the result was the invading army was thrown completely off schedule and would arrive at the border several days later than intended. General Montrose would have more than his requested three days.

The Royal Palace of Telluria is located on an island cut by a loop of the Dire River, at the city of Caprice. Toiling away inside that palace, Murdoch found himself handling dozens of details concerning transition and war preparations. One such minor detail came to his attention when his bodyguard, Finnegin, inquired about a blademaster named Oscar Wyndham, who was found to be a prisoner in the dungeon.

Murdoch knew nothing of this person, but Finnegin was insistent and gained permission to release him. Upon finally entering the cell, Finnegin found Oscar near death. His arm had been hacked off at the shoulder and the wound crudely treated by searing flame. He was then left to rot in an underground cell, forgotten by his captors.

Finnegin called for a Healer and learned that none were available for prisoners. He appealed to Murdoch.

Murdoch, thought the matter a relatively minor one compared to the problems he was contending with, but also having reason to be grateful to Finnegin, gave permission for all prisoners in King Elric's dungeons to be released and suggested to Finnegin that his person was reasonably safe inside the palace, if Finnegin wished to seek out a healer.

Thus it came about that a young girl, dirty, with matted hair and filth encrusted clothes saw sunshine once more.

Twila Lyestehr, the last of her family, cringed in terror when her cell door was opened. Having been taken by Master Fairchilde, and kept alive as a future plaything, she had been forgotten when Fairchilde departed on his quest for power. She had spent all this time in near darkness, with meager rations of stale bread and cold broth, a slop bucket, and rats to keep her company.

The first time a rat had crawled across her face, she had screamed. Screams were generally ignored in that part of Elric's palace. Twila had tried to maintain her wits at first, by remembering her lessons in the art of healing, and reciting all the sagas and poems she could remember. But alone, in the dark, with no way to measure the passage of time, her mind had begun to dull into a kind of cold numbness. She had no idea how long she had been there; hours, days, or years.

Then there was the clank and creak of the opening cell door, and the pain of lantern light, and the accompanying fear that her end was now approaching, for hope of release had died a lonely death within her.

Twila put a hand across her eyes to shield them from the burning lantern and felt herself jerked to her feet by rough hands. A gruff voice told her to come along and began leading her steps out of the cell. Blindly she stumbled along, guided by the firm grip on her elbow. Her eyes were watering and adjusting to the light and Twila began to dimly make out the stone floor and walls of the corridor. She was being led by one of the jailers, to she knew not where.

They stopped in a small chamber, and Twila stood swaying unsteadily as the jailer made a mark on a list lying on a small desk. She was pulled again, down a long hallway and then made to climb some stairs. They stopped once again, and she was handed off to another jailer. Her vision now restored, but mind still numb, she watched vacantly as a mark was made by her name on another list.

While standing there, Twila dimly heard a voice that caused a stirring in her mind. Someone was asking about her and then giving orders. The voice was one she ought to know, but the clouds in her mind were too thick. Still she knew something was happening. Again she was led down corridors, but the hands were gentle and a soothing woman's voice began talking to her as if she were a crying child needing to be soothed. It was not far from the truth.

Finnegin watched the servant he had summoned lead the wretched girl away. He had come down here to personally see to the transfer of Oscar to guest quarters in the palace and had seen another prisoner, whom he first thought was some street urchin, in the process of being released. Something about the wretched boy had caught his attention and looking closer, he had finally recognized Lady Twila, now the Duchess of Lyestehr, beneath the filth and rags. He had last seen her on the High Bridge as a Mage had cast a spell at him, pushing him off the bridge to what should have been his death.

This bedraggled creature was a far cry from the wholesome young girl he had escorted out of a burning castle. She had shown pluck on the journey and he thought she might well have the strength of spirit to recover, once she had the bath, food, and clothes he had ordered and was safely in guest quarters of the palace.

It occurred to Finnegin, that the girl was a healer, and had shown real skill during the battle at the castle. She would make an excellent attendant for Oscar in a day or two. And he would not need to bring in a Healer from the city and let such become knowledgeable about Oscar's survival. Finnegin thought it likely that Oscar might well recover and be very useful to the new corps of Dragoons that had been recruited. Pleased with himself, he whistled a few bars of "The Drunken Goblin and the Dog" as he turned to seek out Murdoch once more.

Two days later, Finnegin and Murdoch looked in upon Oscar and found him being tended by the girl Finnegin had known at the castle. She now looked like herself once more, and although she was thin and occasionally unsteady on her feet, she was practicing her craft to Oscar's benefit.

The arm could not be regrown, but she had healed the massive wound at the shoulder, and he was rapidly gaining strength, as one could tell by the coloring of his face.

Twila was pouring tea into the traditional handleless cup when the two of them entered. The sound of Finnegin's voice caused her to drop the cup. "Ye look right well after such an ordeal."

Hearing the cup shatter on the stone floor, Oscar rumbled, "I always thought you had that effect on pretty young ladies."

Twila had turned and was staring at him, not even noticing Murdoch. Then she found her voice. "I thought you were dead. I saw you fall from the bridge."

Finnegin just smiled and shrugged. Oscar said, "Lit on his head, no doubt. Takes more than a mere fall to kill this stubborn fellow."

At that, Finnegin spoke up. "Nay, gentle lady, I was close

to death but spared by a new found friend. I am pleased ye look so well and are of some help to Oscar here."

Twila gave a polite curtsy and stooped to clean up the fallen tea cup. Murdoch put his hand on Finnegin's shoulder to remind him they did have pressing business. They took their leave and left the chamber.

While walking down the corridor, Murdoch mused, "Now there is a lady full of sweetness and grace."

Something in his tone caught Finnegin's attention. It was the first time Murdoch had ever said anything about the fair sex. "Aye, she is that. A bit too gentle for my taste, but she has shown courage." He gave a quick glance at Murdoch, who seemed to be turning something over in his mind.

A few paces further on, Murdoch said, "Some men might value such gentleness, if they were fortunate enough to be of the proper background." They both then walked on in silence, each listening to his own thoughts.

Twenty-Three

"Those who would defend the past, are unwittingly fighting the future."

—The Book of Vehdahs,
Sacred Text for the Temple of Isis.

Murdoch had a headache. The new King, after a brief flurry of dictated orders, had returned to his original habits of drinking, dallying, and having Murdoch handle most of the affairs of state.

This was more than exhausting to Murdoch. The responsibility was frightening. He, at least, knew that he didn't really know what he was doing, whereas Christopher seemed obviously unaware of events or their meaning.

It took only a few days for the courtiers and the bureaucracy to begin treating Murdoch as a significant power. That morning, on the King's orders, he had issued arrest orders for an odd collection of nobles, merchants, and just plain nobodies who were even now being escorted to the dungeons.

This latest step was bound to alienate even more of the rich and powerful, as some of those arrested were connected to powerful families.

Also, Murdoch could not help but notice that having issued the order, he was now right in the middle of things. Should Christopher provoke an uprising by his too sudden and too sweeping actions, poor Murdoch could hardly escape being a target.

Thus, as he lay awake in his bed, early that morning, Murdoch reluctantly decided he must do something to make this bugwit, Christopher, understand the consequences of his actions and the danger he was creating for both of them.

The guardsmen admitted him to the King's private chamber with a dispatch that only served to remind him of the growing power he was unwillingly collecting to himself. King Christopher was lounging on a couch, being tended by three quite pretty dancing girls while a fourth fanned him with a great plumed fan. He appeared to be completely free of care or worry.

Murdoch, who never stopped worrying about the coming invasion, plots by the nobility, his own uncertainty, and the threat of the Outsiders, gritted his teeth, which only made his headache more intense.

Walking forward, Murdoch gave a most elaborate bow and spoke. "Your Highness, I am bound by duty to call certain matters to your attention. May we speak privately?"

Christopher accepted a grape from one of the dancing girls, and frowned. "More of these tiresome details? We thought being King meant we could do anything we wanted to do, and would not have to do anything we didn't want to do. Now several times a day, you interrupt Our little moments of pleasure with gritty and dull matters that simply are not fun." He stroked the cheek of a dancing girl and gave a pleading look to Murdoch, as if begging him to go away.

"Your Majesty, these matters require your attention."

"Oh, you always say that. Why don't you just take care of them, and leave us to our own devices?"

Murdoch felt a nearly irresistible urge to hit this idiot with a chair. By act of will, he stifled the impulse, as he had been forced to stifle many such impulses since his Master had assigned him to this clod. "Your Majesty, only you can attend to these matters."

With enormous reluctance and some petulance, the King waved the girls away. When they were gone, he turned to

Murdoch and in a sulking tone asked, "What are these crucial matters that only I can manage?"

With a sigh, Murdoch launched into his list.

"Your orders regarding the army have displeased most of the officer corps, and turned many against you. In like manner, the disbanding of the Privy Council has angered the nobles. Abolishment of slavery, raising of taxes, and the outlawing of compound interest has infuriated the merchants and money-lenders. Your cancellation of the building of war galleys and order for these new ships called caravels has outraged most of the naval officers and seamen."

He paused, got only a bored look for a reaction, then continued. "The edict on religious tolerance has cause five of the main temples to begin preaching against you. Your refusal to meet with the guildmasters to discuss their concerns of lost privileges has cost you their support. When a group of students presented a satirical play that old Elric would have roasted them for, you simply laughed and let them off with a lecture on plagiarism, causing many of the university faculty to believe you were simply half-witted."

He paused again, looking for some glimmer of understanding on the face before him. None showed. "Sire, you have done all of this in just one week's time. It is just too much. Each action by itself has merit and would be acceptable if people were given a bit of time to consider. But this is too much, too fast." Murdoch paused. breathing heavily.

The King popped another grape in his mouth and burped. "My good, hard-working Murdoch, you do worry too much. Just what is the point of all this?"

At that moment, the door opened by itself and the cat came sauntering in, as usual looking like it owned the place. The door closed behind it. Murdoch had not seen the cat in several days, since it had taken to keeping company with his bodyguard Finnegin, but he didn't enjoy the sight of it now, presenting as it did a distraction for the grasshopper mind of Christopher. Manfully, he continued. "Sire, I believe you have placed yourself, and me in danger. These reforms are giving cause for an uprising."

The cat walked over to the lounging king and lightly leaped into his lap, calmly making itself comfortable and curling up. Murdoch lost his train of thought. The King seemed amused and lightly stroked the cat. "Friendly, isn't he? My guards have been be-deviling me about him because they can't seem to find any way to keep him out of any room in the palace. I mean, doors just open for him, have you noticed?"

"Sire! We are in danger! Please attend, and forget the damn cat."

The King looked up at him and gave him a broad wink. With a negligent hand gesture he caused the room to grow dark with black clouds suddenly covering walls, floor and ceiling. Then, in a well-remembered voice, he chuckled. "Why Murdoch, I thought you liked Fang."

The face and form of the addle-witted King Christopher suddenly flowed and shimmered, like one's reflection in a pool when the surface is disturbed, and there sat his master Sahm-el the Sorcerer, known to the public as Deathwind.

Murdoch stood there, gasping like a fish out of water, then felt himself gently pushed backwards until he fell into a large arm chair that had positioned itself to catch him. He found his voice. "Of all the dirty low down tricks...So I've been a puppet, dancing to your strings, working my head off, worrying myself to death over this fop who didn't have the brains of a sandcrab, so you and your friends could enjoy a hearty laugh. All that about the Outsiders was just a ploy, to let you play an elaborate game of Jannisaries. I take it ill, sir. I have been ill-used."

Sahm-el was calm, smiling, waiting for Murdoch to stop and breathe. When he finally did, Sahm-el spoke. "Oh ho! So you have found some pride in yourself through all this. 'Tis a bonus I had hoped for."

Murdoch was about to launch into another outburst of indignation when this caused him to pause. In calmer tones, he said instead, "I believe I am owed an explanation."

Sahm-el laughed, "You are indeed, and perhaps an apology as well." He waved his fingers and two drinks appeared, a crystal goblet for Murdoch and the old familiar goblin mug in front of himself. Murdoch took the goblet and found it filled with his favorite light wine. He sipped it, and leaned back, ready to listen to the man who had once saved him.

Sahm-el spoke. "First, the threat is real. All that you have been told was true. We are approaching a crisis. Second, the deception was necessary, and I apologize to you for it. Elric made it needful to hasten his departure and the rightful king is not yet selected. A stand-in was needed and I had to supply it. Time permitted no other solution. This Christopher mask is very temporary and will be gone from the scene as soon as the rightful king is ready. You could not be told, because your honest reactions helped the believability and you have a too honest face to play a double role."

Murdoch sipped his wine, turning over in his mind what he had just been told. Little pieces fit together for him. His doubts and anger dissolved. "But why the mad course of reform? You have deliberately set out to make enemies of nearly everyone in Telluria. How does that fit in?"

"Verily, you have grown quick-witted in these matters. Let us travel that path for a bit and see where it leads." He took a long swing from the goblin skull mug. "Now we begin with an evil tyrant who is nevertheless profitable to certain factions and he dies. One of the factions puts up a stooge to replace him. The stooge turns on them and begins making real reforms. Do you deny that each of the measures is a good one?"

"No...It's not the measures but the suddenness. Spaced out over a few years each stands on its own merits."

"Very well. Now, suppose this stooge, who is suddenly grown very unpopular with everyone is replaced by a true and rightful heir, unquestioned in legal right? Might the new King be welcomed warmly as a reasoned and even-tempered fellow compared with the idiot Christopher?"

"Well yes, but what of the reforms? He could hardly support the policies of his unpopular predecessor."

"He need not. The reforms have been introduced. They will not be forgotten. At the right time, when the support truly does exist for each, they can be brought back."

Murdoch sat silent for a moment, sipping his wine and thinking. "I believe it will work, if handled cleverly, it can be done."

Sahm-el laughed. "I see you have read the books we gave you. How nice it is to see a man who can actually profit from reading books these days."

Murdoch smiled and gave him a mock salute of acknowledgment, lifting the crystal goblet high. In the shared warmth of the moment, Murdoch suddenly realized their relationship had changed, and would never be the same again. They were no longer master and former slave, but rather colleagues, respectful of each other. He promised himself silently that he would always remember this moment.

"Having, as you said read those books, I dare say there is more awaiting me, further little surprises. Knowing the subtlety and care for detail that mark all of your ventures, there is some purpose in having me in this place at this time. May I know what it is?"

Sahm-el laughed again. "Well done! You have just won another wager for me. I told Chiang that you would be able to see deeply enough to recognize that very fact. Yes, you have a crucial role to play. Today you are to be knighted, and then named Royal Spymaster for the Great Christopher. He will make it plain that you are, to be treated as his Chancellor. Most of the Court are already doing that, it will cause no major stir. There are some who will underestimate you and think to use you as a puppet. They will fail."

Murdoch nearly dropped the goblet. "Knighted? Me, a member of the nobility?" The thought was too large to grasp.

"Yes. Your real purpose is to protect the rightful King and guide him in the protection of the realm from its real enemies. By being recognized as Chancellor to Christopher, you will be in position to aid the succession and step into the new role. All that has happened with you has been to lay the foundation for this endeavor on behalf of the new King. Do you understand?"

A broad grin slowly spread across Murdoch's face. He, former maker of mud bricks while a slave, was now to become kingmaker. There was an element of whimsy in this that was enhanced as he realized the faith in his abilities that this situation now implied. All his life, he had felt inferior, awkward, and stumbling around other people. For the first time, he understood some of his true worth. Murdoch leaned his head back and laughed a full rich laugh, of the kind that only a truly relaxed man can produce.

♜ ♜ ♜

Far across the sea, the sorcerer Fairchilde stood upon a parapet, overlooking the crater of an extinct volcano. Directly across from him, on the opposite rim of the crater, he could see another parapet, jutting out from the crater wall, empty.

This was the Place of Challenge on the Isle of Enigma. For centuries, Sorcerers had fought duels in magic at this place, sometimes in the harmless game called Lights, more often in spectacular duels to the death. Fairchilde's vision had brought him to this place.

He didn't know quite what to expect, but stood confidently, holding his wizardry staff, waiting for what was to come.

He permitted himself a smile when little sparks of light started forming in the air over the center of the crater. More and more of them winked in, forming a cloud that began to rotate like a cyclone. As it got brighter and stronger, this funnel cloud of light began producing heat that he could feel on his cheek, until it burst into flames and became a pillar of fire, rising from the crater floor and extending out of sight into the sky.

A common tradesman or simple fighter might have felt fear in the presence of the roaring blast of flame and heat. But Fairchilde was an experienced sorcerer and knew well that he could create such a thing himself if he so chose, so he just waited, admiring the artistry of the spectacle.

When the flames had become most fierce, a deep and powerful voice was heard, so loud that it was almost painful to the ears. *"WHY HAVE YOU COME?"*

Fairchilde felt a thrill as he faced his destiny. "I but follow my visions to seek my appointed place in the universe." He spoke calmly, confident that he would be heard, and that all was going as it should.

"DO YOU SEEK THE CHALLENGE?"

Recognizing the ritual phrase from the prophecy he had studied, Fairchilde answered properly, "I am chosen! Test me!" The prophecy had stated that The Chosen One would be tested by a dragon. Fairchilde was certain there was an Imperial Dragon producing the pillar of fire, and he had slain more than one such dragon in the past.

"HAVE YOU THE STRENGTH FOR THIS ORDEAL?"

"More than enough for victory, I am certain." He had been charging himself with energy, and ensuring his staff was at full power, and in doing so had accumulated a truly awesome amount of strength.

The voice from the roaring flames then intoned. *"THEN YOU SHALL JOIN YOUR COMPETITORS FOR THE TEST."*

Fairchilde was startled. "Competitors? What competitors? The prophecy made no mention of…."

At that moment, the island, crater, pillar of fire, and sky, in short all that he could see, suddenly twisted around him and the world went dark.

Twenty-Four

"Even the most formidable of warriors, in full armor, have oft times been killed by an angry farmer swinging a well bucket in the defense of his family."

—The Decree of Salamanca,
Sacred Text for the Temple of Leto.

Murdoch was knighted, that evening at supper, and his appointment as Spymaster announced to the court by a somewhat tipsy King Christopher. There was no applause.

He arranged for the belongings of the deposed Miriam to be packed and shipped to her, and took over the office of the Spymaster the next morning. Miriam's known agents were suspended, on probation, until such time as they could each be examined to Murdoch's satisfaction.

He had much to do and was ably helped by that strange little fellow, Flettcher, who had an uncanny talent for finding and recruiting people who were both talented and honest. In this way, Murdoch acquired able assistants and began organizing a new bureaucracy in a matter of days.

There were chests of old papers and letters, found in the Spymaster's chambers that hinted at dark secrets and past intrigues, and Murdoch made note of them, to be read after the crisis, as there was not time to do so now. In like manner, he had found even such simple things as finding his way about the palace, and locating the nearest privy, to be difficult in the huge place. It was not surprising that he was completely unaware of hidden chambers and passageways that existed throughout the palace.

One who was not unaware of them was Miriam, the deposed Spymaster, who now had additional reasons for wrath against Murdoch. For on top of her personal grievance, and the humiliation of having been replaced by this mousy little scholar, there was also the fact that certain documents left in her palace chambers could prove harmful to her and others.

Miriam, dressed in a commoner's cloak, made her way to the riverfront area, and in particular to the Broken Tooth Inn, a haven for sailors, dockworker, pickpockets, and harlots, that nonetheless had acquired a reputation for the quality of its eel chowder.

Instead of entering the common room by the main entrance, she quietly slipped into the attached stable and moved from stall to stall until she reached the back corner. Here, she brushed hay aside and removed two floorboards, revealing a flat stone with an iron ring set into it. A tug on the ring, easily moved the stone, which seemed to have no weight at all. Underneath, there was an angular gemstone, a sapphire, about the size of her fist. She turned this stone, releasing the magic it contained.

Immediately, the wall in front of her vanished, replaced by a dark vaporous cloud that glowed with tiny blue sparks. Miriam replaced the flat stone, and carefully covered it with straw once more, then stepped through the magic portal that had been created. It closed behind her, becoming a wall once more.

As she expected, she found herself in a roughly cut underground chamber that exited into a long sloping tunnel. This was originally one of the escape tunnels from the palace, created through sorcery centuries ago and known but to a very few. She was now going to use it to return to the palace, in hopes of finally settling with the upstart sage.

Miriam picked up one of the small oil lamps from a shelf and lit it with tinderbox, striking steel across flint. Then she entered the tunnel. Although she had inspected this tunnel several years ago, and thus knew its features, she moved very carefully, for going into an escape tunnel can be quite different from going out of one. Particularly one as well guarded as this one. She knew of several traps, and at least one guardian defending this tunnel.

Searching the stone paved floor cautiously, she found the almost minute scratches on stones she was seeking and began a peculiar dance, as she proceeded up the tunnel. Step, step, pause, hop, pause, step, hop. She continued that way for a full minute, moving irregularly according to a memorized pattern. Timing, especially of the pauses, was critical. Her life depended upon doing this without mistake.

This end of the palace escape tunnel had one of the dreaded tunnel traps built into it. Her strange dance was to prevent the trap from becoming armed, and then sending the solid rock of the ceiling crashing down upon her once she reached the middle of the trap. The rhythmic tapping of her feet worked their magic and she was safely allowed to proceed.

Two more such traps were passed by safely. One would have twisted her into another dimension of time, the other would have instantly transported her directly to the palace dungeons. Both times, she knew the safeguard that allowed her to bypass them.

After traversing a long stretch that went under the river estuary, Miriam finally came to the end of the tunnel and the guardian chamber. Here, she paused, uttering the Ritual of Calming. The three long deep breaths composed her for this most difficult task. Although skilled at the Master's Level as an assassin, she knew will that she was no mage, and she knew this guardian to be a demon.

Miriam stepped to the opening of the guardian Chamber. The flickering light of her oil lamp showed a round chamber, just three meters across. Inscribed into the floor, and covering the entire floor of the chamber, there was a pentagram. It would be necessary to step into the pentagram in order to cross the chamber. The pentagram was occupied.

The chamber was freezing cold, and the cold emanated

from the center of the pentagram. There, Miriam could see a dark lumpen mass, slowing stirring. Two glowing red eyes suddenly opened and turned in her direction. The mass was unshapen, turning and boiling like a thunderstorm cloud, yet solid and hard, not vaporous. The eyes were rising in the air, about an arm's length apart. In the flickering light, she could make out either horns or large pointed ears above the eyes. All else was shifting darkness and cold.

Such a sight, along with the waves of cold that streamed from it, would have given pause to anyone, and Miriam was no exception. It was commonly known that a demon bound in a pentagram could not leave the circle. But here, the room was so constructed that she would have to step into the circle, with it.

Had Miriam not had her overpowering rage to fire her determination, she might well have despaired. But she had come to hate the little scholar, whom she blamed for her present circumstances. Her anger was enough to balance the terror of the cold. And, it must be admitted that Miriam had her own kind of courage and was prepared for this challenge.

She drew a spill of parchment from a pocket in her gown, unrolled it, and, keeping well back in the hallway, away from the edge of the circle, shifted her gaze to the writing it contained. Even while reading, she could feel the eyes of the demon locked upon her and its mass continually shifting as if it was crouching for a leap.

Satisfied, Miriam looked up to meet its gaze, and stepped to the very edge of the circle. Then in a commanding tone she cried, "Chakha Neh Rahvit!"

The demon stopped moving, as if frozen in place by its own well of cold. Miriam gritted her teeth and stepped into the pentagram. The demon did not move. She quickly slipped around it and hurried out of the pentagram on the far side, entering another tunnel.

Once safely past, she turned and clapped her hands four times, in an odd off-beat rhythm. Instantly the demon moved, twisting around to see her, then silently settling into a dark mound on the floor of the pentagram as it became aware that she was safely out of it's reach.

Miriam laughed, a small laugh of triumph. The Charm of Further Binding had cost a small fortune, but it had worked. Now there was nothing between her hand of vengeance and that worm-tongued scholar, who even now resided in her place at the palace.

Murdoch put down his pen and reflected once more on the good fortune of working for a sorcerer. The dispatches he had just written were, clear, clean and dry, without smear or smudge. The pen he used was enchanted, never required ink, and produced writing that was instantly dry to the touch. It had been a birthday gift from his master a few years earlier.

The thought brought other thoughts, of his past and change in fortune and finally his sense of acceptance as a man, rather than a slave. It had suddenly occurred to him that he was no longer thinking of himself as a slave, or even servant, but rather as a colleague and even friend to his benefactor, Sahm-el.

Murdoch turned in his chair, and picked up the small bag of licorice nibblets that he liked to chew on. Absently putting one of the little bits of dark candy in his mouth, he enjoyed the burst of flavor as he put the dispatches in the little metal casket that he reserved for orders to the Dragoons.

He was alone in the Spymaster Chamber. A protesting Finnegin had been sent with an important message for Develon. Murdoch had insisted that he was perfectly safe here in the palace. A new crispness in his manner and tone had impressed Finnegin and swayed his judgment to agreement. Murdoch had found he enjoyed the sensation.

Now, his meditations had brought him to a personal decision, a new resolve. He had spent his entire life depending upon others, deferring to others, even having others like the good Finnegin fight for him. This recent rush of events had altered him, awakened in him a new person, one that he rather liked. It was a bit like stretching and suddenly becoming aware of new muscles, feeling a new strength. A very pleasant feeling, indeed.

Miriam made her way along well-remembered secret passages inside the Palace of Telluria. She had assumed that the upstart would not have had time yet, to learn of these passages, and certain tell-tale signs she had left confirmed that no one had made of use of the secret ways since she last passed through them.

From time to time, she passed by little branches and alcoves off the narrow tunnel. Each of these led to spy points, or secret doors in various parts of the palace. She continued along the passage, occasionally going up narrow flights of stairs, until she reached the particular alcove that she knew led to the Spymaster Chamber.

Here, she stopped. Her plan was simple, as all good plans must be, yet it showed the subtlety of a master assassin. Miriam intended to entice Murdoch into drawing a weapon. That was all. It would be enough.

Miriam, herself, had designed the magic defenses of the Spymaster Chamber, and the Royal Sorcerer, Fairchilde, had executed them with skill and power. Inside the Spymaster Chamber, anyone drawing sword, or dagger would be instantly bathed in liquid flames, roasted to a crisp by a fire hot enough to turn a troll to ash.

She was confident that he knew nothing of the special enchantments of the palace, since only she, Fairchilde, and the now dead Elric had known of them.

Being cautious, however, she had thought of a fall back plan, in case something went wrong. It was the fall back plan that required her to stop and make preparations with extreme care.

Setting the little oil lamp on a small ledge, Miriam withdrew a glass vial from her sleeve pocket. She opened it and used a tiny brush to completely paint the fingernails and fingers of her right hand with a clear substance that dried invisible. This was the shielding potion. It was intended to protect her own hand from what came next. She used it very liberally, consuming the contents of the entire vial.

When her hand was dry, she replaced the little vial and with the utmost care opened another potion vial, setting its glass stopper on the ledge by the lamp. This was WizardBane, and even its touch brought instant and total death.

Miriam held the small glass vial, and performed the Ritual of Calming. Then with steady hands she dipped the coated fingernails of her right hand into the black poison, just enough to get it on the very tips of her long fingernails. Then she stood while it dried, watching the black color fade until it could not be seen. With great care, she replaced the stopper, checking a second time to insure it was tightly closed.

Now all she need do was touch him, anywhere on bare skin, and he was hers. So even if the thin-necked, bald headed, potbellied, little wretch was too craven to draw a weapon, she would be rid of him, without drawing sword or dagger herself.

With a grim little smile, Miriam eased up to the secret portal that would admit her into the Spymaster Chamber.

Murdoch was at his desk, and did not hear the soundless opening of the secret portal behind him. But a very slight breeze on the back of his bald head drew his attention from the documents he was reading. At nearly the same instant, he heard the voice of the dagger, Miranda, inside his head.

"Danger! Danger! Danger!"

Murdoch leaped from his chair, knocking it over onto the stone floor, and turned to see the former Spymaster, Miriam, standing against the wall, smiling a leopard-smile.

With a chill, Murdoch realized that she could have only one purpose in appearing here like this. His first panicky thought was of the absent Finnegin, sent away on an errand because Murdoch felt so safe here.

Miriam stood composed, taunting him with silence. He glanced about the room, painfully aware that he did not even know how to set off the alarm from this room. She took one step forward.

Then, the very chills of fear reminded him of the last time he had experienced something like this, and he thought of the magic dagger, Miranda, who had just warned him. All he need do is summon the dagger forth and he would be safe.

As he opened his mouth to speak the name, Miriam spoke for the first time. "What now, mister high and mighty Spymaster? Where are your guards and protectors? Who will fight for you now?" Her voice dripped with hatred.

Murdoch, on the point of calling forth the dagger to save himself, now gave pause. Standing rigidly still, breathing heavily and with sweat dropping from his head, he nonetheless hesitated. Something in her tone of absolute contempt brought to mind his earlier train of thought about himself. He found he could not say the name that would bring rescue. He stood silent, blinking, hands shaking, facing the assassin.

She took another step forward. Again her voice rang with challenge and contempt. "In sooth, you are no Spymaster! I doubt you even know how to handle a dagger yourself. You are but a clerk with trembling hands, who has others do the fighting because you are too craven yourself." She took another step forward, and was now almost in arm's reach.

As the seconds passed and he found himself still alive, Murdoch began to think, rapidly but clearly. He could see no weapon on her. What was she doing? She could have killed him at once instead of talking. Why was she so slow and deliberate?

Miriam taunted him again. "There is a dagger just inside the right side of the desk. Have you the nerve to draw it? Go ahead! I'll permit it. There is no gain in killing a wretch who will not even defend himself."

Murdoch knew she was being truthful about the dagger in the desk. He now recalled seeing it there earlier. It only increased the mystery for him. She seemed to be goading him into going for the dagger. He could not fathom why.

On her part, Miriam found her disgust with this creature growing. As he stood before her, trembling, silent, she decided he really was too craven to defend himself. He would draw no weapon. She must use the poison prepared on her fingernails, instead.

Murdoch had no idea as to what to do in this situation, but he did have an intuitive sense that by delaying and not doing what she seemed to want him to do, he was upsetting her. This, in itself, seemed a worthy goal. As casually as possible, he pulled the kerchief out of his sleeve, and used it to mop the sweat from his head.

Now it was Miriam's turn to hesitate, and wonder. Her victims, sometimes tried to flee, often begged for mercy, sometimes fought desperately, but never had she encountered one who simply stood there silently wiping his brow. Was there something she did not know about this man? Glancing about the chamber, she took half a step back. He may have invisible guardians, or some unknown power of his own. Why was he just standing there?

Murdoch noticed that slight move backward. He deduced from this that he was not completely helpless. There were things she feared. A sudden memory of childhood confrontations appeared in his mind. Yes, this was a test of wills. Who will back down? He paralyzed by fear, or she held by growing doubts? The tension was so great that this could not last long.

Miriam reached the limits of her patience and began to move forward to strike, finally deciding there was no secret protection or it would have acted by now. She took a step forward and swung her right arm up, as if to slap him, knowing that the least touch on his face would bring him death.

Murdoch seeing her move, reacted instinctively. He had been holding his kerchief by one corner, and as the assassin moved, he flicked the kerchief, as he used to flick towels in the bathhouse when a boy, snapping the cloth with literally blinding speed. His kerchief caught her in the face with an audible snap.

Miriam instinctively blinked, felt the kerchief sting her closed eyelid and, without thinking, put her hand to her eye. It was the wrong hand. She just had time to realize her error and recognize that the wretched clerk had brought about her death. Then she crumpled to the floor. Her body went rigid, and her skin began turning a glossy black.

Murdoch stood there amazed. One moment he was threatened by a deadly assassin. The next moment she lay dead at his feet and he hadn't any idea as to what had happened.

He carefully stepped away from the body, and looked wonderingly at the kerchief he was holding in trembling hands. He could not recall it being a gift from his master, but it might have been. Murdoch had never heard of an enchanted kerchief as a secret weapon, but this one appeared to have awesome powers. At that moment, the long delayed reaction to the crisis surfaced, and Murdoch found himself running for the privy to vomit.

Twenty-Five

"Success always brings vulnerability."
—Drury's Primer for Princes,
A book of advice on the acquisition and uses of political power.

The Imperial Dragon Ginseng soared high above the mountains. He was flying for the first time in a very long time and relishing the physical experience. The air whistled past his ears, and the stretch and flap of leathery wings were most pleasant.

Ordinarily, he would have used the trans-dimensional magic of sorcery to travel to his destination in the blink of an eye, but on this day he allowed himself the small pleasure of actually flying. Like the larger birds, he was actually soaring on thermals, with only the occasional flap of wings to shift to a new air current before spreading his wings and holding his tail at precisely the right angle to take most advantage of the currents. It was this merging of self with the natural flow, so like the practice of sorcery, that he really enjoyed.

At this great height, he had little to fear. Having dared the rite of passage of Khaleehl three times in his long lifespan, and thus progressed from hatchling to full dragon to royal dragon and at last to Imperial Dragon. He had few natural enemies now. In each ordeal, he had risked death or madness in order to increase his abilities potential. Each time, he had awakened from the hibernation that followed with massive changes in body and spirit. The changes included changes in size, color, and even sex, at different stages in his growth, but each change brought him greater power.

Now, creatures that were dangerous to him in earlier stages were beneath his notice. Only the great sorcerers or other dragons could pose any real threat to him, and he would know if any of those were about.

On this day, Ginseng was answering a call from Chiang and meeting him at the Great Lair. Chiang had informed him through direct mind-talk that the time had come to test candidates for the true heir to the Dragon Throne.

Now, as he approached Bald Mountain, rising by itself just to the south of the land of the Mist Wizards, Ginseng rolled to his left and half folding his wings, swooped downward, gathering speed, as he dived toward a broad rock ledge, scored by deep claw marks worn into the rock over the centuries. At the last possible moment, he curved his spine, flaring his wings out in rounded arches and tipped upward to slow his descent, landing on the stone as light as a feather. It pleased him that he hadn't lost the knack of it.

Now through the long sloping tunnel, a quick dip in a lake of fire much larger than his own, then, with gleaming golden scales, a sip of clear cold water and an easing onto one of the sloping stone resting benches, and a chat with Chiang.

Chiang was already on a dragon-bench, using the very tip of his scaly tail to turn a spit over a roaring fire. The spit, itself, was of considerable size and held half a carcass of mammoth on it, sizzling and dripping fat as it roasted. Chiang had spent enough time among humans to have acquired a taste for cooked meat. Ginseng had to admit that the aroma was enticing.

The two huge golden and black dragons felt no need for idle small talk. Chiang immediately spoke. "On this entire world, there were originally five humans who had some legitimate claim to the Dragon Throne, either through birth or ability. Of those five, two are still in contention for it. Two of the others proved to lack the courage for the challenge, and the third had a mind of such shallow depths and so full of fear and loathing that I deemed him not suitable."

Ginseng nibbled a bit of anthracite from the nearby pile and felt the stirrings of hunger from the smell of the roasting meat. "Then we have two who are willing to face the challenge?" At a nod from Chiang, he continued. "Do they know the risk?"

"Each has been informed that this is a life or death test. Each for personal reasons has accepted that."

"Truly? I have not heard of humans being willing to risk life for anything but gold. These must be unusual specimens. Tell me of them." He nibbled another bit of anthracite.

Chiang gave the roasting spit another turn. "'Tis true that each is somewhat unusual. One is a sorcerer of advanced degree, the other is a young girl, not yet aware of her real abilities. One is clearly brimming with strength, the other is notably lacking. The sorcerer is at the height of his profession. The girl was sent by her father to live and study among the Elves and has much of their temperament, both good and bad. Yet she also has artistic gifts that cannot be ignored."

"You sound as if the choice is a clear one between the obviously strong and the weak."

Having met them, I believe the choice will be clear. However, they have not met The Challenge yet." Chiang, too, was feeling the pangs of hunger and casting a longing eye at the roasting spit. But he added, "Naturally, only one of them will survive that."

Ginseng nodded, and without further discussion, they put the matter aside and turned to enjoy a good meal. Any humans who might have seen these two mighty beings feeding would have found it to be an appalling sight.

Fairchilde the Feared, mighty sorcerer, was feeling impatient. After being whisked from the volcanic island known as Enigma to this unknown place, he had been given little information and left alone in a small chamber with just a chair, and the usual stand to hold his staff upright by the chair. He had not enjoyed the experience.

This was the sort of thing sorcerers did to other people. It was galling to have one such as himself blithely carried off by another who kept control so effectively and so easily. Worse than galling was the fact that he actually could not discover where he was.

He had obviously traveled across more than one dimension in time and space, and was in one of the infinite parallel universes. He had traveled thusly himself many times. He had no doubt he could return to his world by his own abilities. But it had been a shock to him, that all of his power could not tell him where, or when, he was. Sorcerers do not take kindly to beings who show more power than they.

When the world had come into existence around him once more, he had found himself in a velvety fog. He could feel surface under his feet, but not see any ground. Into the fog he stretched forth his hand and found he could not see it at the end of his arm. This was not troubling to him for it was very minor magic, and the sort of thing he had expected.

He was troubled though, when he found he could not cast a simple light, nor clear any of the fog, nor even draw power from his staff. This, too, was not a mystery to him. It meant he was inside a stasis field that would dampen or prevent the flow of any magic. Such was not harmful to him, but it effectively left him helpless as a peasant.

He could not tell how long he remained in this gray void. It could as easily have been an hour as a minute. Fairchilde thus composed his thoughts and calmly disciplined his mind to rest in a waiting state until something happened.

At some point, the fog began to clear, and he found himself in this small chamber, with just the chair. When he sat upon the chair, and rested his dormant staff in its rack, a writing table appeared before him, bearing a sealed scroll of parchment. With an anticipatory smile, he broke the seal and read:

To Ye who would seek the Dragon Throne:

Know ye that the Challenge has Begun.
It is, in essence, a test of strength.

Nearby to this chamber there is a mages Laboratory, stocked with all manner of useful things. The servant will show you in, presently.

The stasis field is being withdrawn, and you are free to make use of whatever ability, wit, and strength you may possess.

At that moment, Fairchilde felt a change in the atmosphere and the return of the normal tingling sensation that emanated from his fully charged staff. His magic was working again.

Within that other chamber, there is a large crystal, the purest of gems. It is a Jewel of Universal Power. Your challenge, is to make use of it, to its best effect. The servant will come for you shortly.

Fairchilde leaned back in the chair. So, the challenge was a typical problem in sorcery. Whoever his rivals were, they were not likely to be better prepared for such a test than he.

He sat in thought, turning over the information contained in the scroll. A Jewel of Universal Power. He had never heard of such a thing, but certainly found the name to be of interest. There were many possibilities. It might allow the user to draw energy from any source, in unlimited amounts. Or, it might be a tool of domination that would work on any target of any power. It might lend magic strength to the user in amounts sufficient to move entire worlds. Or, it could have something to do with the higher arts of dimensional and time magic, allowing its user to control the stress of time itself. Anything was possible.

Fairchilde was completely confident of his ability to master the jewel. Failure at any task in magic was unthinkable to one such as he. Certainly there would be risks, enormous risks, as there always were when brushing against enormous power. But, in magic, the higher the risks, the greater the gains. Fairchilde allowed a smile to spread across his face.

Suddenly remembering that the stasis field had gone down, the grinning sorcerer grasped his staff and took the three long breaths of the Ritual of Calming. He then began to practice his craft.

He drew forth from his staff, a small amount of energy in the form of a sphere the size of a grape. This he patterned, using various the concepts of *perception, connection,* and *mobility,* until it could function as an eye for him. He then sent this invisible eye out through the open doorway and across the hallway to the door of the Laboratory.

There, he made a minor shift in the molecular structure of the door and passed the eye through it, and into the mage Laboratory. There, he paused to observe.

The scene was quite familiar to him. On the floor, there was the great ritual pentagram inlaid in the stones in bright metal. There were the usual work tables, shelves, and supplies. As he looked on, it became apparent that it was the most complete and well stocked laboratory he had ever seen. Every possible tool, raw material and the most rare of ingredients were ready to hand. He even saw a huge vat made of glass tiles that had to contain Entropic Acid, since glass was the only substance the acid would not consume. One whole wall was filed with books and scrolls, and many a secret must lie hidden there.

Of chief interest to him, was the great crystal and the person occupying the room. The jewel was the size of a pumpkin and resting on a pedestal. It was diamond bright and shimmered with an inner light. Upon examining it, Fairchilde found it appeared to fade and return, as if it was only partially existing in this dimension. This alone hinted at great power.

The occupant of the room was a disappointment to him. Instead of a mighty dragon or awe-inspiring sorcerer, it was simply an old man in peasant clothes, cleaning up. He was industriously polishing various lenses, and laying out tools in an orderly fashion, replacing candles and kindling fires in the standing braziers that surrounded the great pentagram. This obviously was the servant.

Fairchilde turned his attention back to the jewel, and began studying it. He moved the magic eye in close to it and began to discern extremely complicated patterns of magical energy flowing around it, and through it. If he could unravel these patterns of flow, he could learn its secrets and master it. So Fairchilde began an intense study.

After some several minutes, he had recognized the pattern of flow associated with the stream of time, and was trying to see how it connected with other patterns when his attention was drawn from the crystal by something happening nearby.

The servant, in carrying a log to one of the round sunken fireplaces, had accidentally bumped a release lever, and the huge glass vat of acid was beginning to tip.

It was major catastrophe in the making. Fairchilde leaped from the chair, grabbing his staff and raced to the hall. He could still see through the magic eye. The vat of acid was clearly going to spill. The servant, unaware of it, was arranging logs on the fire, directly in its path. More to the point, the Jewel, resting on its pedestal, was also in the path of the acid spill.

Entropic Acid was more than just a powerful acid. It was one of many naturally occurring magic substances in the Universe. Fairchilde was moving fast because he knew the acid actually sucked material into another dimension, rather than simply consuming it. Even a small splash of the virulent stuff would begin gradually drawing anything it touched out of this world.

Throwing open the door, Fairchilde pointed his staff into the center of the room. There was time to grab just one thing out of that room before the room itself was consumed. The old servant, suddenly discovering his peril, screamed and backed away, as the acid splashed out on the floor and began taking the very stone of the floor, then one of the fireplaces, flame, logs and all.

Fairchilde did not hesitate. He directed a stream of energy from his staff to the crystal, surrounding it and lifting it from its pedestal, just as the pedestal collapsed under it, into the spreading black pool of acid. He pulled the free floating jewel to him and cradled it in his arms, as he heard the old servant scream again, then suddenly stop in mid-scream as he was taken by the acid.

Fairchilde backed out of the room, carrying the precious jewel along with his staff. Instead of returning to the waiting room, he rushed on down the hallway, fully aware that there was enough acid back there to consume the laboratory, hallway and waiting room, if not much more.

The hallway stretched out in front of him for considerable distance, and Fairchilde hurried on, turning a part of his mind to the question of what he should do next. By saving the crystal, he made it possible to take the challenge test in a safer location. But he didn't know how to get in touch with the Master of the Challenge. Still, the Jewel of Universal Power was in his possession, and he intended to keep it regardless of what happened next.

This train of thought ended abruptly when the hallway disappeared and he found himself surrounded once more by the velvety fog of a stasis field. The great gem disappeared and a familiar voice suddenly spoke.

"THE CHALLENGE IS CONCLUDED. THE TEST IS OVER!"

Fairchilde, taken completely by surprise, both by the loss of the Jewel and the message just spoken, could only stammer. "Wait! Wait! Did I not win? What is the result?" There was no answer, but he suddenly felt his surroundings change once again, and found himself on a high pedestal, surrounded by a void.

The Gem of Universal Power was floating in the air just in front of him. As he watched, it shimmered and changed its form, becoming the well-known emerald and gold Dragon Crown of Telluria. The crown moved of its own accord to rest upon his head. He heard a voice proclaim:

"YOU HAVE NOW EARNED POWER OVER ALL WHO WOULD BE LOYAL TO YOU."

It was the final confirmation of his visions. Master Fairchilde laughed exultantly.

Twenty-Six

"Evil knows not itself. For all beings, regardless of their actions, believe they are in the right."

—The Korakorahm,
Sacred Text for the Temple of Dhao.

The officer in the flowing red cloak addressed Twila as Lady Lyestehr and informed her that her services as a healer were needed. The new title sounded strange to her ears. Her mother had always been Lady Lyestehr. That was almost as strange as the chain mail and red cloak of the officer. He was one of the new Royal Dragoons being created by King Christopher, and his uniform looked quite different from the traditional ornate green and gold of the Tellurian Army.

Twila picked up her healer's bag and followed the dragoon. She assumed that her one and only patient, Oscar Wyndham was probably experiencing the itchy-ache from his stump and needed another appliance of the poultice balm she had been using for him. Since he had felt well enough to get around, Oscar had insisted on offering his help in the training of the new dragoons, and she no longer attended him full time.

Twila was led through the palace, and into a wing she had not seen before. When she was finally shown into a chamber, she did not see Oscar, but rather that funny little man who had been with Finnegin when they visited Oscar's sickbed. She could not remember his name.

He was just standing there, fingering a kerchief in both hands and seemingly lost in thought. She observed him with the eye of a healer and could see no immediate illness or injury. As she looked closer, Twila began changing her first impression of him. She had originally placed his age as older than her bodyguard Finnegin, perhaps in his early fifties. But now, closer examination indicated, that despite the bald head and round tummy, he was probably younger than that, perhaps in his forties, but had a hard life. The small wrinkles about the eyes were more the wrinkles of stress rather age.

Murdoch looked up, saw her and silently motioned to the floor beyond his desk. Twila stepped forward and gasped. There was the body of a woman, probably once beautiful, but now rigid and hard with skin the glossy black of obsidian. Twila had seen this once before, and briefly closed her eyes at the painful memory of her dead brother.

She opened them again, blinked back one small tear and spoke. "This person is beyond any help from me. I know of no cure for Bai Hara Chi." The man was clearly startled, looking almost in panic at the kerchief he was holding in both hands. Twila had never seen such a strange expression on a man's face before.

Murdoch balled the kerchief up and thrust it back into his sleeve, cleared his suddenly dry throat and found his voice. "Am I to understand you believe this death came from WizardBane?" There was a very strange intensity to his voice.

Twila nodded. "That is the common name. I have seen it before. My own brother died this way. The poison is so virulent that its effects cannot be reversed. I am quite certain."

Murdoch looked down at the body again, and Twila noted the muscles in his face moving as he clenched his teeth. He was suddenly very frightened, and she could not understand why, since he clearly had not been frightened a few minutes before.

Murdoch was thinking, "I faced a master assassin armed with the deadliest of poisons with nothing but an ordinary bit of cloth from my sleeve! Fortune does indeed smile on the foolish. Never again will I allow my pride to lead me into such folly?" Then, he turned his attention back to the healer.

"Good Lady, your pardon, for my ill manners. Your information was ...a surprise to me and forced the recasting of my understanding of this event. You need spare no sympathy for this dead woman as she is almost certainly the one who brought about the death of your brother, as she just tried to bring about mine."

Twila looked at the body again. Even as it was, with the twisted rictus grin of death upon the face, she could tell that the woman had been beautiful. "Who was she?"

"This was Miriam, Elric's Spymaster and Master of Assassins."

Twila looked again. The twisted face now seemed colder, as though what beauty there used to be was a mask now cracked. "Master of Assassins? And you were alone with her? 'Tis a daring thing you have done here."

Murdoch gave a snort of laughter. "'Twas a mixture of blind luck and foolishness, good Lady. I would not willingly do it again."

Expecting the usual kind of boasting that men attach to dangerous acts, Twila was surprised once again, by this strange little man. She now found that he did not look old to her at all, merely tired and carrying a great weight. She smiled.

"Good Lady, you have answered my questions of the moment. Now I have much to do and will not ask you to remain in the presence of that any longer. Now that I know what happened, I know how it must be handled. I thank you for your assistance."

She was dismissed. As she turned to leave, Twila asked, "May I know your name sir? I know we met on one occasion but I have lost your name, if I ever knew it."

Murdoch, in a tone of self-mockery, said, "Your pardon, again, good lady. I am Lord Murdoch," and he gave her a half comic bow. Clearly he did not take the title seriously.

She answered in kind, using her new title for the first time, herself. "And I am Lady Twila Lyestehr." They both smiled. Sharing a small joke.

Twila turned, and went to the door. She decided she liked this man. "My Lord Murdoch, I perceive you are heavily burdened with affairs of state. Such cares can sometimes lead to knotted muscles and aches in the head. My small skills as a healer may provide relief to you and lift some of the burden, if you find such is the case."

Murdoch simply nodded wordlessly to her and watched as she left. He could not remember any incident in his life, aside from the family and servants of his master, when a pretty girl had spoken as kindly to him.

The pleasant feeling vanished when his assistant, one of the new dragoons named Woolf, came in with the news that the main Ruritanian forces had finally arrived on the south bank, across the river from the city.

The entrance to High Bridge, on the Ruritanian side of the river is guarded by a barbican, with two strong towers and a solid gatehouse. The dragoons on guard there, had watched for the last few days, as first light cavalry, then mounted infantry troops had arrived and began entrenchments for a major legion camp. Now, as they watched from their towers, full legions, in shiny white armor, came marching into view and taking up positions in the fortified camp.

The dragoons, watched and counted, sending hourly reports back by runner, across the bridge to the palace. From the size of the camp, it was estimated that it would take three days for the entire army to arrive, then the war would begin. It would begin, of course right at the gatehouse and towers of the bridge.

Word had also come, and been confirmed by the sorcerer Develon, that a second huge army was crossing the river hundreds of leagues to the East, threatening the neighboring country of Sardonicus. The jester country was known to lack anything that could be called an army, being as unwarlike as a country could be. Thus, King Christopher had dispatched the sorcerer Develon, accompanied by Finnegin as bodyguard, to Sardonicus, to assist in their defense.

There were many who had protested this, as Develon was the last remaining major sorcerer known to the court, since Fairchilde had disappeared, and Develon was thought to be needed in the defense of the city. But His Majesty had insisted that Sardonicus was an important ally and refused to change his mind. Those who already were critical of the King, and this number was growing, now had new reasons for their opposition, and the name usurper was first connected with Christopher's name. Henceforth, to many, he would be Christopher the Usurper.

The Tellurian Legions, had been sent into the hinterlands, supposedly to prevent disorder. This meant the force actually available to defend the capitol was the newly created Royal Dragoons, numbering less than a full legion. Sentries had already counted at least four full Ruritanian legions and more seemed to be coming. The tension in the city became tangible.

An exodus began among merchants and nobility, those with a place to go and enough wealth to make the trip. Large caravans were hastily assembled and left Caprice by the western and northern gates. Noble families surrounded themselves with their own private household guards, and packed what treasure they could into wagons, coaches, and pack trains.

When Murdoch pointed out that all these household guards could be conscripted into the defense force of the city, Christopher refused, declaring the city was better off without them.

Among those quietly slipping out of town, were the Earl of Lancaster, Baron Ahrlehn, and Baron Simsohms, together with their holdings. Each found reason to move to summer estates in the north at this precarious time. In like manner, General Montrose had followed the army into the hinterlands, declaring they would need a strong hand to command them in such arduous work. Christopher just smiled and let them go.

The leaders of the cabal had found their final plans to be falling apart. Prince Roderic the Simple, their next choice for puppet, had disappeared and was assumed to have fled the country. Of greater significance was the sudden disappearance of Miriam. Dark suspicions arose concerning her possibly being in league with the missing Fairchilde. The city was now expected to fall to the Ruritanians, and their hopes for a long stalemated war and huge profits seemed doomed with it.

The Earl of Lancaster was particularly angry as he had begun entertaining thoughts of himself standing behind the throne, as the savior of the people. Who else would have deserved it, after all. Even so, prudence demanded following the course of safety, and he left the city to retire to safety and begin planning anew.

Unaware, as yet, of this nasty little group of nobles, Murdoch continued with his hard work. In answer to a summons from the King, he went to the Private Audience chamber for what proved to be a final council of war.

Upon entering, Murdoch felt the tingle of magic, and once again found himself enclosed in thick clouds, covering the walls, floor and ceiling. His master, Sahm-el, had dropped the King Christopher pose for the moment, and was seated in one of the heavy oaken chairs, sipping a drink. The other person present was the elf, Sinueh, dressed as always in gray leather. Murdoch was motioned to a chair, and with a polite bow to the elf, joined them.

Sahm-el stroked his thick red beard and asked, "How stand our forces now? The attack comes on the morrow."

Murdoch gave a concise and accurate appraisal of their defense force, including the Royal navy with its sea-going war galleys. He made it clear that they were woefully short of military strength to oppose the invasion. He finished with, "Now if you had permitted the conscription of the household guards from the nobility, we could have defended the city against a siege of virtually any size. Since that is not the case, I am waiting to hear what use of sorcery you intend to use to balance our numbers and repel the enemy." He smiled, certain he had guessed his masters plan.

With a twinkling eye, Sahm-el returned his smile. "Now how could I cast spells, whilst pretending to be this lunkhead Christopher? He is not a sorcerer. Oh, 'tis true that on the sly, I can add strength to the barbican and gatehouse at the far end of the bridge, but I expect them to eventually break through and seize the bridge. How would it look if at the last minute, the bugwit King suddenly turned into a sorcerer, slaying by the hundreds? What effect would that have on our over-all plan?"

Murdoch dropped his smile, and after a moment of indecision followed by furious thought spoke again. "Your pardon, Master. I should have known better than to try to outguess you. Yet, I am confused. We cannot allow the city to fall to the Dominican Fanatics. The whole point was to establish a stable government here. We have created conditions where we do not have the military might to prevent them taking the bridge. If they capture the bridge, they will pour across it in their thousands, and the city cannot be held."

"At the same time, I know you. You have planned for this and have some solution that I do not see. Can you not enlighten me?"

Sahm-el turned to the Elf, who thus far had said nothing. "What does the Eldar Race think of this? Should we alter our plans at this late date?"

Sinueh, momentarily distracted by Murdoch's confusion, sipped some kind of green wine before answering. "The Eldar race takes no part in the wars of man, and truthfully cares not who governs in a city. We think it is like two fleas arguing over who owns the dog they ride upon. I have no advice to offer on the military realities of this situation. As you well know, I am here, as a representative of the Elven Council because of the greater crisis that looms ahead. My people must decide soon whether to abandon this world or remain. What happens here will have an effect on that decision." He resumed sipping his wine.

Anyone with knowledge of Elves would have expected such an answer. Elves were convinced that the striving for power among humans was the worst sort of vanity and folly. Sinueh was present then, merely as an observer, and did not offer Elven aid.

Murdoch turned back to Sahm-el. "Well?"

Sahm-el laughed. "Well, indeed! You are correct. I have made plans."

Murdoch leaned back in the chair and waited expectantly.

Sahm-el continued. "We are here to bring about the succession of the rightful King of Telluria. This little war has complicated that task but not changed it to any degree. This must be kept in mind. In order for this to happen, King Christopher the Usurper, shall have to depart the stage, and the rightful King be brought in. Thus Christopher must die. What better way to die than in glorious war?"

Murdoch knew Sahm-el's true thoughts about war and recognized the intended irony. He gave a brief nod to indicate that, and Sahm-el continued.

"It is my intent, to arrange a battle at the far end of the bridge, so as to be convincing, but to allow the Ruritanians to succeed in breaking on to the bridge. I will then destroy the bridge and die a hero's death. You do agree that with the bridge down, they will not be able to invade and the war will end?"

"Oh yes, The Royal Navy is well able to keep them from crossing the river by ship. Without the bridge the war will end. But I thought you were not going to reveal yourself as a sorcerer. How then, destroy the bridge?"

Sahm-el laughed aloud. "That is the simple part. It will require no magic from me, merely wits. And I promise you, it shall be an action in character for Christopher, and a most suitable final act of his reign."

Recognizing that tone of voice, Murdoch knew his former Master, now colleague, would keep his little secret, enjoying the surprise when it happened. There was no point in pursuing it further. In this, he was quite correct.

Twenty-Seven

"Force should not be met with simply more force. This merely uses up lives and escalates the conflict. Always meet force with wit, for any opponent can be defeated if he can be out-thought."

—The Decree of Salamanca,
Sacred Text for the Temple of Leto.

The Ruritanian attack began with the dawn. Enslaved troll auxiliaries, each with enchanted iron collar of slavery about its neck, moved toward the gatehouse of the bridge in orderly ranks, marching in step and holding their shields together in a shield wall. The front ranks formed a wall, and the next two ranks lifted their large rectangular shields over their heads to form a roof against arrows. The result was a moving box of shields, shiny white. Since the Armor of Blessedness was able to turn most magic, and was equally tough, the attacking trolls were reasonably safe as they moved up to the bridge.

It was an awesome sight from the parapets of the Bridge. Many a man would be forgiven at losing heart at the thought of facing a single troll in combat, and here were many, organized as an army, and protected by the very best in armor.

Yet, none of the new Dragoons bolted and fled back across the bridge. This was due in part to the fact that King Christopher had told them exactly what to expect in each stage of the battle, and thus far, the Ruritanians were doing precisely what had been described. It must also be said, though, that these men had been selected by Flettcher, in part, for a strong sense of duty. Many, no doubt, were afraid. None left their post.

Instead, they looked beyond the immediate enemy troops, trying to get a glimpse of what they knew was coming. The trolls began shooting showers of arrows, in an effort to clear the battlements. Warned of this, the Dragoons crouched down and their officers employed hand mirrors to observe the battle from behind the stones.

Arrows were being shot in volleys, and even though it did little good, the Dragoons began returning fire, shooting the same arrows back, by timing their volleys between those of the enemy. This was to discourage attempts to simply rush the walls with ladders and scale them. From time to time, a shot would pass between the troll shields and a troll would fall, only to have his place taken by another and his body passed back through the ranks and carried out of bowshot. Once the arrow was removed, the troll would begin healing itself with remarkable speed, and in a very short time, be able to return to the battle.

The Dragoons had no such ability, and thus took every possible precaution. If hit by arrow, they were likely to simply die on the spot. It was one of the major disadvantages in fighting trolls. On the other hand, trolls have their weaknesses as well. As soon as they had been sighted, a message had been sent to the Alchemy Guild in the city.

Very soon, a low rhythmic chant could be heard over the din of the archery battle. From the heights of the barbican, a long dark shape could be seen being pushed forward. Oscar Wyndham, who had become known to the Dragoons as Oscar One-arm, and who now commanded the troops at the gatehouse, thought it looked like about six coaches had been lined up, one behind the other, and then the whole line had been covered with a single blanket of sewn together hides. The monstrous thing was being pushed straight toward the barred gate of the bridge by means of long poles shoving against it at the back. Each pole was manned by hundreds of troll slaves, chanting as they shoved. It had to be massively heavy, whatever it was.

Had they not been warned about this, by the King, the sight of it might well have brought terror to even the stoutest heart. But they had been warned, and as they watched they timed its progress toward the gate. As expected, the white wall of shields facing the Dragoons, suddenly split and separated, following orders called out by centurions, leaving a pathway wide enough for the thing to get through.

When he judged the time to be right, Oscar, used a whistle to make a signal. Instantly, the Dragoons, with red cloaks flapping, cleared the walls of the battlement and hurried to places of shelter below. Oscar watched with his mirror as the hide covering was removed from the thing, revealing a great pillar of black stone, lying on its side on a dozen set of wheels and axles. At the front was a large shiny metal ball, more than three meters thick. The ball was bathed in flickering green sparks that crackled and zapped loudly. This was "God's Holy Hammer of Wrath" from the Dominican Temple, and it was intended to ram the gate.

As Oscar watched, the Patriarch of the Dominican Temple, along with his bishops and cardinals took position behind God's Hammer, forming a wedge with the Patriarch at the point. They began a new chant, which was quickly picked up by all of the Dominican forces. This was a prayer for power and its results could be seen. Flashes of green light came from the sky like lightening, striking the head of the hammer. Each strike bathed the head of the hammer in green light that became gradually brighter and brighter, with more numerous sparks and sparks that were greater in size and intensity. The Temple was calling forth power from their God and directing it straight into the Hammer.

Oscar made another signal with his whistle, and a small group of Dragoon archers came out of their safe chambers and joined him on the battlements. At his command, they directed a volley of arrows at the group of priests behind God's Hammer. As he expected, the arrows were stopped short, in mid-flight by an unseen wall, and dropped harmlessly to the ground. He would waste no more arrows on such a protected target. He could do nothing until the alchemy potion arrived, that he had ordered.

The priests continued to draw power from their god and pour it into the great hammer. The green aura around the head grew brighter and brighter. Oscar ordered his archers to begin harassing fire at the enemy, not expecting it to do any real damage, but simply as a demonstration that the defenders had not lost heart at the sight of the awesome hammer. Then they waited.

As the chanting was reaching its peak, a light chariot came racing across the bridge from the city, carrying a keg that bore the crest of the Alchemy Guild. The keg was carefully opened and Dragoons began dipping javelins and arrows into it, coating the points with the potion it contained. They then returned to their shelters.

The chanting abruptly stopped, and there was a rushing of wind and a mighty blast as God's Holy Hammer of Wrath leaped forward and struck the gate with a fiery flash of green light. The whole gatehouse shuddered, and Oscar was knocked off his feet, on the battlements. If any of the stones had been loosened he surely would have been crushed, but the gate house held together, strengthened by magical forces of its own.

The Dragoons were badly shaken in their shelters, but suffered only minor bruises. Everyone held their breath, waiting to see if the massive gates would break. The gates held.

As soon as he was sure of this, Oscar signaled with his whistle and the Dragoons rushed to their appointed places on the battlements. The great hammer was once more resting on its carriage and the priests were beginning to chant again, preparing it for another blow. Oscar was certain, that an assault would be tried while the Hammer gained new strength. This certainty had been the reason for his preparations and signals.

Sure enough, horns blared and the troll slave army surged forward, many of them carrying ladders. There was no need for the magic control of the slave collars, for the trolls blood was up and they were now eager for the kill. As they ran toward the gatehouse with its two small towers, snarling and growling in the troll manner, showers of arrows and thrown javelins dropped upon them.

This time there was a dramatic difference. Each troll struck by arrow or javelin, dropped kicking on the ground then screamed as their bodies burst into white hot flame. The Dragoon weapons had been coated with Trollbane, a magic potion first developed by the Elves during the ancient troll wars. This potion was amazingly expensive and not normally produced in any large quantity, except by the Elves themselves. So the attack came as a surprise to the Dominicans. Someone had to have spent a major fortune to have TrollBane made by the Alchemy Guild. Only Murdoch knew that Sahmel had simply changed a few ordinary bricks to pure platinum to pay for it.

The troll attack broke up before it even reached the walls, as trolls, who are accustomed to rapid healing from the most grievous wounds found they could actually die in this battle. Some of them, who refused the commands to advance, were killed by their slave collar, tightening about their necks due to their disobedience. In any case, it was apparent that the troll assault would not succeed in storming the walls. They were withdrawn.

By this time, God's Hammer had renewed its strength, and the Dragoons barely got to shelter in time to withstand the second great blow against the gates. This time, damage was done. Cracks appeared in the stonework, and one of the hinges broke. Some of the stones fell from the battlements. The magical force put into the gatehouse was not equal to the great hammer.

Again, the Hammer returned to its carriage and horns announced another assault. This time it was human troops from the Legions, wearing the Armor of Blessedness, that glossy white armor that turned magic back. Again they surged forward, carrying ladders and were met with showers of arrows and javelins. This time they reached the base of the fortifications and erected their scaling ladders. The battle gained in intensity as some of the Ruritanian legionnaires reached the top of the wall. Fierce hand to hand fighting with sword and shield kept them from coming over the wall, until they were recalled for another blow from God's Hammer.

This time, instead of seeking the shelters, Oscar ordered his Dragoons back out onto the bridge itself, forming a shield wall and slowly backing toward the center of the bridge.

Again his judgment proved sound as the third great blow shattered the gates, turning the gatehouse to rubble and opening the way for the invading legions. Scattered among the broken stonework were bodies of Dragoons and much spilled blood. Tellurian losses appeared severe. Yet when Oscar turned his gaze to the Dragoons, in their orderly ranks behind him on the bridge, he could see none missing from rank and file.

The Ruritanian Legions came through the rubble of the gatehouse and onto the bridge, marching six abreast with shields locked together in a shield wall. Oscar had pleaded for a delaying action to be fought at this point, intending to defend every foot of the bridge and make it costly to the enemy in blood. But the orders from His Majesty were very exact and firm. Reluctantly, he followed them and backed his force of Dragoons out across High Bridge toward the waiting city.

High Bridge is supported by two tall columns that divide it equally into three parts, with the center span being high enough that a caravel in full sail could pass under it. Oscar and the Royal Dragoons inched backward across the arch. He had been told to make it clear they were retreating, but to also do it as slowly as possible to delay the enemy. He did not know why. Thus, step by step, the two armies crossed High Bridge, separated by a gap of about one hundred meters.

Oscar had been given no instructions as to what should happen next, so he was ordering in his mind, disposition of his troops at the very gate of the city, when a hand clasped his shoulder from behind, and he turned to see Murdoch there, and

His Majesty, accompanied by an Elf, standing right behind him.

With a strangely reassuring smile, Murdoch told him. "You may stand fast now, we retreat no more from this point. You have done well." Oscar gave the signal to stand fast, and turned back to ask why they were going to stand out here on the bridge when either end would be more defensible. The Tellurian defenders had just passed the second support column and were less than a third of the bridge length from the city. The leading Ruritanians were just past the peak of the arch. Before Oscar could speak, King Christopher had stepped past him and was walking toward the enemy.

Oscar started to follow but was stopped by Murdoch, just as the King signaled for a parley. Murdoch whispered, "It is part of the plan. We must wait here."

The King took just a few steps, then stopped, waiting for a herald from the opposing side. An officer, resplendent in his armor stepped forth to inquire if the King wished to surrender the city.

His Majesty answered in a booming loud voice. "Nay! I come to welcome you. As soon as I learned of your arrival I ordered my loyal troops to escort you into the city." He gestured back toward the Royal Dragoons, in their disciplined ranks, scarlet cloaks flapping in the breeze.

The Ruritanian officer looked confused, then smiled to himself. He, too, answered loudly, but in a tone of mockery and arrogance. "By your leave then, Your Majesty, show us into your city." His men laughed.

The King also seemed amused. "There is but one small matter, that of the toll."

The officer looked blank. "Toll? What toll?"

And King Christopher responded, "The toll you must pay for the crossing of this bridge. I, King of Telluria, do hereby charge you a toll of one silver piece for crossing High Bridge."

The officer blustered, "Is this some joke? Do you dare to mock me?" But King Christopher had already turned his back and rejoined Oscar and Murdoch, and the silent Elf.

There was no time for a reply in any event, for a grating and grinding sound began somewhere below, rising in loudness on all sides. They felt the first tremors and saw small cracks begin to form in the stonework of the bridge.

King Christopher ordered the Dragoons to stand fast, telling them they would be safe. Oscar wondered at the crisp tone of command and decisive air of strength being displayed by His Majesty, so unlike all the reports of him.

The Ruritanian officer commanding the lead cohorts of the legion, hesitated, unable to quite believe what was happening. As major cracks suddenly appeared in the bridge structure, he bawled out an immediate retreat, and his soldiers turned and tried to make it back off the bridge.

Oscar could hear large splashes in the river below, as huge chunks of masonry fell into the river. The bridge was breaking up. Still, King Christopher held the Dragoons in place.

Murdoch, was bringing to the surface of his memory something about an old legend that no toll shall be charged for crossing High Bridge or the bridge would fall. He suddenly laughed aloud.

As they watched, the center span suddenly dropped into the river, taking Ruritanian troops with it. Then the second support column toppled and the rest of the length of the bridge, all the way back to the Ruritanian shore, fell with a resounding crash. One third of the bridge remained standing, the third that held the King and the Royal Dragoons.

The King motioned Murdoch to step aside for a private comment, while all else watched in awe as the Ruritanian invasion come to an end.

Murdoch leaned close and heard Christopher speak in Sahm-el's voice. "Word has reached me from Master Chiang that the rightful heir has been found. It is time for Christopher to depart." Murdoch nodded his understanding and was suddenly pushed backward, by the King, into the Dragoons, as a heavy stone, loosened by the shocks, suddenly tipped and fell onto the King, delivering a crushing blow.

Murdoch and the elf, Sinueh, rushed forward and Sinueh

took the King's head in his lap as Murdoch tried to stop the bleeding from the crushed chest with just his kerchief. They both heard a low chuckle from the King, and leaning down so only they could hear, heard him say. "Relax, this is but play-acting. Now, good Murdoch, give me some heroic or at least noble last words to say."

Murdoch, still shocked by the illusion of blood and injury could only mutter, "Have we really done it, then?"

With a snort that might have been pain or laughter, the King cried out loudly, "Have we really done it then, good friends? Is the city saved?" Then he collapsed and spoke no more. Murdoch pronounced him dead, and runners went through the streets of Caprice, bearing the double news of salvation for the city and death for the King.

Twenty-Eight

"Strength can be measured in many ways, some of which are quite subtle."

—The Chronicles of Deathwind, Vol. IX.

The Imperial Dragons, Ginseng and Chiang, once more rested on the sloping stone benches. The Dragon Challenge was concluded. The selection had been made. There would be a Queen in Telluria for the first time in centuries. A girl named Anastasia had passed the test where the Sorcerer Fairchilde had failed. Fairchilde no longer held any existence in this reality.

Ginseng had been privately amused at the expression on Fairchilde's face, standing on the pinnacle, and wearing the supposed Tellurian crown, when he had been blandly informed that he had failed. The sorcerer had protested, raging, as Ginseng had asked him who he thought could possibly be loyal to a monarch that would sacrifice a subject for a mere thing. No doubt, he would be raging yet, if allowed to do so.

The two Dragons were in complete agreement, and had no doubts at all, although Chiang seemed to be enjoying some private amusement. An ancient prophecy had been fulfilled, just as Chiang had expected, but he knew of at least one human who would be utterly shocked by the result.

At a nod from Ginseng, Chiang fluttered the clawed fingers on one large hand, and summoned the girl to their presence, from the fold in reality where the testing had occurred. Instantly, she stood before them, a sleight girl with long red hair, dressed in the Elven manner in a maiden's gown of forest green, that nearly matched the green of her eyes.

She looked up at the two mighty serpents in defiance. "There is no need to prolong this, I am ready for my fate. I agreed to the test, and I failed. Do with me what you will, but do not play with me, Oh Great Ones, it would be unworthy of you." She faced them directly, without quivering and meeting their gaze directly. Both Dragons knew that few humans could do such.

Ginseng gave her answer. *"SILENCE! YOU KNOW NOT WHAT YOU SPEAK."* His voice was near deafening, and this time she recoiled from them, clasping hands over ears. Then she stood straight and faced them again, this time waiting silently, in the Elven way.

The Chiang spoke. *"TELL US, HUMAN, WHEN YOU SAW THE VAT TIPPING AND UNDERSTOOD THE DANGER, WHY DID YOU SAVE THE OLD MAN INSTEAD OF THE VALUABLE CRYSTAL? DID YOU NOT UNDERSTAND THAT THIS CRYSTAL OF MAGIC WAS IRREPLACEABLE? THE SERVANT WAS JUST AN OLD MAN. THE WORLD IS FULL OF THEM."*

She pause, then answered in a quiet voice, the flush of embarrassment on her face. "I ...acted without thought, from my heart rather than from my head. I saw only an old man, who might have grandchildren, who needed to hear wisdom from him in bedtime stories. The crystal was a thing. Not alive. True, it was of great power, but it was not alive, and in my foolishness I chose life over power. I cannot replace your lost crystal, and I am sorry to have lost it for you. For that I face grievous punishment."

Again, she faced them directly, willing to accept their punishment.

Ginseng let her stand there in silence for a moment, under

intense scrutiny, then spoke again. *"AND NOW, WOULD YOU MAKE THE SAME CHOICE AGAIN, NOW THAT YOU HAVE GIVEN THOUGHT TO IT? KNOWING THE RESULT THAT YOU FACE?"*

The girl named Anastasia did not answer immediately. She gave serious thought, knowing the answer they wanted to hear. It would be easy to speak the words, denouncing her former judgment and proclaiming her understanding of the power and value of the magic crystal. Such an answer might, even now, save her life.

Yet she could not bring herself to say those words. Although she did not clearly know why she had saved the man instead of the gem, she did know that she would do it again. It did not occur to her to try to lie to an Imperial Dragon. "I would make the same choice again.'

"WHY?" There was an intensity in Ginseng's question that was obvious to the girl. For some reason, this was important to them.

She shrugged her shoulders. "I don't know why. It just feels right." She felt it was a stupid answer and had probably doomed her.

Both of the awesome dragons stretched their necks out, and Anastasia closed her eyes, expecting to be blasted to nothingness. Instead, she heard the roar of great flames and when she opened her eyes, they were both facing straight up, breathing roaring flames that joined into a single column of white fire. The sound was deafening, and she could feel a great blast of heat. She crouched down on the floor and covered her head with her arms, praying that this be over soon.

The noise suddenly ceased, the heat stopped, and sulfurous fumes dissipated. Anastasia found herself still living and both Dragons staring at her in that still way that she had sometimes seen cats use with humans. She slowly stood up, smoothing her gown, and with growing curiosity returned their steady gaze.

One Dragon turned to the other, she did not yet know their names, but was beginning to suspect that she now might live long enough to learn many things. He spoke. *"I BEGIN TO UNDERSTAND YOUR FASCINATION WITH THIS SPECIE."* The other nodded.

He then turned to address her, for the first time in a respectful tone. *"MOST GRACIOUS LADY, I CONGRATULATE YOU. YOU ARE THE CHOSEN ONE! YOU SHALL RULE TELLURIA AS QUEEN."*

The girl was seen to shiver, then grope for words. "But...you said it was a test of strength. I cannot have been the strongest. I am but a young girl who has never cast a spell."

Chiang explained. *"OF THE SEVERAL KINDS OF STRENGTH, THAT WHICH COMES FROM THE HEART, THAT SOME CALL SPIRITUAL AND OTHERS CALL LOVE, IS THE TRUEST AND MOST DEPENDABLE. IN THIS, YOU WERE THE STRONGEST. AS TO THE CASTING OF SPELLS, THERE IS MUCH IN YOU THAT YOU HAVE NOT YET LEARNED."*

Ann bowed her head in embarrassment. She found she could not speak. Overwhelming thoughts were pouring through her as the import of these words struck her. She looked back and forth at the two golden Dragons and grew afraid, feeling very small for the burden they were placing on her. She said nothing.

The Master Chiang spoke. *"THUS PROPHECY IS FULFILLED. THIS IS YOUR DESTINY. DO NOT REJOICE, FOR THE THREATS ARE MANY AND THE PROBLEMS DIFFICULT. MORE THAN YOU KNOW."*

Anastasia gave him the nod of a very hesitant sovereign, still unable to find words, but he noticed the beginning of a truly regal manner in her stance and bearing.

Ginseng carefully stretched out a foreclaw, inviting her to take it in hand. *"COME, CHILD OF MAN, WE WILL GO TO THE POOL AND SEARCH DOWNSTREAM IN THE RIVER OF TIME, TO SEE WHAT AWAITS YOU. YOU HAVE WON THE RIGHT TO BE QUEEN, TO THE SURPRISE OF MANY, I SUSPECT, BUT YOU MUST PROVE YOUR RIGHT TO THE HUMANS OF YOUR COUNTRY."*

Ann shyly took the curved claw in her hand and began walking with the Imperial Dragon toward a large tunnel. He continued to explain as he led her out of the chamber. *"FOR MEN TO ACCEPT YOU, YOU MUST FULFILL ONE OF THEIR PROPHECIES AS WELL AS OURS. TO DO THIS, YOU AND I MUST MAKE A SHORT JOURNEY TOGETHER. WE WILL OBTAIN THE LOST SCEPTER OF TELLURIA AND IT SHALL BE YOUR PROOF TO THE PEOPLE OF YOUR LAND."*

"You and I journey together, where?"

"I SHALL TAKE ON HUMAN FORM AND WE WILL TRAVEL AS ORDINARY PEOPLE THROUGH A PART OF YOUR LAND. THIS WILL ACQUAINT YOU WITH SOME OF YOUR PEOPLE AND BEGIN YOUR EDUCATION AS A RULER. HAVE NO FEAR, WE SHALL SUCCEED IN THIS MINOR QUEST AND YOU SHALL BE CROWNED QUEEN IN BUT TWO WEEKS TIME."

They turned the corner and were gone. Chiang smiled, a ferocious tooth filled smile. The girl truly was the rightful queen, and he felt certain that once she discovered her own latent ability, she would make a great queen. Telluria would be stable when the real crisis came. And he looked forward, with relish, to his next meeting with Sahm-el.

The sorcerer Sahm-el stood on the balcony of his mountain retreat, overlooking the valley he had named Xanadu. He sipped his favorite pepper drink from the goblin skull mug and was feeling mightily pleased with himself. The plan, which had seemed so difficult, had actually worked. Telluria would have a strong and stable King when the real crisis finally arrived.

It had been a near thing, especially at the bridge. He had nearly lost his temper there. The fools had angered him with their arrogance and simple-mindedness. The blessed armor that turned magic back was folly, in his estimation. Any novice with a tea cup worth of wits could have beaten it. Like so many defenses, it offered no protection against the more subtle form of indirect magic.

He had been tempted to direct his magic at the ground under their feet, causing it to open and swallow them in fiery chasms. Had he wished to, he could have destroyed not only the troops on the bridge, but the entire legion encampment. If he had been the idiot they thought he was, thousands and thousands of men would have died, instead of the few hundred who fell with the bridge.

The fools! Stupidity always angered him. Well it was, for all sides, that he was not the fop Christopher that he was portraying. A few hundred men had died, but a war was averted that would have imperiled the entire world. It was a cheap price to pay.

Then, as his mind turned to the details of the battle of the bridge, Sahm-el smiled. He particularly liked the little detail of Dragoon bodies left among the rubble of the gatehouse, suggesting heavy losses. Not one Dragoon had died. The illusions he created were done with an artist's touch.

And, he would do the same on the morrow, for the State Funeral of King Christopher, especially during the public cremation ceremony. The common man would never know how well served he truly was by this kind of theater and trickery. That was a thought that brought him a private amusement he shared with no one.

In the palace, at Caprice, Murdoch was once again writing in his journal, reporting to Sahm-el the minor events that had followed the saving of the city.

> *The Will of Christopher was found, and after much discussion has been accepted. I have been named Regent on the promise that the lawful heir will arrive and provide proof to the Title, and this within a month's time.*

I have received a letter from Chiang, telling me that the new monarch is all we could have hoped for and will easily be here within that time limit.

I have also received the strangest letter from Master Develon. He and Finnegin, and your cat, are all well. It seems the Ruritanian Legions that attacked Sardonicus have been utterly defeated. He hinted at bizarre happenings and suggested the jesters of Sardonicus had not needed any help from him. He should have an interesting tale to tell when he returns.

The city is still in turmoil. Some of the faint-hearts who left before the battle are returning. Merchants have complained about the loss of the bridge. Such is to be expected from those who think only in terms of profit. One of my officers has come across evidence that some of our nobles might have been in league with the Ruritanians, in some way. We are beginning to investigate.

The Ruritanian forces, on the far side of the river, are withdrawing. My spies report that they have decided the fall of the bridge was in indication of God's Will to them and fate did not intend them to succeed in the conquest of Telluria at this time. Machis may be in serious trouble with his own priesthood.

As to my own person, I am well, although much changed from the quiet scholar of Xanadu. I have read in your Chronicles that once the "whisper of the ax" has been heard, the quiet life loses its appeal. I think I have come to prefer the thrill of riding in the runaway coach more than merely reading about it.

By the by, I have met a person here that I should like you to know. She is a remarkable healer, one of Elric's victims, a most unusual lady.

With that, Murdoch closed the book. And if his thoughts lingered on a certain healer for a few minutes, it was nobody's business but his own.

Twenty-Nine

"A good surprise, from time to time,
is beneficial to the health of the mind."
—The Book of Vehdahs,
Sacred Text for the Temple of Isis.

Three weeks passed. Sahm-el had paid little attention to events in Telluria, since arranging the supposed death of King Christopher. He had complete faith in Murdoch, Flettcher, Develon, and the others to manage a Regency until the new King was crowned.

Most of his attention went to the far off Empire of the Khan, the most critical of the remaining two areas of instability. His beloved wife, who liked to be called Crickett, was there now, posing as a harem girl and keeping an eye on Suliman the Dread, a major sorcerer who was capable of much evil.

It was a position of great danger. Although Crickett was a sorceress in her own right, she could not hope to face this Suliman the Dread should her presence be discovered by him. Only Sahm-el himself would stand a chance in a duel of sorcery with one of such power.

Thus, Sahm-el kept close watch on his wife, and talked with her daily by arcane means. Her reports on this Suliman indicated he was trying to build a power base by using the

Great Khan as a puppet. Of greater significance, was the fact that this Suliman had been showing interest in the forbidden TEK associated with the Great Cataclysm. It was a most perilous situation, with the return of the Outsiders now predicted.

Fortunately, Sahm-el could take heart in the fact that his other source of pride and love, his young daughter, was safely out of any such fray, pursuing scholarly studies with an old family friend, the elf sage, Sweevey. She, at least, he did not have to worry about.

On this day, he had just finished enchanting a large cooking kettle so it would heat itself without fire and clean itself upon command, when Leslie informed him that horns of alarm were blowing in the valley.

Sahm-el grabbed his staff and used it to instantly flash to his balcony. The Dwarven clan that lived at the other end of the valley of Xanadu, under the mountains, were blowing horns and sealing up their tunnels. The reason was obvious. Swooping down the valley, on outstretched wings, there came a gold and black Imperial Dragon. Chiang had come unannounced, scaring the wits out of the dwarves. It was something he enjoyed doing.

Sahm-el took up position by the roosting bar and waited until the dragon had flared his wings and landed, gripping the bar with taloned feet, then steadying himself and calmly stepping down into the stone balcony at Xanadu.

Sahm-el gave him a mocking and over-elaborate formal bow. The dragon replied in kind, folding its wings and dipping its head down to touch the stones, chuckling all the while.

Sahm-el spoke in greeting. "Hail to thee, oh winged one, who has just terrorized my Dwarves for the umpteenth time! I see you still indulge in dramatics when the mood strikes you." He then gestured toward the door, bidding his guest to enter.

On previous visits, Chiang, had out of courtesy assumed a human form, and entered the home of his friend. This time, he remained his true self, and thus stood still, on the wide balcony. When the dragon did not immediately change, Sahm-el became curious, for this was very unusual behavior.

Chiang spoke, making an effort to restrain the volume of his true voice. *"GREETING TO THEE, OH MASTER OF THE ART! I WISHED TO BE THE FIRST TO CONGRATULATE YOU ON THE SUCCESS OF OUR VENTURE."*

Knowing Chiang as he did, Sahm-el now became very wary. The dragon was in enormous good humor. In the past, this had always presaged some colossal practical joke.

On one occasion, Chiang had secretly cast a spell upon him of such devious subtlety that no matter what Sahm-el attempted, his magic produced hundreds of carrion crabs. As he attempted to correct each flawed spell, more and more of the scavenger crabs appeared until his home was literally crawling with them. He had been forced to make use of spells stored away for an emergency, to travel upstream into the past, in order to correct the situation. He then had to do a thorough house-cleaning to get rid of the two million or so crabs. These he had sent to a goblin lair that he knew of.

Then there was the time that Chiang had managed to attach an invisible aura to him that had the effect of making any horse he encountered fall in love with him. That had caused major inconveniences. Crickett had roared with laughter over that one.

It had not been all one sided, of course. Sahm-el had struck back in his own way. He had once filled Chiang's entire lair with molasses, floor to ceiling. On another occasion, he had secretly cast a spell of the dragon that resulted in Chiang being caught in a time loop and having to experience the same unpleasant experience 732 times, before he got out of it. Since the experience involved an encounter with stench producing gas spores, it was most memorable.

Now Sahm-el was wary, for the great dragon was obviously up to something. "You did not have to come here to deliver a simple message." He paused, gripping his staff and eyeing Chiang steadily. Chiang affected an air of nonchalance.

"Come now, old drake, what else is on your mind?"

Chiang's tooth-filled grin widened ever so much. *"I THOUGHT YOU MIGHT ENJOY WATCHING THE CORONATION IN TELLURIA WITH ME."*

Now Sahm-el was worried. "What have you done?" He drew power from his staff and instantly sent his mind's eye streaking across the sea to the city of Caprice.

Chiang murmured something about just doing what they had agreed upon in finding the rightful monarch.

In his mind's eye, Sahm-el saw the city of Caprice, looking much as it did on the day the bridge fell. He knew that coronations in Telluria took place at Temple court and his vision flashed to that place, only to see the court beginning to empty as the Royal Procession headed back toward the palace. Clearly the new king had just been crowned.

His view passed along the honorary rear guard, now composed of the new dragoons, and up through open carriage after open carriage bearing various dignitaries, and nobles. He saw Lord Murdoch, riding in one of the palace carriages, with a slim girl by his side, no doubt this healer his writing had mentioned.

Looking further ahead in the procession, he could not find the new king. Whatever, Chiang found to be so humorous had to be something regarding this new king. Near the front, there was a royal carriage, but it had a single woman in it, not a king. As he looked closer, he noticed the woman was wearing the crown of Telluria. So it was to be a queen instead of a king. Surely that was not sufficient to provide Chiang with such amusement.

He was about to pass on to observing the palace, when something about the new queen caught his notice. She had long red hair, much like Crickett's. In fact it was the exact same shade as Crickett's hair. He knew Crickett to be on the other side of the world. It could not be her. Still …

Suddenly it hit him. "Anastasia? My daughter? You chose my own daughter to be Queen of Telluria? Damnation to you!" There was a rumble of suppressed laughter from Chiang.

Then did Sahm-el the sorcerer take on the aspect of the fearsome and mighty Deathwind. He seemed to grow larger in size, although it was only his wrath that made it seem so. With a look of absolute fury, he launched a bolt of pure energy at the dragon, one of immense power.

Expecting precisely this response, Chiang had prepared a barrier of force, and the energy bolt, which resembled dark purple lightening, simply bounced off and shattered the south end of the stone balcony in a thunderous explosion.

Another blast followed, with the same result. Then the universe twisted around them as both of them suddenly left the dimension that men call reality and flashed through time and space locked in a struggle.

They were, in fact, evenly matched, and it must be admitted that the Dragon withheld attack and merely countered the various onslaughts launched by his furious friend, until that worthy finally calmed down, the explosion of temper having passed.

When that occurred, both were standing on a gray featureless plane, a no-where and no-when kind of place. They both stared at each other, each heaving, trying to catch his breath, for such a struggle is exhausting when carried on by such as they.

The Chiang spoke. "*COMPOSE THYSELF, AND HEAR ME OUT. I HAVE DONE NOTHING TO WARRANT THY WRATH. SHE TRULY IS THE RIGHTFUL RULER OF TELLURIA.*"

He paused, watching the sorcerer master his own volcanic temper and bring it under control. They stood in silence for a moment.

Finally, Sahm-el found his voice. "Show me!" was all he said.

Swiftly, Chiang spread before him the River of Time, and took them both upstream into the past. There, he showed Sahm-el all that had transpired in the search for the rightful heir. The combing of archives, consultations with other dragons, including Ginseng, the approach to different candidates, the challenges, and the results.

When he had finished, in order to insure against trickery, Sahm-el then actually traveled to each of those events himself, watching them unseen, proving to himself that what had actually occurred and that Chiang was not in any way deceiving him. Then returned to the same instant that he had left from, and they both returned to the balcony at Xanadu.

Sahm-el took a deep breath, then upon further thought, went through the Ritual of Calming. While he was doing so, Chiang quickly gathered stones, reshaped them, and smoothed them into place, repairing the damaged balcony.

When man and dragon faced each other once more, Sahm-el spoke in quiet tones. "I am satisfied. She is the genuine heir to the throne. I would not have wished it for her."

Chiang shimmered, seemed to change to a vaporous cloud, then took on human form, that of an elderly man in golden robes. "And why not? Is she not worthy?"

The red-bearded sorcerer leaned against the stone parapet of the balcony. "Of course she is worthy, none better, as you well know. But there is both hardship and danger in this. What father would wish that for his daughter?"

Chiang moved next to him. "And would you weaken her so? You know the result of shielding someone from life. Is that the act of a father to one he loves?"

Sahm-el let out a long sigh. "No. You speak wisely, old friend. I would not have her remain dependent on me. She must face her own trials to find her own strengths. How long have you known?"

Chiang drew forth a long stemmed pipe and watched as it instantly filled itself with pipeweed. He flipped his thumb up, producing a flame, and lit his pipe, drinking in the smoke, and letting it out in a variety of geometric shapes, one after the other. "I have always known the rightful ruler would be a flame-haired female of your specie. Such was described in the original prophecy. I was not sure it would be Anastasia until she actually passed the test the others had failed."

Sahm-el nodded. He drew forth his own pipe and puffed it alight and the two of them enjoyed drinking smoke in silence for a moment. When Sahm-el did speak, it was in a wistful tone. "I have never searched Anastasia's future timeline, for fear of foreknowledge might tempt me to interfere too much in her life, and thus ruin her. I had no idea. It was probably just as well that I did not, I suppose." He signed, again. "The dilemmas of parenthood among humans never seem to change."

Chiang had no response to that, and just puffed his pipe.

Sahm-el put his hand on the other's human-assumed shoulder. "Forgive me old friend. I thought you might have endangered not only our plan, but this world for some small joke at my expense. I should have known better." And he turned and began to lead Chiang into his home.

Chiang replied with a chuckle, "'Tis well that you were not angry at me for cause, or we would both still be out there tying knots in time and space."

They laughed together and went in for some refreshment, each to his own taste.

Thirty

"There is no such thing as a conclusion. Each ending brings a turning to a new path."

—The Book of Vehdahs,
Scared Text for the Temple of Isis.

The Imperial Dragon Ginseng stood in the center of the circle of protection etched in the floor of his lair. Recent events had stirred his curiosity and he was about to attempt something he had not done for a very long time, a Cosmic Visualization.

More than just exploring the River of Time downstream, this was an attempt to grasp the universe as a whole, to merge with it in order to know this moment in time totally.

To prepare for this, Ginseng had fasted for a week. This was done, not so much to deprive his body, but more to simply clear his mind. He could have gone without food for months at a time had he needed to. The fasting simply brought focus and greater concentration.

Now he reached out with his powerful mind and touched the very fabric of the universe, expanding infinitely, throughout all of space and time, through an infinite number of dimensions, steadily allowing his spirit to grow until he could feel himself, not only as a part of the universe, but also as being the universe, the unnumbered cells in his body being first swirls of stars, then star systems, then individual worlds, then individual beings on all of those worlds, all at the same time.

He absorbed this experience for an unknown amount of time, feeling himself to actually be the cosmic reality. Then he turned his attention to various portions of this reality that was himself, and began to learn. He could now experience everything occurring at this moment in time everywhere.

Through prodigious concentration, he came to focus on just one of those whirlpools of stars, moving his attention into it, focusing ever downward, smaller and smaller, until he could observe a war taking place in the void.

The creatures called Outsiders were moving implacably across this swirl of stars. Their advance was steady, delayed only a little, here and there as they encountered opponents attempting to defy them. Ginseng was interested to note that many of those daring resisters were of the human specie, who thus far had managed only to delay the spread of this infectious-like conquest. The advance of the Outsiders would bring them to the World of Three Suns, which men called Eridani Trianus, in but a matter of years.

He shifted his attention down even finer, to the world upon which he stood, the World of Three Suns. Seen from the outside, the world was a ball with an ugly streak carved into it, like a knife gash in an apple. This was the Great Rift and was actually a wound inflicted by the Outsiders during their first visit. Commoners believed the Rift to be the edge of the world, for if one stood on its edge, one looked out into fog-bound nothingness, the other side being beyond the range of human sight.

Upon this world, there were many countries, ruled by kings, beings of power, or in a few cases parliaments. The majority of them were at war. It had been nearly a thousand years since the devastation known as the Great Cataclysm. But the hatred, the fear, the impulse to fight remained as a legacy of that event. Such worlds do not heal easily.

Ginseng now turned his attention to the ripples and whirlpools that disturbed the surface of the River of Time locally.

He saw just what Chiang and the human Sahm-el had seen. There were three broad areas of disquiet on this world. They were located in the land of Cetshiwego, the Empire of the Khan, and most importantly in Telluria.

The recent game played in Telluria had set that problem on the right path, for the moment. The new Queen, aided by a handful of most loyal followers, would prove to be strong and firm, wise in judgment. There would be many plots, conspiracies, and attempts to assassinate her, executed by those compelled to defend the past because they were too faint-hearted for the future. If she overcomes these difficulties, she may well succeed in stabilizing Telluria.

The King of Cetshiwego faced similar problems. A shrewd and strong monarch, well established on his throne, he was aware of the challenges and keeping close watch on all parts of the land, and even beyond to the very limits of the continent known as Carpathia. Still he faced powerful foes of great wealth and hunger for power. Then too, agents of Suliman the Dread were attempting to introduce a cult of the forbidden TEK into that land that would prove most dangerous.

Finally, in the Empire of the Khan, there was Suliman himself, regarded by many as the most powerful sorcerer in this world. He was posing as a trusted advisor to the Khan but secretly building his own empire. He had ambitions of making himself a god, and heading a new religion. He also harbored thoughts of trying to make an alliance with the Outsiders, expecting to bend them to his will and use them as tools in his own plans. In the long run, he presented the greatest danger to the humans of this world.

Then there were these humans themselves. Certain of them had come to his attention recently. He saw Lord Murdoch, who was spending much time in the company of the healer Twila. This Murdoch was just beginning to become aware of his real abilities. The sorcerer Develon was also demonstrating the beginnings of real ability, although he must guard against pride, for he was vulnerable to it.

And of course there was Sahm-el. Chiang was right about

nim. He was an equal in every way to the Imperial Dragons themselves. Sahm-el's greatest danger, other than the sorcerer Suliman, was himself. There were grave risks in striving to do what he was attempting. It would be easy to lose oneself in the glory and the power, and forget that strength of heart that was so essential to a real leader.

As Ginseng prepared to pull back from his visualization, he briefly glanced at a few others on this world. There was a Duchess of Lancaster who sought to dominate the world through banking. There was a mutant troll in the mountains of Carpathia, attempting to forge a Troll empire using old TEK weapons. There was the secret world wide organization of shapedancers known as the Black Brotherhood, who worshipped chaos and did their best to destroy all order and sanity. And there were the Mist Wizards secluded in their domed refuge by the upper end of the Great Rift. These could not be seen clearly, even by Ginseng's visualization.

Ginseng gradually withdrew from the trance, returning inside himself until he was once again standing in his own lair. He scratched behind one ear with a hind claw, and stretched out full length, unknotting muscles that were beginning to cramp from the long trance. Then he slowly ambled from his ritual chamber and sought rest upon a dragon bench.

He was feeling pleased. The one thing dragons dread most is boredom. He felt assured that, for the foreseeable future, he would be living in interesting times.